Published by Lulu.com

The mon●dreme

For Jill and Sarah

Contents

Contents

1
The End of the World

I never think of the future. It comes soon enough.
- Albert Einstein

We ran for our lives.

It was Pee's fault.

At first we were just frozen, crouched there in the dark, barely able to breathe, just staring at something that had changed our world in an instant from one that we knew, and understood, into...something else. We just stared.

But then he ran, snapping our paralysis like a rib, and we just got up and chased after him. Fear clogged our throats, oozed out of our pores, pounded in our brains. A mindless panic expanded inside us like an airbag, pushing our personalities out. We weren't ourselves anymore, just running things.

And all the while I was dimly aware of a small part of myself, a silent observer that was actually excited. But my mind was a muffled voice now, sent out of the room for its own good. Survival was everything. Luxuries such as thinking could come later – if there was a later.

I was in third place, behind Pee and Osmo. I stumbled endlessly over the uneven ground because I couldn't see a thing, but once we got past the perimeter fence, and in amongst the warehouses, I started to make good speed. I was about to overtake Pee, who had slipped into second place behind Osmo, when my inbuilt chivalry started to kick in, just as automatic as my running. I couldn't leave any of them behind, especially someone as little and helpless as Pee. It's not that I'm brave or something. I know I'm not. It's just that my body decides things for me sometimes. So I slowed down, expecting Sal to catch up and overtake at any moment, because she was easily faster than Pee. Then if anyone were going to fall victim to what was behind us it would be me.

But Sal didn't catch up.

We were all the way to the hole in the wall that leads back onto Brookland Common by the time I realised. I had to shout to the other two to stop. Otherwise they would have run all the way home without looking over their shoulders once. Our throats were dry and tight from breathing the cold air so hard. The streetlights on the far side of the wall coated us in an unhealthy yellow brown light.

"Sal's still back there." My voice sounded like somebody else's, so serious.

5

I sweated clammily under my coat, while above the neckline my ears glowed with the cold. Osmo swore. Bits of gravel and broken glass crunched loudly beneath our feet as we started back the way we had come.

We didn't speak at first. There was no question of us carrying on without Sal. So we jogged wordlessly back in amongst the warehouses and commercial units. Osmo and Pee were looking wide-eyed and haunted.

"Is it me or are we dreaming this?" I muttered eventually. Osmo nodded. Pee had a fixed frown on his face, as if he was sitting an exam, or as if he were constipated or something. He kept making this mewling sound from way back in his throat. I don't think he realised he was doing it.

"What are we going to do? I don't know what we think we're going to do!"

"Shut up, Pee. I'm scared enough as it is."

"Just don't think," said Osmo. "Just shut up and don't think and keep on going."

It was the only sensible idea.

When we got back to the fence I crouched down and took the lead, still playing the protector. I kept low behind the overgrown weeds and bits of wall, working my way forward. Every now and then a glimpse of the golden light caught me, and I reeled in disbelief that we hadn't imagined it, some kind of group hallucination. But I still wasn't convinced that I wasn't dreaming.

We could leave her, I thought to myself, cringing at my own cowardice but following the thought anyway. Maybe it was too late to help her. Maybe it would be more use to go and get help. But my body decided to keep going forward.

We finally got as close to where we'd left Sal as we were going to get without giving ourselves away. I inched my head over the edge of some crumbled old brickwork, trying to keep my face in the shadow of a spindly old bush that was leaning over from the other side. When I saw what I saw my chest started to shudder, and I couldn't stop it for the life of me.

My god, it was really real.

•

Sal liked science fiction and I think that had a lot to do with why she hadn't followed us. I don't know how many girls are into science fiction compared to boys, maybe more than you'd think, but Sal loved it. I know she believed in life on other planets because she'd told me. As far as she was concerned it was simply a question of when the human race would be mature enough to receive our visitation from the stars. That's if the aliens weren't already here: learning about us, guiding us, helping us to evolve. It seemed plausible to both of us.

But where we disagreed, me and Sal, was the bit about how ready we humans were for first contact. I thought it should be any day now – well, I felt ready, personally, being an evolved, well-balanced individual. And though Sal seemed to agree that I wasn't the most stupid example of the human species she'd ever met she didn't have that much faith in the rest. As far as she was concerned it would probably be another thousand years before humanity got over itself finally and grew up.

"Human development," she said, "if you average it out around the globe, is about equivalent to that of a teenager. Or in other words: we're pretty messed up."

I liked Sal. Well, that might be a bit of an understatement. Actually, saying 'that might be a bit of an understatement' might be a bit of an understatement. She was a deep thinker, a fast runner and she liked Star Trek. And yes, she was cute. So cute, in fact, that she could have got away with having a horrible personality, if that had been her bag. And, let's face it, most cute girls try that on for size, for a while at least. She was way too cute to hang around with me. But somehow, through some weird space-time anomaly or something, she'd inherited the geek gene. She was talking about learning how to speak Klingon so she'd be able to swear at Mr. Michaels without him realising. I didn't think it would work. Ask somebody if they want a nice cup of tea in Klingon and they'll think you're swearing at them.

But yeah, out of the four of us, she was definitely the most likely to ignore popular opinion. Even if it meant hanging around on her own to face something potentially dangerous. Even if her three friends were in the process of running for their teeny little lives.

I peered over the top of the wall from the safety of my shadows and I saw Sal kneeling in front of the thing that was glowing with that golden light, the thing that had floated down from the sky.

"Do you think it's taken over her mind?" whispered Osmo.

•

I was George. Back then I was what some people would call 'precocious', at least in some areas of my development, meaning my head. For a fourteen year old I could knock out a pretty deep short story, the kind that made my English Teacher, Miss Schneider, think the sun shone out of my notebook. These days, because of what happened to me, I'm not the old George anymore, precocious or otherwise. There are moments, like right now, as I write these words, I don't even feel human. But I shouldn't get ahead of myself.

It was back in the olden days – not just a different century but a whole different millennium – back when we still watched Friends, back when my 10-gigabyte hard drive still seemed pretty impressive. I lived at Number

Nine, Iron Street, Banford. I went to Penrose High School. I hung around with Sal and Osmo and Pee. On Saturdays we'd go ice-skating at the rink in Kurtsholme and then wander around the market, eating butter pies and trying to avoid anyone from school. The dockland waste ground at Five Elms marked the northernmost point of our wanderground. To the south we wouldn't normally go further than the woods at Hensley Edge, although now and again, just to shake things up, one of our random end-of-the-line bus journeys would take us further. And occasionally we'd take the train to Blackport, of course. Never dull.

By evening we'd be piling heavy-eyed into my house, or Osmo's or Sal's – not Pee's – for our tea. We'd doss around indoors for a while, but sooner or later a morbid compulsion would draw us back outside to see who was out and about that was worth avoiding. Banford was a buzzing place. There was always something, at least on a Saturday, anyway. I'm not saying it was always something nice, but there was always something.

Sundays, on the other hand, tend to be deadly boring wherever you are. Well, you canna change the laws of physics can you? On Sunday we would zombie-walk from one morose limbo moment to the next. Well, that's how I remember it. This particular Sunday was the most boring ever - Granddaddy Sunday - right up 'til 7:40pm, when we saw the light in the sky from Openshaw New Road and we set off chasing it. It's funny how the most overwhelming events in life always seem to be preceded by quiet moments.

We followed the light from the far side of the cemetery. It drifted slowly enough for us to keep sight of it as we ran down the main path that splits the cemetery in half. We were scared we'd lose it as it fell behind the trees near the perimeter, and there was a lot of cursing and scuffling as we fought with each other to be the first to get through the gap in the fence. But as we emerged from the trees we saw that its descent had slowed. It hung in the air, seeming lost, seeming to wait for us. In the end the timing was perfect. By the time we crossed Brookland Common and passed through the old industrial estate, and were pulling up behind the protective cover of the bit of wall on the waste ground near the docks, we were just in time to see it land barely ten metres in front of us.

It drifted down from the sky like the first star leaf of some great universal autumn. We could see what it was now, in the centre of all that shining: an inhuman figure, clutching a smooth golden ball.

It was impossible to tell whether it was the ball that was shining or the figure or both. We watched from the shadows. It floated gracefully down, but when its feet touched the ground it tipped backwards drunkenly, falling against the low remnant of another wall. The brickwork crumpled beneath its weight. All was still for a moment. The figure didn't move. Maybe it was dead. We held our collective breath, despite all of the running we had just done. Then it looked directly at us.

8

It's funny that we had run all that way there, and then, at a panicked squeak from Pee, we turned around and started to run back again.

All of us except Sal, of course.

•

From the safety of my shadows I could see Sal kneeling on the floor, looking into its face.

"Do you think it's taken over her mind?" whispered Osmo.

They were both completely still, just looking at each other, and this did seem scary to me – as scary as if it were chasing after her with a ray gun. I couldn't even summon the courage to answer the question, I was so afraid of being heard.

Pee put his back against the wall, slumped down onto his bum and moaned.

"We're going to die," he croaked.

I was dimly aware of him puking up. Me and Osmo continued to watch the scene in front of us. And that's all we did. We should have been working out some plan to rescue our friend, but we didn't even try. We just cowered there in the shadows and waited. It makes me feel sick when I think back to it.

What broke the spell in the end was Sal herself, standing up and turning around and walking towards us. The light was behind her and all around her, casting her face in shadow so we couldn't see her expression. We had no way of telling if it was our Sal or if she'd been taken over by a telepathic nightmare from the stars. A bit of drool at the corner of her mouth would have been enough for me. I would have been off and running again.

"Come over," she said as she drew near. "He knows you're here. It's alright."

She sounded pretty normal. As she reached the wall I was able to make out her face. She did have something of a stunned expression, wonderstruck I'd say, but I could tell at once that it was the real her in there.

"Are you alright?" asked Osmo, and for a moment I felt bad that I hadn't asked first, but then he said, "You're not going to turn into a bug-eyed monster, are you?"

"I'm fine, honest. You've got to come over. It's amazing. You'll regret it if you don't." Sal's voice was alive, I mean, really alive – I'd never seen her so switched on. She was having the biggest moment of her life.

Me and Osmo looked at each other. It was one of those looks that only happen now and again, that you share with someone who's in the exact same extreme situation as you, when you're both feeling the same feelings, thinking the same thoughts. We both nodded minute little nods at the same time. I turned to Pee who was still on the floor.

"Do you wanna stay here, Pee?"

Pee looked like a trapped animal, like a mouse that's been caught and you can see its heart fluttering through its ribs.

"Yeah," he managed. "Just for a little bit." None of us blamed him. I nearly got down there and joined him. Sal smiled.

"Come out when you're feeling a bit braver, Pee." Pee nodded seriously, and his eyes rolled in their sockets, scanning the darkness behind our little wall, making sure the rest of the world was still normal. Sal turned to me and Osmo. An excited light danced in her eyes, but her breathing was measured, her body language calm.

"It's okay," she said levelly.

She took the time to look each of us in the eye, to communicate her confidence. I felt myself stand up straighter. The small part of me that had been excited all along suddenly stepped forward, elbowing my fear to one side. Osmo managed to raise his eyebrows high and puff out his cheeks. He shrugged in a mock devil-may-care way and the three of us relaxed a bit, looked more like our old selves.

"Come on," said Sal.

She beckoned with her head for us to follow her. I've got to say that with the golden white light behind her, and my bloodstream pumping with adrenaline and everything, she did look beautiful in that moment. I'm sure me and Osmo were both ready to faint on the spot - with the intensity of the situation, you know. I feel like fainting every time I think about it.

We shuffled out from the shade of our barricade and into the beams of an alien light.

"By the way," Sal said, conversationally, "he's telepathic."

2
The Fallen Angel

When you sit with a nice girl for two hours, it seems like two minutes. When you sit on a hot stove for two minutes it seems like two hours. That's relativity.
- Albert Einstein

It watched us approach. We were walking just about as slowly as we could but that didn't stop us from drawing closer and closer. Its eyes met mine, and I suddenly felt like I was a dust mite or something. Those eyes belonged in an angel's face. The intelligence there was golden and deep; it seemed a million miles away, not because it was cold and distant and alien, but because it was so here and now, and could see so far into me...further than I could.

I wondered what other things those eyes had seen. I wasn't sure if I wanted to know. The mind behind those eyes understood things, things that were beyond me, things I was glad were beyond me. The hairs on the back of my neck stood on end in a Mexican wave that travelled up the back of my head and over the top. My skin crawled, and the world slowed down. I'm gonna say it, though I don't know if it's wise: I wet myself a little. I managed to stop it almost straight away, but I was still glad I was wearing a long coat. What can you do?

We stepped up close. Sal knelt again. Osmo and me remained standing.

The creature hadn't moved a muscle, except to tilt its head a little as we drew closer. The position it was in looked uncomfortable. I guessed it had exhausted itself. It's going to die, I thought.

It was short and stocky and powerful looking. I think it must have been almost as wide as it was tall. It didn't have much of a neck to speak of, and its thick short limbs and torso seemed to consist entirely of solid muscle. I looked down and two things surprised me. The second thing was that it didn't have ankles. Its thick legs simply ended in a flat pair of feet, reminded me of elephants' feet. Put it this way, if it had come to Earth to be fitted for a pair of designer jeans they were gonna have to be flares. This angel was built for standing. With those feet planted firmly in the ground it could have stood for a hundred years without ever being knocked over.

But the first thing that surprised me was that, although it was completely naked, it didn't seem to have any rude bits – not as far as I could tell, anyway. It was hairless and smooth all over and it didn't seem to be a boy or a girl. It was a nothing. For some reason this sent an extra big shiver along my spine.

Its nose and ears were small and button-like, its mouth little more than a slit. Its design was very simple. It was beautiful really, in the way a shark or a stone is beautiful.

And it was shining with such a light.

It was shining so much that our retinas should have curled up and rolled away in agony, but somehow it didn't hurt. I could keep my eyes open wide. That light should have lit up the clouds above. It should have lit up the air itself for miles around. But it didn't. Spangles twirled in the golden white beams but they only penetrated the night for two or three metres. It seemed full of activity, that light. Looking into it got my mind whirring. It felt like I was thinking so fast that I was having ten different thoughts at the same time, all fitting together like a jigsaw. It was like my brain was upgrading. I didn't come up with a solution to war or anything, but it felt like I could have, if I'd spent some time on it.

- Hello, said a voice. It seemed to come from all around me. I instinctively looked around for the source, Osmo did too, even though we both realised already that the voice was in our heads. It was gentle, warm, filled with knowing, filled with understanding. It reached right inside me. It was almost as if an angelic part of myself had finally decided to speak for the very first time. There was an inflection of curiosity, a hopeful shyness, like it had always wanted to say hello, but had only just built up the courage. My heart ached. I felt myself falling in love after one word.

- Hello, I said, but the word didn't come out of my mouth. I heard Osmo's thought like an echo of mine. We both knelt down.

- He needs our help, said Sal's mind.

- He? asked Osmo's, beating me to it. We were speaking telepathically, as if it was the most natural thing in the world.

- Well, he's not a he or a she, but I'm not calling him 'it', she stated firmly.

It seemed a bit rude to be discussing the creature as if it wasn't there, but this issue of 'it' or 'he' or 'she' seemed important. I was aware of the alien observing this exchange closely. Osmo and I quickly agreed with Sal. Its mind was more feminine than masculine, but there was just no getting over those muscles.

- Okay, said Osmo.

- Yeah, I said. *He* it is. I looked at the alien and gave a little shrug. Sorry.

- It's okay, George.

He knew my name. I guessed he could know anything he wanted to know about me. All he had to do was look inside me.

- What's your name? asked Sal.

- My name?

He seemed to stop, like a film on pause. His golden gaze lost its focus, became empty and lifeless. A moment passed, and another, until I began to think we might all remain like that forever, just waiting. Suddenly his shoulders twitched and he grasped at the ground as if he were falling. I had a sudden sensation of falling myself, like when I'm almost asleep sometimes and the world seems to be pulled out from under me. There was a great darkness out beyond the light somewhere, just out of sight. It was yawning like a bottomless well, calling me. A nameless terror reached out and gripped my heart and I wanted to scream something to make me wake up, a spell that I knew didn't exist. I was going to be lost forever. Then he took a big gulp of air and shook his head and the feeling cascaded away into the night. We all looked at each other with haunted eyes.

- **What the hell was that?** asked Osmo, his thoughts like window shards. The alien breathed deeply and seemed to recover.

- **I'm sorry. Forgive me. I'm not used to your minds. Bathing in your thoughts is a rich experience. It's a little overwhelming. And I am not well. I will try to maintain my equilibrium.**

We didn't recover immediately. The memory of that boiling blackness wasn't easy to shake off. Sal was first.

- **That's okay**, she said: calm, soothing, motherly. **It's okay.**

This had a tremendous effect on him. He sat up straighter, his thoughts radiating solidity. He gave Sal thanks, poured a golden waterfall of heartfelt gratitude over her until she seemed to glow from within like him.

- **Hey, don't sweat it**, she said with a wink. I couldn't believe how cool she was.

He told us his name, but it was more of a feeling than a word. It was like a slow river filling a deep pool with heavy water…and round, yellow hills, somehow. There was a scent on a breeze in there too. It reminded me of antiseptic cream. I realised suddenly that he hadn't been speaking to us in English at all. He was transferring knowledge directly into our minds. We were translating his thoughts into English, out of the habit of thinking in that language, I suppose. But there is no English word that his name could be translated into. We could think his name, form its essence in our minds and repeat it back to him, but we couldn't turn it into a word.

- **Would you like to give me a name in your language?**

I shrugged.

- **We may as well call you by your real name.**

- **I would like you to give me a name in your language.** There was a significance to this that escaped me.

- **How about 'Fred'?** said Osmo.

Somehow the alien knew this was funny and burst into a kind of mental laughter that was a stream, sparkling with diamonds, washing through our minds. Everything about him was like light and water.

I suddenly felt a bolt of inspiration.

- **What about Milton?**

- **Milton?** asked Sal and Osmo together.

- One of my poets.

They both pouted unenthusiastically.

- **I like it**, said the alien. I knew he had dipped into my mind and absorbed my knowledge of Milton's poetry, small as it was, and the meaning it had for me here in this situation. **Thank you, George.**

Sal still wasn't convinced.

- **I was hoping for something a bit more science-fictiony. Something like, I don't know...'Nebulon'!**

- **Hey, that sounds pretty cool**, said Osmo. **That could be his first name. Nebulon Milton!**

This started the alien off laughing again. I don't know why but I was amazed he had such a good sense of humour.

- **No. 'Marvin Milton' is better**, said Pee's thoughts.

- **Pee!** we all shouted.

He had crept up quietly and the alien had allowed him to listen in on our mind-talk.

- **I like that**, said the alien. **But we should make it one word I think, with two capital ems: 'MarvinMilton'. Then you will never confuse me with the other Milton, or the other Marvin, by only calling me by one of my names.**

Pee had chosen 'Marvin' because of Hitchhiker's Guide to the Galaxy, of course. Pee wasn't a big reader but Sal's mum had given him the radio series on CD for Christmas, and his favourite character was Marvin the paranoid android.

We shuffled sideways on our knees to make a gap for him. He walked out of the darkness and knelt down in the welcoming glow like somebody joining a campfire in a desolate place.

- **Hello, Pee**, said MarvinMilton. Pee blinked bravely, but being less used to affectionate feelings than the rest of us he couldn't stop the two thin lines of tears from stretching down his face. They glittered in the light like they were veined with gold, but he didn't sniff, and he didn't look away very much either.

- Hello, MarvinMilton, he thought.

Osmo patted him on the back, then turned to the alien.

- So what's happening, MarvinMilton?

MarvinMilton seemed to brace himself. A little wave of sadness then, and I knew instinctively there was more where that came from. There was a strange, far away tremor of the blackness we had felt. It seemed to rumble over a vast distance from somewhere inside him. With a slight grimace of discomfort he suppressed it, and it was gone. He held up the sphere.

- **This is a monodreme.**

For some reason he didn't speak the word 'monodreme' in his own mind-language. It came straight to us as a word we could say out loud, or spell, in English: no capital letter, as if the word was too fundamental to need one.

- If you are willing this is what will happen: we will wrap it in George's coat. We will wrap it up tight so that no light can escape. You will have to finish the wrapping for me because as soon as the last ray of light is blocked out I will die, and you will have a task to perform.

MarvinMilton paused there. I don't think any of us were surprised. Somehow it seemed inevitable. Looking down on this small, naked figure, lying motionless beneath an alien sky far from his home, it was clear that, no matter how much light he radiated, he wasn't going to last long. Sal started to cry, even though she wasn't surprised.

I suddenly felt old. My insides trembled. Of course it had been too good to be true. But I didn't know if I was ready to lose something so good so soon after I'd found it.

We sat there and absorbed the impact of MarvinMilton's words. There was no use questioning them because they weren't really words. They were facts, hard and definite, being inserted into our knowing.

- So what's this task, then?

Osmo was just as affected as the rest of us, but he was also the least sentimental. I already knew he was better equipped to ignore his own pain than we were.

- The task is simple. MarvinMilton paused, almost unable to go on. The darkness seemed to be rushing in again, gathering into a wave of sheer black force, intent on sweeping us away into a cold, endless nothingness. It surrounded us completely, just beyond the circle of light, but somehow MarvinMilton was holding it back, keeping it from touching us. I was shocked that such a serene being could experience such a horror. Then I realised that it was there constantly, always on the edge of his awareness, that he was shielding us from it all the time, with every drop of his strength. Only sometimes his strength faltered and we caught a glimpse, just the merest glimpse. Sal put a hand out and touched his arm lightly, and he looked up at her and rallied again. The task is simple, but it could still go wrong very easily, in so many different ways. It is of the greatest importance that it doesn't go wrong.

As I say, there could be no misunderstanding MarvinMilton. We knew right down to our very bones, there and then, that we had to do this task, and we had to get it right. The consequences of any mistake would be terrible beyond anything we could imagine. He placed this knowledge inside us like a boulder.

As you finish wrapping the monodreme in George's coat you must take care not to touch it with your bare skin. Those of you that are wearing gloves should not trust them to give you the protection you need. The weave of the wool isn't tight enough to guarantee your safety. When the monodreme is sealed in the coat, and I am dead, you must take it away and hide it. I think Sal's bedroom will be best, if you can get it there without arousing the suspicion of Sal's mum. Place the monodreme, still in the coat, into your old leather suitcase, Sal. Lock the suitcase. Hide it under your bed. Your mother is not the sort of person to go through your things without your permission, so it will be as safe there, for a short length of time, as anywhere else I can think of. Once it's safely under the bed you must all save up what money you can, until you have enough for two of you, I suggest Osmo and George, to take a trip on a ferry. You will have to find out the details of this yourself. Plan it carefully, so that nobody is worried about your whereabouts. Take Sal's suitcase, with the monodreme and George's coat still inside, and drop it into the sea when you are half way into your journey. Make sure nobody sees you do this. The suitcase will sink quickly. I'm afraid you will not see your suitcase again, Sal, and you will not see your coat again, George, and none of you will see the money you have saved again. I need you to sacrifice these things.

Once the suitcase has been dropped into the sea, and you are confident that nobody has seen it, your adventure will be over.

MarvinMilton allowed a dramatic pause there. It was a great adventure, but we would go un-rewarded. We had to understand that. Once it was over our lives would be as ordinary as ever. There would be no keepsakes to remind us of the time we met an alien. In short we had to be grown-up about this.

From the moment the monodreme's light is sealed inside George's coat you must not look at it again. The coat stays sealed. And once the coat and the monodreme are sealed inside Sal's suitcase the suitcase is locked and stays locked - no opening it up for one last peek before you get rid of it. This is of the greatest importance.

As I say, this is a simple enough task, but there is a great deal that could go wrong along the way. The responsibility I'm offering you is enormous. You must understand that. You don't have to accept it. You can say no. I can find somebody else to do it. You must decide between yourselves, and your decision must be unanimous. If one of you is not willing then I will move on. I will not blame you or resent you for deciding not to accept the task. I will applaud your honesty, to yourself and to me. I want you to take the time to think about it carefully. Ask what questions you need to. Don't rush into a decision. I have speeded up time within the reach of the light. Outside, in the night, the world is moving so slowly it is almost at a dead stop compared to us. We have this time together. There is no need for haste.

- I don't need any time, said Sal almost immediately. I know what my answer is, and all the time in the world won't change it. I accept.

One down, three to go, already. Osmo turned to her.

- Sal, you really are the queen of cool. I bow before you.

She nodded.

Osmo turned back to MarvinMilton and frowned.

- I've got to ask this.

MarvinMilton smiled.

- Why is the monodreme so dangerous? And seeing as it is so dangerous, why are you going to trust us to take care of it? Osmo pointed to either side of himself, indicating the four of us: not exactly children anymore, but a good distance from being capable, confident adults.

- The monodreme is so incredibly dangerous that the difference between an adult, a child or a young teenager almost pales into insignificance. Faced with the enormity of the danger held within the monodreme the oldest, wisest, most responsible adult in the world would be as capable of using his or her judgement as a newborn baby.

There are a lot of people on this planet I would not trust this task with, for one reason or another, but there is *nobody* I can trust one hundred percent. I touched down in this area by random chance. I have chosen to offer this task to you because I have looked into your minds and decided that a gamble on you is as good a gamble as I'm going to get. I'm putting my trust in what we are sharing right now. It's not that you are more special than anybody else on Earth. There are many that could offer me something just as good, just as rewarding. But there is nobody - adult or child - that can offer me more. I will put my faith in the bond we have formed. It will be enough or it won't. But I can't continue with this burden any longer.

Our heads were swimming. MarvinMilton paused and smiled mercifully, and sent a thought that was like a refreshing breeze through our minds, blowing away the cobwebs and revitalising our spirits. I smelt the scent of mountain top airs, morning meadows and turning tides. It was a world I could lose myself in, except it purified my thoughts so perfectly that I was acutely awake, effortlessly aware of everything around me. We stirred and looked at each other with bright eyes. It was so good to see each other like that. Darkness, all darkness, seemed a distant memory. He continued, knowing that we couldn't be more ready, more able, to hear every single nuance of what he had to say.

As for 'why is the monodreme so dangerous?' I'm not going to tell you. To tell you would be to make it even more dangerous. What you need to know is that it is terrible and that the worst thing that could happen is that you or anybody else should touch it with your bare skin. If I give you the details of what the monodreme does I will be turning it into even more of a Pandora's Box than it is already. And believe me, it *is* Pandora's Box. Your choice is simple: keep it sealed and safe from contact with any living person or unleash the evils of the universe into your world. It sounds melodramatic, but it is no exaggeration.

- Where did it come from? I asked.

- Irrelevant. Try not to be curious about it. And if you can't stop yourself from forming questions about it then the least you must do is resign yourself to never having answers for them. Everything depends on your self-control, all four of you. You must be cool, detached, uninterested in anything but achieving the objective of getting the monodreme into the sea - if you choose to accept the task.

- Well, I know that I'm going to accept, said Osmo. But I'd like to carry on talking about it though. I mean, if we're frozen in time anyway, more or less, I'd quite like to stretch this out, you know. He smiled a tight thin smile and I thought sentiment was going to get the better of him for a moment, that he wouldn't be able to continue. I'm not exactly in a hurry to say goodbye, you know.

- Thank you, Osmo.

Two down, two to go. Then Sal's thoughts rose up.

- The monodreme has given you the power to reach here, and it's keeping you alive, but it's also doing something bad?

I thought that she had been quiet. She had been doing more of that deep thinking she was renowned for.

- Sal, I know I can't stop you from thinking about this, but I'm not willing to give you information that will cause more harm than good. Please respect this decision.

- I'm sorry. I don't mean to be pushy. It's just I can't help wondering if it's really necessary for you to die. If the monodreme's got enough power to keep you alive, and bring you all the way here, isn't there some way we can separate the part of it which does good stuff like that from the part of it that you're afraid of?

- No. The monodreme does not have separate parts. It is a single whole that cannot be divided. The best we can hope for is that it will lie out of reach until the sun destroys this planet in millions of years time, and that it then becomes part of a black hole. The chances of that happening here are quite good. It is the best chance I've been able to find.

- Why don't you drop it in the sea yourself, or in a black hole for that matter?

Sal's imagination was alight. I could see that she wanted to understand – not simply because of curiosity but through a desire to be equal to MarvinMilton. She wanted to be fully developed, fully evolved, to have the mind, the aspirations, of an angel.

- Sal! MarvinMilton's head flopped back. He jerked it back to look at her, but his gaze seemed to slide away from her face and into the night. His muscles spasmed suddenly, making his entire body go rigid. The remains of the wall crumbled still further beneath him. Sal! And his voice was filled with, I don't know. Anguish. But that word isn't enough, nowhere near. I felt him struggle to master something. With a horrendous flex of willpower he managed to find his voice again. I'm not good enough Sal. I am weak. That is all. I cannot let go of it on my own. I don't have the strength. I don't have the spirit. I'm just not good enough.

Sal stared at MarvinMilton, aghast at the pain she seemed to have triggered in him, horrified by the strength he needed to force it back. She bowed her head, ashamed, face crumpling, shoulders shaking.

- I'm so sorry.

- Don't be sorry, Sal - any of you. Being here with you will enable me to let go. It is through your presence, your strength, through your sanity, that I will be set free. Accept that, as poor an explanation as it is. To give you too much detail is to endanger you more than I am doing already. I won't have that on my conscience as I die.

- Okay, MarvinMilton, said Sal. Of course I'll help. I'm sorry I pushed you.

- No apologies are necessary. If anybody should be sorry it's me. This has all come about because of my actions. But I am not sorry. There's no purpose in sorrow for me anymore. Instead I will take two of your English words with me as I go: 'I accept'.

MarvinMilton turned to Pee.

- **No,** he said, flatly, calmly, without hesitation. A stunned silence.

- **But, Pee…** said Sal, forlorn.

- **Come on, Pee…** said Osmo, not believing his ears.

- **No,** said Pee again, simply. **Not unless…I get a kiss…from…** he pointed his finger, swung it round to Sal, paused and then moved it on to Osmo. **…Osmo!**

Pee giggled hysterically at our stricken faces. **Oh, you poor babies! Go on then, I suppose I accept.**

I couldn't believe it. The kid had no respect for anything. Osmo called Pee something unsavoury.

- **We absolutely can't take you anywhere!**

Pee hugged himself and fluttered his eyelashes.

- **Thank you darling. The pleasure was all mine!** Then he laughed hysterically and twitched as though he'd eaten too much sugar. What a time for him to revert to his usual mode of behaviour. MarvinMilton smiled a slow, deep smile but didn't seem to have the energy to laugh.

- **Pee!** hissed Sal, incredulous.

- **So sorry,** sighed Pee, and he flopped onto his back and giggled helplessly for a good minute and a half.

Eventually he settled down and they all turned to me.

- **No,** I said, and they could tell I wasn't joking.

3
Goodbye MarvinMilton

Gravity cannot be held responsible for people falling in love.
- Albert Einstein

- But George, said Sal, why?

I shifted uncomfortably.

- It's just too much responsibility. What? The safety of the whole universe! Us four?

They stared at me, disbelieving.

- Come on, George, said Osmo in a whiny voice. Don't be such a coward.

- Nice, Osmo. Thanks. I suppose letting you bully me into saying yes would make me brave?

- No, he coughed indignantly. Doing the right thing might though.

- We'll mess it up. You know we will. Let MarvinMilton find someone sensible and reliable. I mean, don't you think we kind of owe it to the rest of the universe?

- I can't believe this! 'Find someone sensible and reliable'! Have you forgot what planet we're on?

- Look, I'm sorry. I know you want to be a hero and everything...

- A hero! Well, I suppose if doing the decent thing makes you a hero, then yeah, I do. You can sue me.

- Osmo...

- Hold on, hold on! cried Sal, sticking her palms in our faces. Pee was watching us with wide eyes. MarvinMilton was watching us calmly. Cool it Osmo, and she turned to me. She put her hands on my arms and looked carefully into my face like I was a little kid who needed to have something explained to him very carefully. George, Osmo's right about one thing. Who else can be trusted with this? You know how stupid everybody is. That's why you don't like it when the news is on. Remember? If MarvinMilton's prepared to put his trust in us who else is he likely to settle for? This is our chance to make sure the least stupid people we know of get to have a go, instead of some crazy people.

She was making a lot of sense. I struggled not to weaken, but it was nice having her touching me and talking to me like that.

- 'Least stupid people we know of?' Have you forgot about Pee? No offence, Pee.

Pee shook his head philosophically. He didn't trust himself either.

- Well, yeah, sure, we'll keep an eye on Pee. But, George, don't put our fate in somebody else's hands.

She said it with such a deliberately solemn, pretty face. I felt my own face twist in anguish as my defences began to sidle away casually into the night.

- Sal, what are you doing to me?

She suppressed a smile and started to stroke my left ear.

- Come on, George, she said softly. You know it makes sense.

- I don't know, I mumbled. Maybe.

- Huh, said Osmo, shaking his head coolly. I should have tried that.

•

- What should we do with your body? asked Sal.

- Leave it here. It will be found and it may cause a sensation. That's not important. Your mission is the one and only importance.

Once the monodreme is sealed in the coat go directly to Sal's house. If anybody asks tell them you hung around the streets and the cemetery for a while before walking Sal home. Keep it simple. There shouldn't be any connection between any of you and the appearance of an alien body here.

- It doesn't seem right, to just leave you here, said Osmo.

- It is right, Osmo. It is the only right thing to do. By doing it you will be taking care of all the living everywhere. And by doing as I ask, leaving immediately, you will be honouring me and my memory.

- Okay, said Osmo quietly.

Sal nodded.

- We'll do a good job, MarvinMilton.

- I know you will.

•

After that we talked – about other things. We asked MarvinMilton what his home was like. He fed knowledge of his home world into our minds, and we were as good as there, experiencing it with his emotions, his own nostalgia. We could smell the air, feel the breeze on our faces. A specific rock or field or waterfall would haunt us like a memory from an old sunken dream. We found ourselves longing to return to a place we'd never been.

We stood on rocky desert plains, and we could feel the density of the planet beneath our bare feet that were now broad and flat like MarvinMilton's. We felt the crushing weight of the atmosphere pulled down onto our broad, muscular shoulders by the powerful gravity, and we understood why MarvinMilton was the shape he was. Only something as squat and strong as he was would be able to get out of bed in the morning in this place.

He asked us to give his homeworld an English name so that we could talk about it after he'd gone. Sal was really struck by the huge single ocean that dominates the planet. She suggested 'Oceana'. It seemed to fit perfectly. MarvinMilton loved it.

We asked to see some of his people. Did they live in big cities like New York? Did they travel in flying cars? But he said he didn't want to show us any of his people or how they lived. It would give us clues about the monodreme, he said. This made us intensely curious, which he picked up on straight away.

- **Let it go**, he breathed. So we let it go.

We stayed there for about twelve hours while the world back home held its breath, waiting for our return. We invented names for animals and all of the planets in Oceana's solar system. We named its sun 'Los', which is 'Sol' backwards. This seemed a bit sad, it sounding like 'loss', but MarvinMilton thought it added something poetic.

He delighted in our company during this virtual tour. I got the feeling that by seeing his home world through the eyes of four British teenagers he was discovering it again for himself.

We didn't get any more glimpses of the darkness that we knew was surrounding him, waiting for its moment to come, when it would close in and snuff out his light like a black ocean dousing a match. But during all of our mind sharing we were always aware of a little knot of his self-control that he kept clenched tight and apart from us. We knew it contained all of his secrets, but by now we had learned to tactfully ignore it. And MarvinMilton's gratitude for this was worth all the secrets of the universe.

- **Do you believe in an afterlife?** asked Sal.

For the first time he seemed stumped. It felt like a long time before he spoke.

- **I don't know**, he said. **Perhaps the memories that this body has stored will wink out when my body shuts down. But the universe may remember me, remember the things I did, after my body has forgotten. Is that like carrying on? Is it another kind of life? I don't know.**

Sal frowned.

- **So you don't believe in a soul then?**

- **A soul? A soul that has my name and essence attached to it? A little ego that refuses to die? I don't know.**

Sal chewed on that silently. We suddenly knew that we were almost out of time. We had named enough things.

We shared a silent moment then, where we didn't exchange any more conversational thoughts. We just looked through each other's eyes straight into our communal soul, blissed out in the glorious golden sorrow of preparing to say goodbye when we'd barely begun to say hello.

It's a funny thing, sharing a telepathy like that – and difficult to describe. It's like being in a hall of mirrors. You're looking into different reflections of yourself, but each reflection is at a slightly different angle. You can barely tell where one person ends and you begin. Pee, Sal, Osmo, even MarvinMilton himself, they looked like me, looking back at myself, laughing in their eyes as if to say 'what am I doing over there?' Before that night I would never have volunteered for telepathy. Who needs somebody else snuffling about inside your mind, seeing all your faults and weaknesses, your most embarrassing thoughts? But, thankfully, details like my most embarrassing thoughts, my secret crush on Sal for instance, were not visible to the others unless I consciously projected them. But our emotions blurred into each other. And I don't know if MarvinMilton made it that way, or if it's just a natural thing, but right then our emotions were all about wonder and joy and loving each other. It sounds pretty squishy, but we didn't have to be embarrassed about anything. We were what we felt, and we all felt the same thing.

I loved it.

MarvinMilton looked into us and tried to soak up every last crumb of knowledge about what it felt like to be us, to have lived our lives. It was almost as though, now that he knew he was about to die, he wanted to experience as much life as possible – anybody's life, even four kids from Banford. I guess at the end of the day life is life.

He asked us to take him on virtual tours of our worlds, in our minds, just as he had shown us his. I took him out onto the streets of Banford and showed him the pavements, wet with rain, lit by orange streetlight. We stood by shop windows and bus shelters, smelt the chips and pies of the Openshaw Fish Bar, watched headlights tinged with blue moving down Rigby Street, kids flipping their skateboards in the college car park, heard the sound of sirens warbling down Salford Road and the cry of a gull that had followed the canal inland, felt the vibration of the Number 36 from the top deck as it wended its way home from town, tasted Mars bars outside Chigley's News, and let Coke-Cola bubbles fizz on our tongues, went inside to slouch on the sofa and watch telly late into the night, drinking Dad's beer, trying to make the weekend last forever.

I showed him my bedroom and what it is like to stay up into the small hours of a Wednesday playing Homeworld on the PC. He saw my alarm clock in vivid detail, down to every last scratch, my bedside cupboard and the dark tacky patch where I had peeled a Spiderman sticker off because I was trying to make my room look more grown-up. He saw a small, poorly painted space marine terminator standing dead centre in a coffee ring amidst a landscape of bootleg CDs, frozen in mid-step, assault canon idling casually at his side, wondering how he'd got there. He saw the texture of the wallpaper, four little stains where four tiny balls of Blue Tac had held a postcard of Felix the Cat. A hundred details.

He felt the exact sleepy bewilderment that I felt whenever I saw the screensaver come on and gradually realised that Sal had managed to change it, yet again, without me noticing. And he felt all of the subtle shades of my furious admiration at seeing the words 'GEORGE IS A PANTY PAD' trek slowly across the screen.

I love living in the modern world.

So MarvinMilton saw us. And he saw how we saw ourselves. He saw that I am pompous and arrogant and completely insecure, all at the same time. He saw that Sal is a weird humanist girl who's totally irritated by humanity. He saw that Osmo should rightfully be one of the popular kids in school but had decided to hang around with the half-geek-half-cool kids for some reason. He saw that Pee, with his scrawny body and his big wet eyes, was some kind of street urchin from a Dickens novel – the kind that always dies early on in the story. Poor old Pee, youngest boy in the year – he was always the last one in everything. He wasn't even fourteen yet.

And MarvinMilton saw that our favourite superheroes are:

Me – The Incredible Hulk or The Thing

Osmo – Spawn or Cerebus

Sal – Tank Girl or Peppermint Patty

Pee – Homer Simpson or Nigella Lawson (she can save him with the kiss of life and then make him a pie)

He saw how we looked after each other, and how we loved Christine, Sal's mum, who was our beautiful grown-up friend who took us on trips in her beaten up old Saab and told us tales of being young and wild, and who was divorced, and how we had vowed to protect her from picking unsuitable boyfriends. He saw all of the weird ordinariness of our little lives and how they overlapped with each other.

Poor old MarvinMilton saw it all.

•

When the time came I took my coat off. MarvinMilton wrapped the monodreme in it until the lights were all out of sight except for one beam that he kept directed at himself. His lifeline.

- The time has come, friends. He had wrapped the monodreme in such a way that the sleeves of my coat were left loose, one on either side. His hands were shaking. We felt the fear bubbling inside him like it was our own. **Who will finish the job for me?**

- Well, it's my coat, I started.

- No, let me do it, said Sal urgently. **I want to do it.**

Well, she was the one who had stayed after we'd all run away.

- Thank you, Sal, said MarvinMilton. **I accept.** Then he began to cry suddenly, and I thought my heart would break. **Please**, he said, **hurry**.

The moment was unreal, one of those moments that you have anticipated so much that when it finally arrives you're expecting it to be familiar and you're surprised it's actually a stranger. We all became disconnected then as we braced ourselves. MarvinMilton withdrew his mind. The light was about to go out.

Pee's face was white and pained. He said goodbye to MarvinMilton and turned his back. Me and Osmo stayed as we were, offering our smiles, thin as they were, for MarvinMilton's comfort. Sal had to look down in order to tie my coat sleeves into a knot. The last ray of light was gone. She looked up quickly to catch what she could of MarvinMilton's fleeing spirit but he was dead already. His body had slumped like a puppet whose strings have been cut, the moment the touch of the light had left his body. It was over just like that.

She hadn't been expecting it to be so sudden. I couldn't see her expression because my eyes needed time to adjust to the sudden darkness, but I could see the tension in her silhouette. She made a noise that sounded like something small inside her was being crushed.

"Oh god," I said, but Osmo was moving. He was braced and ready, businesslike even. He stood up, lifting the monodreme in the coat and tucking it under his arm.

"George, bring Sal," he said in a clipped voice. He clapped Pee on the back. Pee jumped as if he'd had cold water thrown in his face, and he jerked to his feet. "Come on, Pee," and Osmo was striding away. I was glad he was so galvanised, so able to squash his emotions down. We needed that.

"Come on, Sal," I said, guiding her to her feet and turning her away from MarvinMilton.

I cast a last look at him as I walked her away. He looked ghoulish and fake, a hoax alien made of wax, left by pranksters. Now the golden light was gone from his eyes he looked more like a grotesque gargoyle than an angel. I turned away with a shudder and urged Sal to pick up the pace. We hurried back into our world of dirty orange lamplight.

•

We didn't see anybody until we reached Rigby Street. We didn't see anybody at all that would recognise us.

"What shall we say to your mum, Sal?" asked Osmo, breaking the silence on Henry Street.

"We don't need to say anything." She sounded okay. A bit emotionless, but okay. "We can go straight upstairs. She probably won't even see us."

"Well, that's cool," said Osmo, "but I think we should prepare something to say, just in case she does see us. I mean poor old George here is shivering like crazy and we're holding something rolled up in his coat. She might have a question or two about that."

"If she asks what's in the coat I'll just tell her it's secret kids' stuff and she'll humour me. We just need to be brazen. Keep it simple, like Marvin said." She caught herself immediately. "I mean MarvinMilton."

Her head slumped forward in utter dejection. I put my arm around her for a while, but then I had to let go so I could stomp around and hug myself. I was freezing. She rubbed my back a couple of times in sympathy but then retreated into her gloom again.

A fog of silence hung around us as we walked. I allowed myself to sink into the pit of unhappiness that was lying at the bottom of my stomach. My mind began to fill with cold paving slabs. They scrolled by beneath my feet and accumulated in untidy piles in the back of my head where the wind could blow through them. They mounted higher and higher until they were pressing hard right-angle corners against the interior of my skull. Then they pressed forward until all that was behind my eyes was a dense world of dismantled paving. It wasn't until we turned onto Sal's road that I roused myself a little and noticed that my face was wet with tears. I caught Osmo looking sideways at me. He looked away quickly, but then seemed to reconsider and looked back again and held my gaze for a moment.

•

We were at the foot of Sal's stairs when Christine came out of the kitchen.
"Hello, you lot."
"Hello," we chimed dutifully, trying to inject a bit of perk into our voices. Osmo was the most successful at this. He had a habit of flirting with Christine. I must admit I had a bit of a crush on her myself.
"Hiya, Mum," said Sal, not bothering with the perk.
"What have you all been up to?"
"Secret kids' stuff," we all droned together. We followed Sal up the stairs as if we were linked by chains.
"You can tell me. I'm young at heart."
We continued to shuffle upwards.
"Thanks, Mum," droned Sal, nicely conveying that cheerful banter was not required at this time.
"George, you look freezing! Where's your coat?"
I shrugged plaintively, not really wanting to give her the cold shoulder.
"Secret kids' stuff," I mumbled. I pulled a bemused face and nodded up the stairs at the rest of the chain gang to indicate that I was humouring them as best I could.
"Oh yeah", she said, and she looked a bit rejected. "I've heard about that." But she turned away and left us to it.
"Okay," said Osmo when we were in Sal's room, "where's your suitcase?"
She pulled it out from beneath her bed. It was old, scuffed, medium-sized but nice and deep. She set the combination on the lock and opened it. Inside were six diaries and a bunch of notebooks and sketchbooks, all of Sal's secret writings and doodles. That morning they probably would have rated

as sacred objects, now she hefted them out and piled them untidily against a wall until the case was empty. Osmo knelt down and placed our special bundle inside. He screwed up his face, not really happy, while I pulled Sal's quilt off the bed and wrapped it around me urgently.

"We could do with packing out the corners with something."

"Yeah," said Sal. She looked tired. "Some scrunched up newspaper."

"Yeah."

"I'll bring some up from downstairs later."

She closed the case and locked it, then slid it back out of sight before clambering onto her bed and flopping there with glazed eyes. I sat down on the floor and let myself keel over. I just wanted to lie there and be warm, maybe pass out a bit.

"Is everybody okay?" Osmo seemed unsure of himself suddenly, now the immediate need for action had passed.

Sal stared at nothing. Pee sat by the pile of diaries and poked them distractedly.

"I think we probably just need a rest," I mumbled from my cocoon.

"Right. I'll...er, I'll...I think some tea would do us good. I'll get us some tea."

I heard him leave the room. My gaze fell on the carpet by my face. It was thick and soft and dark. From this vantage it reminded me of a forest seen from above, or a rainforest, perhaps. I thought of American helicopters flying over the jungles of Vietnam. My eyelids grew heavy and I imagined myself dropping from my helicopter to be swallowed into the depths of the secretive foliage below. I had a jungle dream, but then I woke to the sound of a phone ringing. I didn't know where I was for a moment, and the details of the dream disappeared into the darkness of the room. A small constellation of glow-in-the-dark stars speckled a nearby wall, and I realised I was back at home in my own bed.

•

My mind stalled. I gazed blankly around the dark room. It felt late. The phone was ringing. At last I had a thought. I decided that whatever was going on I didn't like it. I should go back to sleep and face it, or not, in the morning, bright-eyed and bushy-tailed. *Yes,* I agreed, *that's a good plan.* But instead I lay there on my back, staring into the dark. I didn't even have the motivation to turn over and go to sleep. I lay like a zombie that didn't remember who it had been.

Who could be ringing this late? I could see the silhouette of my clock but I'd have to turn on the lamp if I wanted to check the time. *Do I want to know the time?* I asked myself. *No. Go back to sleep.*

My hand snaked out from beneath my quilt and up to the lamp and turned it on anyway, without even checking with me for permission. I blinked stupidly in the sudden glare until I could make out the time: 2:32am. *Must be serious.*

I lay there listening to the distant but relentless ringing of the phone until my body suddenly clambered out of bed without warning. *Maybe I'm still lying on Sal's floor. Maybe I'm dreaming this.* I staggered woodenly to the door. *It feels like a dream.*

I emerged onto the landing just as Dad was doing the same.

"Shall I get it?" I asked groggily.

"Yes," he said, with a frown like a thundercloud, and he closed the door on me. *Charming. I hope it's for him.*

I was sure it would stop ringing before I reached it, probably at the last moment. But whoever it was did seem persistent. I slumped into the big, old armchair in the back room and kicked the door shut so my voice wouldn't carry upstairs. I lifted the receiver.

"Hello."

"George…"

Sal's voice. Something wrong. I waited for her to continue but she didn't. I heard her sniffling, crying maybe.

"What is it, Sal? What's up?"

"I'm going to touch it, George!"

"What?"

"You've got to come. Come and stop me. Please, George. You've got to be quick."

She sounded a bit mad. My mind was moving at a snail's pace.

"You're going to touch what?" As I asked the question the answer provided itself. *The monodreme. She's going to touch the monodreme. It's real. Either that or I really am dreaming. How did I get home?*

"The monodreme, George. The monodreme."

"I don't understand, Sal. I'm still asleep. Why are you going to touch the monodreme?"

"I opened the case. I was going to pack the corners with newspaper. There's a gap in the coat, some of the light's shining out. It's so lovely. It's so amazing. I don't want it to go away. It wants me to touch it. It doesn't want to go to the bottom of the sea."

"Sal…MarvinMilton, don't you remember what he said? Close the case, Sal, for God's sake."

"I can't. You've got to come and help me. You don't understand. It's like he said. He couldn't get rid of it on his own, not while the light was shining. He needed to be with somebody. I can't do it on my own either. You've got to come now or the mission will be over."

My mind was picking up speed at last but I realised there wasn't anything to think about.

"Just try to hang on, okay? I'll be as quick as I can. Can you hold on?"

"I'll try."

33

"Okay. Do your best. I'm coming now."

I put the receiver down, sat there for a heartbeat as MarvinMilton's words came back to me – **Your choice is simple: keep it sealed and safe from contact with any living person, or unleash the evils of the universe into your world.** I swore in the dark and got myself moving.

I couldn't allow myself to rush too much while I was inside the house; a lengthy explanation to my dad about how the safety of the world depended on me slipping out to Sal's house at half past two in the morning would not help matters. I crept upstairs and grabbed my jeans from the bedroom floor, pulled on my trainers and slipped back downstairs again. This was the most painfully slow part of the operation. I was excruciatingly aware that every moment could be one too many. Once downstairs I picked up speed. I pulled on one of Dad's coats and closed the front door behind me quietly, then I was off. I sprinted lightly down the path and vaulted the gate. Leaning into my patented middle-distance pace I felt the cold suburban air clear my head at last.

What am I supposed to do when I get there? What will I say if her mum wakes up? What will I do if Sal has touched the monodreme? Stop asking all of these questions. That's what Osmo would say. Don't think, just keep moving. *Sal should have called him,* I thought as a vision filled my mind of me arriving at her house to find giant, black tentacles wriggling out of the windows and the front door, heralding the dawn of a new age of evil.

Maybe MarvinMilton should have given us a few tips – what we could do if the worst did happen – but then I realised that he would have done that if there was anything we could do. His lack of advice meant that if I did arrive to find Sal holding the monodreme in her hands then that was that, I might as well go back home and go to bed and stay there for all the difference I was going to make. It would at best mean 'The End'. At worst it would mean a horrible new beginning. This was what scared me most: what kind of catastrophe would it be? Would it be painful? I didn't want it to be painful. I could handle the world blowing up, just as long as it didn't hurt.

I turned the corner that brought me out halfway down Pengorse Road. I could see Sal's house at the end of the row opposite. All seemed quiet. No tentacles. As I drew closer I noticed that Sal's bedroom window was dark. That had to be a good sign. If the monodreme were uncovered her room would be lit up like the sun was rising in there. I felt something like relief.

I opened the gate slowly and crept round to the side of the house. I spent a few moments gathering small stones to throw at her window, but when I straightened up she was standing there looking down at me. She lifted the window and leant out. She looked pretty normal.

"Thanks for coming," she hissed.

"That's okay," I hissed back. "Are you alright?"

"You're probably going to be really angry, but I'm okay now."

I looked at her blankly. How could she be okay? I flapped my arms at my sides uselessly.

"You are?"

"Yeah, I'm sorry. I just got panicky. I've closed the case now. It's back under my bed."

I scratched my head and scrunched up my face. Nonplussed, I think the word is.

"I thought you couldn't do it on your own."

"I knew you'd be angry."

"I'm not angry, I'm just trying to understand."

"I know, I'm sorry. I didn't think I could do it on my own. It's just because I was panicking. It's hard to describe. I think that talking to you, and knowing that you were on your way over, helped me to calm down. I'm alright now. You should go back home, George. Thanks for coming though. I really appreciate it. I knew I could depend on you. You're a mate."

The anticlimax washed over me, unnerving me. I had been ready for tentacles. I almost wished the world was about to be overcome with evil.

"Do you want me to come in for a bit, stay with you for a while?"

"No, honest, I'm fine. We'd just wake Mum up. Thanks though."

"Do you want me to take it back to my house, so you don't get tempted again?"

She hesitated.

"I don't know. It seems a bit risky."

"It might be more risky leaving it where it is," I pointed out. She nodded, recognising her willpower was in question.

"Maybe I could bring it round to yours tomorrow. I don't think we should do it now. I mean, if you get caught roaming around the streets with a suitcase at this time of night – well, it's got to be suspicious, hasn't it? And if my mum catches me throwing suitcases out of my window to you she'll probably think we're trying to elope!"

I smiled ruefully in the dark.

"I suppose so. I'm just worried about you."

"I know. Go on though, really. I'll be okay for the rest of the night, I promise. Go home. I'll see you tomorrow."

I didn't want to go home now. I felt too awake.

"How did I get home?"

"My mum took you. We all fell asleep, even Osmo. She woke you enough to get you down to the car but you were all as good as sleepwalking. She wanted to interrogate me about where we'd all been but I was too groggy to answer her questions. She's worried we've been up to mischief."

I thought of my dad's dark expression on the landing. There were going to be questions asked – something to look forward to.

"I woke up at home and I didn't know where I was."

"Poor old George. Go home and get some sleep."

"I'm wide awake now."

"Well, I'm not. Go on, I'll see you tomorrow."

"It's a funny old do, isn't it?" I said lamely.

"Yeah," she said.

I loitered a moment, to give her the opportunity to change her mind and invite me up to her room to comfort and protect her, but she didn't. She wanted me to go. I turned away, deflated, and made my way back on to the road. As I passed by on the far side of the hedge I heard her voice, small in the night.

"Thanks."

With a wave of my hand I headed off through the quiet streets.

4
Fake Sal and the Runabouts

Sometimes one pays most for the things one gets for nothing.
- Albert Einstein

Dad tended to go to work early, thankfully, so it wasn't too often that we had to put up with his miserable presence at breakfast. All the same, I paused at the foot of the stairs and listened for the telltale rumble from the kitchen that would reveal he had stayed late to grill me over my extreme grogginess and coatlessness the previous night. I heard Mum say something to my sister, Emma, and I knew immediately from her voice that he had gone to work.

I walked into the kitchen, put the kettle on and opened a packet of lemon pancakes. Mum was sitting at the table working on a job application. She stopped what she was doing and watched me, her face completely expressionless.

"Good morning," she said in a specifically neutral tone.

Emma's eyes flicked back and forth between us expectantly.

"Hiya."

I put my pancakes under the grill. Mum waited patiently until I was at the table with my breakfast.

"So?"

One syllable, planted like a lead weight, dead in the centre of the kitchen table. I'd been desperately trying to come up with a plausible explanation for our sleepiness that didn't involve anything that would get us in trouble. There wasn't one. I decided my best bet was to be vague.

"You know, it was really weird," I said. "We all just got really sleepy. I thought we were all coming down with something but I feel fine now. I don't know, I can't explain it." I can be very natural and believable when I lie if I'm ready for it, but Mum just stared at me blankly. "Maybe there's a mouldy lump of cheese under Sal's bed giving off vapours or something." Nothing. "Probably too much homework," I said dismissively. "School stress." Emma shook her head in disbelief at my puny performance.

"You haven't mentioned hypnosis yet," she said unhelpfully. "Or maybe you were drugged and kidnapped by slavers but then they brought you back again because you wouldn't fetch fifty pee between the lot of you."

I actually thought that was quite funny.

"George," Mum said in a horrible, serious voice. "If you're not going to tell me the truth, just don't say anything." She gathered up her stuff and walked out. That was it. It was a bit melodramatic for my tastes but still effective. She knew I was a total sucker for that kind of emotional manipulation. But there was no point in chasing after her and unburdening my soul. The truth just wouldn't have helped. And we had our mission. So I just sat there and felt rotten.

I think my expression became seriously world weary because my big sister sat back in her chair and studied me, and she looked genuinely concerned.

"Have you got trouble?" she asked.

I shook my head in mock surprise.

"You really care about me," I said solemnly.

The concern disappeared from her face and I was instantly sorry I'd said it.

"Up yours," she snarled. She got up and followed Mum.

•

I walked through the streets and I thought of MarvinMilton. I hated it that his body had just been left there, discarded like a piece of broken furniture. I realised that I didn't really care about the suitcase or my coat or the adventure of having a mission. Dropping the monodreme in the sea would just be a way of honouring our lost friend. I missed him. The streets seemed more colourful than they had a right to be on such a morning of mourning. Even the tarmac seemed to contain a million colours. What a miserable world of bricks and stones.

I met up with Osmo and Pee at the main gates to the upper school, and they both looked as blank as I felt. We tucked ourselves out of sight round the side of the canteen to avoid having to speak to anybody. I told them about Sal.

"We should move the case away from her house," said Osmo lethargically.

"Well, don't think of bringing it to mine!" said Pee, nearly jumping out of his skin.

"Cool it, Pee. When, in a million years, would we do something like that?" Osmo pushed his eyebrows up his forehead and endeavoured to look strained and sardonic like Robert De Niro.

"Because I'd open it and touch it straight away," said Pee earnestly. "It wouldn't even be worth me trying to stop myself. If I'm not allowed to touch something then that's it, I can't help myself." Sometimes, when a joke is handed to you on a plate, the cool thing to do is let it pass. Me and Osmo looked at each other and rolled our eyes. I had a go at the De Niro face.

We went to our form rooms. Me and Osmo sat in a corner and tried not to attract attention. Pee was in a different form from us, you know the one. Every year has one that's filled with the most severely brain-cell-challenged kids.

There was no sign of Sal until she finally turned up for her mark just as everybody was filing out.

"Are you trying to give us heart attacks?" I asked her on the way to assembly.

"Sorry. I overslept. Look, I need to talk to you all at lunchtime."

"Lunchtime? We can talk at break."

"No. I need more time than that. Don't bother with the canteen, just get Pee and meet me at the Peacock."

"What do you mean, 'Don't bother with the canteen'?" protested Osmo. "I'm not going to the chippy, it's always packed full of squitty little scum suckers like Stuart Towns's brother!"

"Don't worry about that, food will be provided."

Osmo stopped walking and shook his head as if a fly had flown in his ear.

"Really?"

"Yeah."

"What's going on, Sal?"

"Nothing."

"You didn't touch it did you?"

"No, I didn't. Thank you."

"But you're laying on food so we can talk in private? I don't understand."

"Just be at the Peacock and you'll find out."

"But I'll be dead from suspense by then."

•

I couldn't get it together with my lessons that morning. Miss Banks kept twisting my ear in chemistry for looking off into the distance when I was supposed to be monitoring my solutions. It really hurt too. Nobody messes with Miss Banks. She's got calves of rock from playing squash with Mr. Reynolds. She's very sporty and rather cruel. I always found the best way to deal with her was to be excessively wimpy and plead for mercy at the first sign of aggression. This usually gratified her sadistic streak and got her laughing.

But I didn't feel able to play the clown today. Miss Banks stopped twisting my ear eventually. It just wasn't satisfying her.

"Okay, George," she said reluctantly. "What's the matter with you?"

"Teenage depression, Miss."

She snorted contemptuously, but she left me alone for the rest of the class.

At break I found Pee drinking hot Vimto by the mobile outside the main gates. I told him about the lunchtime rendezvous.

"What does she mean 'food will be provided'?" he wanted to know. "If I don't get my butter pie I won't be good for anything this afternoon!"

"You gimp," I said.

"You chimp," he replied.

•

Next up was a half lesson of religious ed', which felt more like a triple. It was terminally dull but nothing was demanded of me.

I wasn't looking forward to the half of drama. I knew there was no way I'd be able to be animated and participate properly, but it actually turned out okay. We were improvising character studies so I invented a character whose motivation had been surgically removed by the government and then just acted how I really felt. Mr. Whyte described it as a 'compelling performance' and praised my powers of observation. Poor guy.

By the time I was heading for the Peacock I felt like crying. I really didn't care what Sal had to say, but then again I didn't really care about going to the canteen either. It was all the same. Nothing could have much meaning compared to what had happened the previous night. I shuffled along and was the last to arrive at the Peacock. Pee and Osmo were sitting at the foot of the statue that guards the main entrance to the lower school. Sal stood nearby looking edgy. I was surprised that she didn't seem to be affected by the same apathy that me, Osmo and Pee were suffering from. I would have thought she would have had it the worst considering her closeness to MarvinMilton.

"Come on chaps," she said. Maybe it was me but she seemed to be studying us carefully, gauging our mood.

"Where are we going?" asked Osmo.

"The sports centre."

"We're going to the sports centre for a quiet chat?"

"Round the back."

"Oh. And you've got food stashed behind the sports centre?"

"Sort of."

Osmo was looking tense, ready to come unstrung. He obviously had the same creeping paranoia as me.

"Just tell me straight, Sal – is it something good, or is it going to make us cry?"

Sal looked as if she had algebra on the brain.

"It's serious. It's important. Come on, let's run!"

It was the best idea I'd heard in ten years. I felt a sudden desire to run myself into exhaustion. Something about Sal's manner was giving me the heebie-jeebies, but the simple act of running gave me some relief from the sensation that our doom was stalking us, just over our left shoulders. It wasn't until we were crossing the sports centre car park that I wondered if we were running in the right direction.

·

Behind the sports centre there was space for the staff to park their cars, but it was always clear during the day because the staff could never be bothered to drive around to the back when there was always plenty of free space in the customers' car park.

It was a roughly square area, one side of it created by the back wall of the sports centre itself, tall and wide, and flat and windowless. The trees that bordered the car park defined the rest of its perimeter. They were about fifty metres deep and would bring you out at the allotments if you had a mind to explore them.

We leant against the wall to catch our breath, except Osmo who paced up and down.

"So what is it, Sal?" he barked.

"Osmo," I cut in. "Are you sure we should actually be eager for an answer to that?" It was starting to freak me, seeing him so highly strung. He was supposed to be the calm one.

"That's a good point," he realised, still pacing. "You should take your time, Sal." He seemed to become aware of himself. "Will somebody slap me or something?" He was speaking too quickly, like the time he drank four espressos in the underground market.

Surprisingly, it was Pee who took him by the elbow and quietly led him to the wall. He sat Osmo down with his back to the sports centre and encouraged him to lean forward with his head between his knees. Osmo submitted to this and followed Pee's instructions to concentrate on his breathing.

I looked at Sal who was watching this scene inscrutably. I had no way of telling what she was thinking, which made me sad after the wonderful connection we had all shared the night before.

After a while she spoke.

"How are you doing, Osmo?"

Osmo didn't lift his head. He gestured with his hand and his voice emerged from somewhere near the paving slab he was looking at.

"Tell me you're not our enemy, Sal." It was halfway between a command and a plea.

I was watching her carefully. She didn't look like an enemy. She looked like she was holding something inside.

"I'm nobody's enemy. But what I've got to tell you is heavy. I think you two should sit down too."

Me and Pee looked at each other. I shrugged. What did it matter? I just wanted the tension to go away. We sat down on either side of Osmo. Sal lowered herself to the ground in front of us, sitting cross-legged.

"Okay. I'm going to tell you something that you'll find hard to believe, then I'm going to prove it to you."

She paused, giving us time to brace ourselves.

"Just listen carefully to what I say, and do me a favour – just please think before you react. Okay?"

She waited for us to respond and wouldn't continue until she'd had a nod or an 'okay' from each of us.

"Thanks. Are you feeling okay, Osmo? Do you want some more time?"

"I'm okay," he said quietly. He didn't look it.

"Alright then, here I go." She sat up very straight and took a deep breath. "Sal isn't here. I am not Sal." Osmo let out a strange high-pitch moan that made my stomach knot inside me. "Sal touched the monodreme last night. It was just before you got to her house, George. She touched the monodreme and stuff happened that is going to take some explaining. I need you to stay calm and listen."

"You told me you didn't touch it," said Osmo miserably. "What's got in to you? You told me you didn't touch it!"

Sal just pushed on with her explanation.

"When she touched the monodreme the light entered into Sal's mind and her body. It was kind of like when MarvinMilton connected to your minds, but instead of a smooth stream of consciousness this was more like a dam bursting. Sal was filled almost to overflowing with the golden light, and it was alive. It became one with her, and she became one with it. She became capable of…amazing things. Things you could barely imagine. She became capable of things that MarvinMilton was capable of. Things he didn't tell us about.

"She's decided to go away for a while, to think carefully about what she should do next. She created me to take her place at home and at school, mainly so her mum won't be freaked out by her disappearance, but also so I could come and explain things to you."

I was grateful that I was sitting down. The sky seemed to be trying to crowd forward over Sal's shoulders and swamp me.

"It's a nightmare," Osmo was saying. Next to him Pee was as white as anybody could ever be.

"In very simple terms," said Sal, "she can cause virtually anything to happen just by willing it to happen. Anything."

Osmo turned to me.

"What are we going to do?" he asked me, his face pinched fiercely.

"What do you mean?"

44

"She's touched it! You know what MarvinMilton said."

"Osmo," started Sal, her voice full of gentle concern.

"Shut up!" snapped Osmo. "You've touched it. You've been changed. Don't speak to me!"

"I'm not Sal. Sal has…"

Osmo ignored her and turned back to me.

"We've got to do something. It's happened. It's taken over her or something."

"I don't know."

Osmo turned back to Sal.

"Why did you have to do it? After everything MarvinMilton told us, and showed to us. All of that and you just throw it away at the earliest opportunity. You didn't even last a night!"

Sal absorbed the attack silently. She didn't look guilty, or defensive, or angry. She looked sad.

"Hold on a minute, Osmo," I said. "Will you just calm down? I mean look at her. She looks all right."

Osmo leant back against the wall in frustration.

"I know. I know she does. That's the trouble. I wish she didn't. I want to believe her because she looks the same as always. But nothing could be more convincing than MarvinMilton. I know for a fact, right down to my bones, that everything he told us was true. I know it."

Osmo was right. I knew it too. I leant over and looked at Pee.

"What do you think?"

Sal sat there, waiting patiently.

Pee's colour seemed to be returning. He frowned.

"I think I need my butter pie," he said.

Osmo didn't know whether to laugh or cry. He made the horrible high-pitched sound again.

"Great," he said. "Pee's acting cooler than me! It must be the end of the world."

"Carry on with your explanation, Sal," said Pee.

"Pee!"

"Well, what are you going to do, Osmo? What are you going to do?"

"I just think it's dangerous to listen to her."

"Well, look, if she is all the evil in the universe I don't know what difference snubbing her is going to make."

"It might make all the difference in the world. Maybe she needs us to believe her."

"But what if she's okay? Maybe *we* need to believe her, if we're going to prevent the catastrophes that MarvinMilton told us about."

"And how likely do you think that is?"

"Well, the thing is, whatever we do is going to be a guess, so we may as well guess that it's best to trust her, because I want to."

"But I don't know if I can."

As Osmo and Pee argued I looked at Sal and she looked at me. She gave me a little smile.

"I'll miss Deep Space Nine at this rate," she said quietly. My heart skipped a beat.

"You said you'd prove it," I said.

"Yes, I will."

"So what will you do?"

Osmo and Pee shut up suddenly and listened.

"It's probably easier if I just do it," she said, and without enough time to fit in a single thought, four large objects appeared in the air behind her. They were glassy and ovoid, each roughly the size of a mini bus. The three of us were on our feet in the blink of an eye.

"I'm sorry, don't kill me!" shouted Osmo shamelessly. He covered his face with his arms and cowered against the wall of the sports centre, snivelling and sobbing uncontrollably. "Please don't kill me! I don't want to die!"

It would have been hysterical but I'd wet myself again. If life was going to be like this I really would have to start going more often.

Sal actually did burst out laughing.

"Osmo, what are you doing?" I was glad she was laughing. It sounded natural and real. I pulled my fleece down to save me from embarrassment and tried to pull myself together. Pee was standing with his back pressed against the wall as if he were trying to push himself through it, very wide-eyed and still.

"I'm sorry," said Sal, as if our trousers had fallen down and now she felt bad about laughing. "I didn't mean to laugh. I just wasn't expecting your reaction to be so extreme." She was completely failing to keep a straight face.

"What's happening, Sal?" My voice sounded shrill in my ears. It was broad daylight and we were being invaded by large glassy objects. The sky looked unreasonably pale and bland. I noticed a crumpled crisp packet on the ground and it looked too ordinary to be part of the same universe as those objects.

"You're not under attack," she said calmly. "I know what MarvinMilton said. I know he was telling us the truth. I know all that. But Sal has touched the monodreme now so we have to face up to that, whether we want to or not. I can tell you what the situation is now, what might be in store for us. But I can only tell you if you're willing to listen. What MarvinMilton told us is absolutely true, but that doesn't mean I'm not your friend. It doesn't mean that Sal isn't your friend."

Osmo raised a shaky hand and pointed at the impossible objects.

"What the hell are they?"

"They're gifts from Sal. One for each of us."

"What do they do?"

"They're runabouts. It's like having your own miniature space ship. They'll fly you anywhere you want to go. But they've got a lot of special features."

She sounded like a car salesman, which couldn't be a good thing.

"Why should we trust you?" I asked.

She shrugged carelessly.

"I don't know."

"And what happens if we don't want to?" asked Osmo, recovering some of his spirit at last. "What happens if we decide to fight you?"

Sal – or whatever she was – shrugged again, not phased in the least.

"Sal is far away from here. You can fight me if you want to, but that won't affect her."

"But what will you do to us if we don't want to accept these…things?"

"I won't do anything, Osmo. The crucial thing you need to understand is this: when MarvinMilton talked about all the evils of the universe being unleashed he wasn't talking about devils and demons and people being taken over by aliens. That stuff comes from our minds. He was talking about how power corrupts the people who have it. Sal has all the power in the world – in the universe! She has all the power she can imagine. That's what MarvinMilton didn't want to happen. He didn't believe that anybody could have that much power for very long before they were corrupted by it and started to abuse it. He's probably right. Sal knows this. Sal believes it too. She's gone away to work out what the best thing for her to do is. She doesn't want anybody to become a victim of her going crazy with power."

My eyes kept flitting to the runabouts as she talked. Having them floating there behind her, like four impenetrable bodyguards, certainly leant weight to her words. Her story was preposterous of course. It couldn't possibly be true. But neither could they, and there they were.

"Anyway, this is all very heavy stuff, and I did promise you food." She stood up and she seemed much brighter than she had done, as if the worst part of her job was done.

"I'll cloak three of these things for the moment. It's making me nervous having them all just floating there in broad daylight."

She waved a hand, and the three runabouts on the left disappeared. As she stepped up to the forth a hatch gull-winged open. Before the hatch had opened there had been no indication of its existence. The surface of the runabout had been perfectly smooth. The whole thing had looked like a giant, semi-translucent, polished stone. The colours beneath the milky surface were deep red tones. It had looked solid until the moment the hatch had lifted, revealing it was actually a hollow pod.

Sal grabbed hold of the side of the newly gaping hole and dragged the runabout towards the corner where the trees met the wall of the sports centre. She towed it behind her as easily as if it were a soap bubble. It slid through the air at a constant height above the ground, approximately one metre.

"Let's tuck it in the corner shall we? What would everybody like to eat and drink? Anything you like."

I was aware as I stepped towards it, craning forward with curiosity, that I was eager to believe her. If it turned out that one of my best friends was an all-powerful being who gave out free miniature spaceships to her mates, then maybe I didn't really mind so much after all. An image of MarvinMilton's beautiful golden eyes flashed through my mind suddenly. Where did my loyalties lie?

"A butter pie and a pint of lager please," said Pee as if he'd just popped out for a pub lunch.

"You heard the man, Tom," said Sal to the interior of the runabout. "Can you manage that?"

- **I'm afraid my programming inhibits me from furnishing you with recreational drugs, my dear,** said a voice smoothly in our minds. **How about a hot Vimto instead?** And I recognised the voice. Sal observed us with a mischievous grin.

"This one's mine. Sal gave it Tom Baker's personality and voice for me." Sal had been addicted to old reruns of Dr Who ever since she had discovered it on cable.

I had so many questions.

Sal clambered inside. The rest of us edged closer and peered in. The interior was much simpler than I had expected. At the nose of the runabout was a large, sumptuously padded chair. It had no legs or base. It floated in there, just as the runabout itself floated at a constant height above the car park. I took one look at that chair and knew that it would be as comfy a chair as ever there was. It was long and low and easy on the eye. It looked leather, but I knew it couldn't be because Sal was a vegetarian. I wanted to sit in it. My body wanted me to sit in it.

From inside the nose of the runabout was transparent. It almost looked as if the end of the pod had been sliced off with a very sharp, very large knife. There was no dashboard, no control panel, just a floating chair facing an invisible dome. The simplicity of design was almost heart breaking.

From the chair back the interior was padded after the same fashion as the chair itself, even the floor. It looked like a cross between a luxurious leather sofa and a lunatic's padded cell. And that was all there was: no buttons, no lights, no computer displays, no speed dial. I loved it. It was a perfectly comfy womb, with a window on the world. I wanted it. I wanted my gift from Sal.

A compartment opened in the padded wall with a butter pie in it. The pie sat on what looked like a real plate with a fork resting on it. There was also a mug of steaming hot Vimto. Sal brought them to the hatch for Pee.

"This poxy thing can't even give me a beer?" grumbled Pee.

"Are you really not Sal?" I asked.

She looked at me carefully.

"Really," she said.

I suddenly missed her – the real Sal. I wondered where she was and if she was okay.

"So what should we call you?"

She gave a crooked smile.

"Call me Fake Sal," she said. "That's what I am. And you can call me Sal for short, at least in the company of others, anyway."

I was about to ask something else but something behind me caught her attention.

"Uh oh," she said.

We turned around to find someone looking at us. He was wearing an orange sports centre tracksuit. He was holding a packet of cigarettes and a lighter, forgotten in his hands.

"Maybe you should get in," Fake Sal said.

"I don't think we should," said Osmo, but Pee had had all the invitation he needed and was halfway in already. Sal grabbed him by the seat of his pants and hauled.

Osmo looked me in the eye.

"I don't know if we should get in, George."

It didn't seem like much of a choice to me: go for a trip in a marvellous, butter pie producing flying machine that spoke with the voice of the all-time greatest Dr Who, or be left stranded around the back of the sports hall to be interrogated by a guy in an awful orange track suit. But Osmo deserved some loyalty. I could see he was trying to stand up for something. He was trying to honour MarvinMilton's memory, even though he was filled with self-doubt.

The tracksuit guy had been standing dumbstruck, looking at us with a gradually deepening frown. I think he was having one of those experiences where you look at something but see something else, and it takes your brain a while to work it all out. He started to walk slowly towards us, looking completely unsure of himself.

"Look, Osmo, I'd really like to get in, I mean, really. But I'm not going to leave you here on your own. If you decide to stay I'll stay with you. It's up to you." *Please get in! Please get in!*

Some of the uncertainty left Osmo's eyes. He stood up a little bit straighter. I was glad. He turned to Fake Sal.

"We're staying here," he said.

My heart sank. Well, it plummeted actually. The hatch was closing already.

"Give me a shout if you change your mind," said Fake Sal. Pee was looking a bit bewildered. He hadn't expected to be going without us. "...I'll beam you up," she called. The hatch closed. It was as if it had never been there.

The runabout disappeared, too.

"You'll beam us up?" I shouted to the thin air. "You can beam us up?" Oh joy of joys! I so wanted to be beamed up. I turned to Osmo ready to beg, but he clapped a hand on my shoulder before I had a chance.

"Thanks for staying," he said seriously. "I don't know what I would have done if you'd got in."

What was happening to my life?

The guy in the tracksuit had stopped walking, about two metres from us. His jaw was hanging low. Me and Osmo looked at him.

"What was that?" he said. You had to admire the directness of his approach. He wasn't scared or aggressive. He didn't seem freaked out at all in fact. He was just curious. My mind whirred. What could we possibly say that would be plausible? Well, there was nothing, of course. I quickly realised the best thing to do was pretend we didn't know what he was talking about. Let him think he'd imagined it. I opened my mouth to speak but Osmo had come up with a plan of his own and he beat me to it.

"It was a runabout," he said. The guy pulled a blank face. "It's kind of like a little spaceship. Our friend just put the cloaking device on – that's why it disappeared."

It was definitely the best plan because the guy gave us such a strange look. I could tell he was aching to say "really?" but he couldn't bring himself to do it. I started to laugh. I couldn't help it, his expression was so funny. And the more I laughed, the funnier his expression became. It was a bit of a vicious circle. Osmo started to laugh too, and I think this was all a bit too sinister for our friend in orange. He was now on the verge of tears. He backed away from us jerkily, then turned and fled. This produced near hysterics from me. Osmo was more sympathetic.

"Poor guy," he sighed. "He seemed quite nice too. I'm sure I recognise him."

I just continued with my laughter. It felt good. It seemed like I hadn't had a good laugh in an age.

"Come on then," said Osmo. "Let's beam up."

My laughter petered out.

"What? You sure?"

"Yeah, course I am. We won't save the world from down here will we?"

I could have sung. Osmo was back.

"I can see your logic," I said, nodding appreciatively. "I think you should do the honours." I couldn't help breaking out in a great big smile. Osmo reflected it back at me and spoke those wonderful words.

"Come in, Fake Sal. Two to beam up."

5
Secrets and Miracles

It may affront the military-minded person to suggest a regime
that does not maintain any military secrets.
- Albert Einstein

Our favourite films:

Pee – Titanic
Sal – The Abyss
Osmo – Akira
Me – Any of the Christmas Carol films, it really doesn't matter which one, they're all perfect.

•

I am walking down our street and I'm wearing paper underwear. Nothing else, just paper underwear. It's women's paper underwear. The net curtains of every single house are twitching. I can't see anybody, just twitching material, but I know they are watching me. I want to get off the street, but somehow it's elongated all the way to the horizon. All I can do is trudge along, rubbing at the goose bumps up and down my arms, hoping nobody will come outside to laugh and point.

It starts to rain, of course. Large dark drops of rainwater begin to speckle my bra and knickers and I'm wondering how long they'll hold together.

But I forget about my underwear concerns for a moment when three enormous, robotic vultures suddenly tear down from the sky and land in front of me, screeching viciously. Their voices are high pitched and synthetic. They loom over me, their metal talons scritching at the paving slabs, and they project their shrill screeches into my head, into my brain, making my skull reverberate. I'm rooted to the spot, unable to make a decision. They're scrambling my thoughts. I realise, with a feeling of inevitability, that my sodden underwear is coming apart at the seams. It's all coming undone...

Suddenly I was staring at the ceiling of my bedroom, my alarm clock screeching at me from the bookcase like a robotic vulture. I hate it when that happens. I knocked the alarm on its head and checked the time. What kind of maniac set my alarm for 6:30? A little voice in my head informed me it had been me, but that didn't seem right. I'd never do such a thing, surely.

Pulling myself torturously into a sitting position I twitched my curtains (but they weren't nets) to catch a glance at the weather. Yes, it was raining. Raining hard from an unforgiving sky. The wind lashed droplets against my windowpane and I felt a cold, damp draft from the poorly insulated frame. It was purgatory out there. I breathed a big, deep lungful of musty bedroom air, slightly sweetened by the draft, and then suddenly realised.

"What a beautiful day," I said out loud. I smiled a big, cheesy grin. "One to beam up, Fleet."

Four days had passed since we'd met MarvinMilton, and I was finding that every day is beautiful when you have your own personal runabout.

There was a short fuzzy moment of transition where I felt my body lift slightly. My skin experienced the, now familiar, tingling sensation as my vision furred over. Then it cleared and I was sitting in my flight chair, looking out over our street from the domed window of my runabout.

"Good morning, Fleet."

- Good morning, George, said Fleet's beautiful, achingly sad voice. Sal – the real Sal – had given my runabout the voice and personality of Fleet Control from one of my all-time favourite computer games, Homeworld. According to the scenario this race of people, the Kushan, discovers an ancient spaceship buried in the desert that proves they originate from another planet. They rebuild the ship, which acts as a mother ship for their fleet, and they set off to discover their homeworld. Their chief scientist makes a supreme sacrifice and allows herself to be wired into the mothership. In effect she becomes its intelligence, its central processing unit. She becomes Fleet Control, guiding the explorers through the vast reaches of space with her lovely, poignant American voice. Sal knew I was in love with that voice. I was touched that she had chosen it as the default for my runabout.

"How are you today?" I asked her.

- All systems are running at optimal efficiency. When I'd asked her if she had a sense of humour she had said, **the calibration of spontaneous humour responses is engaged**, but I think she was just joking.

"Is anybody else up and about?"

- Only Pee. He is located approximately thirty-five metres off the Great Barrier Reef, four point two metres below sea level. Shall I open a hailing channel?

"No, that's okay thanks, Fleet. You're all the company I need."

There was a pause.

- Compliment acknowledged.

The only time Fleet ever had to pause was when she was dealing with input that contained potentially emotional content. For her the laws of physics, or any science or mathematical system, were a doddle. Any request for pure information, no matter how complicated, was answered instantly. The intricacies of human feelings, however, were a whole league of complification and illogicality of their own. Even my quick-minded Fleet had to pause for thought when dealing with one of my jokes, or soul-searching questions on the meaning of girls.

"You're welcome," I said. "Okay, I think an early morning spin to blow the cobwebs away. I'll take the controls thanks, Fleet."

- Autopilot released. You have control.

By golly, life was good.

I pointed the runabout at the sky at an angle of about forty-five degrees. It was easy to do. The runabout didn't require steering wheels or joysticks or anything crude like that. It was connected to my mind. When I took the controls it became an extension of my body. Pointing the runabout at the sky was as simple as making a decision. You decide to point your finger, and then you do it. It was exactly the same.

I decided it was time to get out of the rain.

"Time to fly."

I sent us bulleting up into the clouds. There was no gradual acceleration. We went from stand still to, I don't know, three or four hundred miles an hour instantaneously. .

"Yeeeehah!" I screeched. My chair lagged slightly as I was pressed back into it. If I wanted I could set the interior of the runabout to zero inertia so that I wouldn't feel the effects of acceleration, deceleration, or turning. The world outside my window would whiz past and I would feel as if I was perfectly motionless, as if I was watching it all on TV. But it was more fun this way. Fleet would reduce the effects of the acceleration to prevent me from being liquefied where I sat, but I'd still get to feel something.

I punched right through the clouds and into the boundless blue sky above, where the golden beams of a rising sun caught me and filled the pod with light. I could hear myself laughing as I arced above the world.

I slowed to a crawl and followed a curve, which would eventually have me looking down on the blanket of cloud below me. It reminded me of climbing to the top of the first big drop on a rollercoaster. Gut-wrenching vertigo gripped me as the clouds below slid into view.

"Quick, Fleet! Give me seat straps! Give me seat straps!"

Such a wuss, I thought, as a sturdy set of seat straps suddenly whipped around me, clicked into place and hugged me snugly into the flight chair. I'd been practising like hell, too.

I tore down through the sky towards the clouds, screaming for my mum but loving every second of it. I levelled off and slowed, skimming the upper reaches of cloud because I didn't trust myself not to shoot right through and smash into the ground or a block of flats or something. Fleet's anti-collision protocols wouldn't allow that anyway but my pride would be injured if she had to retake control because I'd become a flying hazard.

I brought myself back down through the clouds at a more sedate pace. Visibility was not great. Dawn was going to be a long drawn out process in this weather. I swooped down and had a bit of fun flying along a motorway as if I was in a car, on my way to work with all the other suckers. It wasn't rush hour yet but there were a fair number of commuters about. I pulled alongside a green Range Rover and peeked in at the driver, wondering what she would think if I de-cloaked the runabout and she saw it, speeding along, a metre off the ground, beside her. It would be a cool UFO story to tell her friends, if she didn't crash. I zoomed ahead, still following the motorway, weaving in and out of the cars and lorries, remembering all of the journeys I'd been on as a passenger, passively counting bridges. *This is crazy*, I thought, *I can't even drive a car!*

Only four days had gone by but already Fleet seemed to fit me like an old trainer. Each day passed in a blink, seemed to be over before it was begun, yet each day was a whole string of miracles, one after another, more than you should be able to fit into a month. It just didn't make sense. But already I was starting to take it for granted.

I lifted back up into the sky, through the clouds again, through the blue, through the atmosphere and out into the glittering black velvet of space.

"Set a course for Saturn please, Fleet," I said.

- **Course set for Saturn.**

She had set the course for me but I retained control of our speed. Fleet could travel at any speed imaginable, and I had a good imagination. She was also able to teleport to any point of space in the universe that could be specified and occupied. But I liked to see the stars shift and turn around us as I executed corkscrews through the Solar System. There not being very much scenery between Earth and Saturn, I didn't dawdle too much and was pulling up by the giant planet after about twenty seconds. I had Fleet rustle me up some scrambled eggs on toast and a mug of tea. I sat in my chair with a floating breakfast tray and I seasoned my eggs with salt, pepper and HP sauce while I examined Saturn and its moons from different angles.

I flew down into the planet's turbulent atmosphere of gases but it soon became too murky to actually see anything. I flew along the rings and felt tempted to fly the runabout right in amongst the chunks of ice and through the other side, but they looked so peaceful and unlikely that I couldn't bring myself to disturb them.

"Take me out to Pluto, Fleet."

- **Course set.**

From Pluto the sun was no more than a particularly bright star in the universe. I positioned myself on the far side and I looked out into the galaxy, beyond the boundaries of the solar system. Fleet could take me almost anywhere. She could answer almost any question. The question was: where did I want to go and what did I want to ask?

"What are you, Fleet?"

It must have been a trickier question than I thought because there was a distinct pause.

- I am a runabout, she said. It was a bland answer, even for Fleet.

"But what does that mean? You're not a machine. No machine could do what you do. Am I hallucinating, or dreaming, or something? Am I trapped in a virtual reality game? Is that what the monodreme has done?

- I am not a machine, George, you are right about that. I am not a hallucination or a dream. I am not part of a virtual reality program. This is real. It is really happening. I'd never heard her say so much in one go. I am an extension of the monodreme.

I sat in silence and quite literally gazed into space for a while. *An extension of the monodreme?* I instinctively trusted both Fake Sal and Fleet, but I couldn't stop myself from coming back to the warnings of MarvinMilton. A monodreme was the most dangerous thing there was, according to him, and here I was sitting in 'an extension of one.' I was suddenly aware that I was a long way from home.

"What's the monodreme?" I asked it slowly, tentatively, not sure if I really wanted to be asking.

- The monodreme is a self-aware particle.

A little voice inside me cried 'Great! A straight answer that doesn't tell you anything! Now, just leave it at that and go home and stop asking questions! You've been brave enough for one day!'

"And what does that mean, Fleet?"

Well, there was no point in stopping now.

- I will try to explain…hold on! I am receiving a signal from Osmo. Do you wish to hear it now, or shall I answer your question first?

Saved by the signal.

"What's he got to say?"

- Patching him through.

Osmo's voice filled my head.

- Hey George. We've got a sweet game of runabout tag going on here at the Great Barrier Reef. Stop skulking around Pluto and get over here. It's rubbish out there anyway.

- On my way, I said.

I sat there for a moment, thinking.

- Shall I lay in a course for Osmo's co-ordinates?

Fleet didn't exactly seem eager to continue our conversation.

"Fleet, who are you loyal to first: me or Sal?"

- I am loyal to you, George, that is how Sal wanted it. But she has placed inhibitors on my performing certain actions and accessing certain information.

"Okay. Is there anything else that would make you want to keep information from me?"

- Affirmative.

"What's that?"

There was another one of those significant pauses. When the answer came it was short and chilling.

- Compassion.

I sat there, stunned.

"Nice," I said. After a few moments of consideration I decided I'd asked enough big questions for one morning. The Great Barrier Reef and my lovely friends were calling me. But suddenly another big question did occur. And it was the biggest one of all.

"Fleet, does Sal love me?"

I suddenly wished I hadn't asked.

- Are you inquiring about Real Sal or Fake Sal?

"Well, both I guess."

- I am unable to calculate the solution to that problem.

"So, can you calculate whether either of them loves me?"

- Negative.

I sighed with relief and turned the runabout around and started heading back to Earth.

"You're not up to much, really, are you, Fleet?"

- Insult acknowledged.

"Sorry, Fleet. I didn't mean it."

- Apology acknowledged.

"I think you're the bee's knees really."

- Acknowledged.

•

"Okay, so are you ready for my important matter?" asked Pee, clapping his hands eagerly.

"Come on, let's hear it," said Fake Sal.

"But please let it be something normal," I whimpered.

We were all sitting in Osmo's runabout.

- I'm waiting to hear about your matter with excited anticipation, Pee. Osmo's runabout had the voice and personality of HAL-9000, the insane artificial intelligence from 2001: A Space Odyssey. Pee hated it. Pee's runabout was Homer Simpson. He grimaced but didn't respond to HAL.

"The thing is this, can I show Gaynor Williams my runabout?"

We hooted uproariously.

- Well, I think that's an admirable pursuit, Pee, said HAL.

"But she loves the Simpsons," Pee explained. "Especially Homer. She'd be putty in my hands."

"Ack! Quick..." choked Fake Sal. "Somebody get that image out of my mind! It's taking over my soul!"

Although we laughed, Pee's question was actually important. Who could we tell our secrets to? What would happen if it became common knowledge?

Of the four of us Pee was most desperate to let a few friends in on what was happening. He would have been quite happy for the whole world to know. At last, after a lifetime of being the runt, the clown, he felt powerful. In truth we all fancied a bit of that dream. To throw off the pretence, forget about school and family obligations, take a few friends adventuring, to be admired, or at least envied, the whole world over. What was stopping us?

I was in favour of caution. No matter how tempting the possibilities I knew there would be consequences to being open. It would mean the kind of instant fame we could never escape from again. Pee had had enough of anonymity, but I saw there was still something to be said for it. I was enjoying having my secrets. I could walk down a crowded corridor at school surrounded by kids who were living a life I had stepped out of. This filled me with a dizzy feeling of freedom. I reckoned it was way superior to Pee's rude cravings for power. I was actually a bit worried about him. The desire to de-cloak his runabout and fly circles around the schoolyard was a feverish gleam behind his eyes. He wanted to wipe the smug smiles from the faces of everybody who'd ever pushed him around – all the bullies that had hit him, all the teachers that had lost their patience with him, all the members of his family that had belittled him. It was something I would have liked to have seen myself. But what would the cost be?

Osmo said that it was something we had to be unanimous on, as if one of us started flying about in public it wouldn't be long before we were all rumbled, whether we liked it or not. Then our families would be in the spotlight too. Everybody would want to know us. Everybody would want us to do things for them. The attention of the governments of the world would suddenly be focused on four kids from Banford.

"So what?" said Pee. He didn't care about his family. He didn't care about the governments of the world. In his runabout he was untouchable, uncatchable. Even we couldn't reach him if he didn't want to be reached.

"And if the world finds out about us," I said, "how long will it be before they know about Real Sal?"

"So what?" said Pee again – it was becoming his catch phrase. "Real Sal is all-powerful. We don't even know if she's on this planet anymore. The only worry Real Sal has got is not going bonkers because she's turned into God. She doesn't care what the world knows."

I was starting to wonder if we shouldn't knock him out before *he* went bonkers.

"Real Sal does care," said Fake Sal. It was the first time she had joined in with the conversation. "She cares about her mum. Please don't do anything that will hurt Sal's mum, Pee."

Pee opened his mouth to speak. I was ready for 'so what' to come out and then I'd have had no choice but to slap him one, no matter how small he was. But for once he stopped himself, closed his mouth. A look of frustration and despair fell over his face, and I felt sorry for him again.

"I don't know if I can last much longer," he said.

We all looked at each other uncomfortably. Fake Sal stepped forward and hugged him.

"We'll think of something, Pee. Just give us a little bit of time and we'll think of something. Can you hold on a little bit longer? Just for us?"

"Okay," he said, "but I want you to think hard, yeah?"

"We will," she said. "We promise, don't we?"

"Cross our hearts," said Osmo.

"Course we do," I said.

"Anyway, Pee," said Osmo brightly. "It'll take more than a runabout with the voice of Homer Simpson to get Gaynor Williams like putty in *your* hands. A lot more."

Pee threw himself onto the padded floor and pummelled it in a tantrum that was only half play-acting.

•

It was time for school. HAL located four empty cubicles in the school toilets and closed their doors with projected fields. We beamed down and stepped back into the mundane half of our lives. Pee wore a scowl, I wore a half smile.

The truth was that Osmo and me had become perceptibly more confident over the past few days. People were noticing that we were always in a good mood, that we had lots of energy. Sudden homework assignments did nothing to dent our smiles, put-downs from classmates rolled off our backs. Pee had too much history as a target for people to start taking him seriously now, just because he was a bit perkier than usual, and Fake Sal was doing a very good job of impersonating Real Sal, so nobody noticed a change in her. But Osmo and me were definitely feeling the benefits. There was nothing that could hurt us.

As we made our way to registration we found ourselves pressed up against a wall by Stuart Towns and Eddie Miars. It did hurt, actually.

"Georgey Porgey and Osmo Cosmo. How about a chat with your favourite uncles?"

"It's good to talk," I squeaked.

- **Can you do something please, Fleet?** I asked through our mental connection.

- **Monitoring the situation,** came the runabout's reply. Great. She wouldn't step in and bombard them with particle beams, or whatever, unless they began to get serious.

"So if we're members of the family, suddenly," said Osmo, trying to be chummy, "I don't suppose there's any chance of getting our protection for free?"

"Nothing's ever free," said Stuart philosophically.

If I could get away with describing him as a caveman I would, but the fact was Stuart was pretty sharp. He just happened to be six foot two, two hundred and twenty pounds of muscle and a bit insecure. Not a good combination in one so young.

"The question is," he said, "what have you got?"

When we started to rummage through our pockets he stopped us.

"No lads, you're too kind, really. Leave your balls of fluff where they are. What you can do is tell me what's going on."

We exchanged looks.

"Well," said Osmo, and I could tell straight away his answer was going to be cocky. I hoped his newfound confidence wasn't going to be over confidence. "I think what we've got here is a case of you bullying us, and us being bullied by you."

"Ostensibly," I added helpfully.

Stuart's beady eyes flicked to mine.

"'Ostensibly'? Did you say 'ostensibly'?"

I realised my mistake.

"I don't know."

"You should know better than to use words like that, Georgey Boy." Stuart sounded concerned. "This just isn't the right environment for that kind of language."

"But you just said 'environment'."

Stuart smiled condescendingly.

"Do as I say, George, not as I do. Now what I want to know is why are you two so happy?"

I looked at Osmo. I could see he was desperately trying to think of something useful to say. He opened his mouth but I beat him to it.

"Well, the thing is, Stu, somebody we know met an alien a few nights ago who gave them the power to do anything in the world. They've gone away to think about what they should do next, but before they went they gave me and Osmo our own private space ships."

Stuart looked at me inscrutably. Eddie's gaze flickered back and forth between Stuart and me while he waited to find out what kind of response Stu would go for.

"So, obviously," I continued, "we're feeling a bit happy about that."

Osmo was looking at me aghast.

"George! What are you playing at? Didn't we just decide that we weren't going to tell anyone?"

Stuart frowned, disconcerted by the authenticity of Osmo's anger.

"It's alright. Stuart's not gonna believe a stupid story like that – are you, Stu?"

Unfortunately Stuart was no dimwit to be toyed with. He ate irony on toast for breakfast. He tightened his grip on my shirt and spoke through taught lips.

"Meet me at lunch time and show me. If I don't see one of these space ships I'm going to crush your skull. Okay, Georgey Porgey?"

- **Fleet?**
- **Monitoring the situation.**

"Whatever you say, Stu."

"The Frog Entrance, five past twelve."

Stuart released me and turned away. Eddie lingered for a while. He looked at us both with an openly mystified expression, then he shook his head and sighed with compassion. He released Osmo and wandered after his master as if he were sauntering through the prettily manicured grounds of a lunatic asylum.

"Nice job, George," said Osmo flatly. "Seriously though – that was smooth."

"It didn't quite hit the spot, did it?"

"Oh it hit the spot all right. And after Stuart's hit you, you'll be a spot."

"I thought I'd try out your technique. It worked on Orange Tracksuit Guy."

"No, no, no. Don't try to blame me. And don't ever try out my techniques. Don't ever do that."

"He'll have forgot by twelve anyway, won't he?"

Osmo shook his head and walked off to registration.

- **Well, thank you, Fleet. Nice of you to help me out there.**
- **You didn't issue any commands. Would you like to specify a course of action to be carried out in the event of subsequent engagements?**
- **Well, I don't know. Are there any non-lethal ways to disable somebody in a situation like that?**
- **Numerous.**
- **Well, next time use one please – something that won't arouse suspicion.**
- **Affirmative.**
- **Thank you.**

I realised I was standing half way down a corridor having a silent conversation when I could be walking. I started off to registration.

- **Can't you use initiative at all, Fleet?**
- **I can only perform actions under my own initiative if you grant me clearance first.**
- **You mean if I give you permission?**
- **Affirmative.**
- **Isn't that a contradiction in terms?**

- Negative.
- But for you to use your initiative I have to take the initiative!
- Affirmative.
My mind boggled.
- What do you think I should do about Stuart?
I realised this was the first time I'd ever asked Fleet for an opinion.
- Refuse his requests for information.
- And if he gets aggressive?
- I will neutralise him at my discretion. There was a pause. **Now that I have clearance from you for the use of initiative in this matter.**
- Okay, Fleet. I get the message.

The prospect of telling Stuart I was keeping the secret of happiness to myself, thank you very much, was daunting, but on the other hand, the prospect of seeing him and Eddie 'neutralised' by Fleet did have a certain appeal. All the same, I could live without these kinds of confrontations. I was beginning to think that Pee's longings for openness made sense compared to the amount of concentration it took to live two lives.

I reached the end of the corridor and turned the corner that led to my form room. I stopped. Something had caught my eye, a flash of colour from the other side of the glass doors that led to the playing field. I backed up and looked. It was gone. Now there was just a man in a blue suit who was preoccupied by a little notebook. He was big and solidly built. He looked about as much like a plain-clothes policeman as is humanly possible. I felt a tingle of trouble. But, still, he wasn't what had caught my attention. For a fleeting moment I had caught sight of something that looked distinctly like a guy wearing a bright orange tracksuit.

•

Having a mental connection with Fleet was very useful in day-to-day situations, especially at school. She could provide me with the answer to any question from any teacher in any lesson. Sometimes I had to pretend I was working out the answer to a question, just so I didn't seem to have become all-knowing overnight. I even gave the wrong answer occasionally – but not too often. She could patch me through, via the other runabouts, to Osmo, Fake Sal or Pee, so in effect we had become telepathic. She could tell me the location of anybody I wanted to find, or avoid. She could even tune me into any radio station, or play me any track from any album that existed in any recorded format anywhere. It was a nice way of getting through the 'occasional' stretches of boredom.

I was watching drops of rainwater race each other down one of the windowpanes in History. Fleet was playing me a Radiohead track. There was no joy in the grey sodden world outside. The rain fell and it fell. It didn't get any heavier. It didn't get any lighter. It just fell, uniformly, monotonously, like the words from Miss Royle's mouth. She was telling us something about the history of the International Dateline, but all I had ears for was Subterranean Homesick Alien. When she noticed me gazing blankly at the window she shot me a question, hard and brittle, designed to shame me with my ignorance. Fleet provided me with the appropriate date. Not even bothering to hesitate I supplied it to Miss Royle. She raised her eyebrows, momentarily speechless.

"Well, I guess you can go back to staring out the window then, George."

I asked Fleet to play me 'Paranoid Android'. It was right in the middle of the big, lovely, crunchy bit in the middle when I got an incoming call.

- Party line request from Pee, said Fleet, putting the track on pause.

- Okay, go ahead.

We called it chat line when we spoke to each other one to one, and party line when more than two of us were connected. Pee's voice entered my head.

- Hey everyone, I've just been called out of class. I'm on my way to Norris's office.

Mr. Norris was our head of year.

- What's it about? asked Fake Sal.

- I don't know.

- What does Homer say?

- I haven't asked him. I got straight through to you.

There was a pause.

- Well, what are you waiting for? asked Osmo.

If we were on party line we only used one runabout for questions. Otherwise there'd be a confused garble as we all questioned our own runabouts at the same time and there'd be eight voices talking back and forth.

- What's going on, Homer? asked Pee.

- Gee, said Homer, in his perky voice. It looks like a government operative called Stephen Armitage has tracked you guys down, because he's waiting in Mr. Norris's office right now, and he's really beefy.

- No way! I can't believe this, said Osmo. How could they have tracked us down?

- I think it might have something to do with orange tracksuit man, I said. I'm pretty sure I saw him earlier on.

- Really? said Osmo. Mr. Orange, eh? But how could he inform the government and be taken seriously?

- What did Mr. Orange do, Homer? asked Pee.

- Oh he's one of those computer geeks! He posted something on his website about seeing Fake Sal's runabout behind the Banford Sports Centre. The guy's a big loser. Mr. Armitage has been sent by the Visitor Project, a top-secret project that's investigating MarvinMilton's remains. He got Orange Tracksuit Guy down here this morning to look at school photos and he identified Osmo and George straight away. He wasn't so sure about Fake Sal and you, Pee, but when he said he'd seen four of you old Norris blew the whistle on you both straight away. He knew it wouldn't be anyone else.

So they had found MarvinMilton. I pictured his body lying cold on some stainless steel table somewhere and had to shake my head to make the image go away.

- So why have they only called me out?

Pause.

- I don't want to answer that question.

- Homer, insisted Pee.

Homer's voice was reluctant.

- Norris told Mr. Armitage that you'd be the easiest push over out of the four of you.

The line was silent for a moment.

- I hate Norris.

- Don't worry, Pee, said Fake Sal. We'll help you out.

- But I've started to sweat. He'll see the fear in my eyes. He'll know I'm guilty. I always feel guilty when I see cops, even if I haven't done anything.

- But Pee, you really haven't done anything. We aren't guilty of anything, asserted Osmo.

- But if they find out we've been mixing with aliens and flying about in runabouts they'll lock us up and study us, and stuff.

- If it comes to that we can just beam out of there, no problem, said Osmo.

- I know, said Pee sadly. But what about Real Sal's mum?

He could really pick his moments to start being sweet.

- Well, we just do the best we can, eh? said Fake Sal. It'll be okay.

- What should I say?

- Just what we agreed: on Sunday night we hung around the streets near the cemetery and then went to my place.

- But he's bound to ask if we were behind the sports centre, I said.

- Let's keep it simple. Fake Sal was cool and collected. The four of us were there, behind the sports centre, but we didn't have any space ships with us. It's more believable than the truth, isn't it?

- I've got a bad feeling about this, whined Pee.

- Where are you, mate? I asked.

- I'm sitting outside Norris' office now. Fat Madge just went in to tell them I'm here.

We could feel the waves of anxiety radiating from Pee's thoughts.

- Look, Pee, I said, angry suddenly, if they think they can push you around then let's let them think they can. Act stupid. Take a long time to answer their questions, talk really slow, give them lots of blank looks. That'll give us time to help you with your answers.

- Yeah, okay, said Pee. He began to warm to this idea. He was always up for a bit of acting. **I'll teach 'em.**
- That's the spirit.
- Okay, they're coming for me. Here I go.

•

We had expected them to use one of the offices as an interrogation room. I somehow had an image of an angle poise lamp shining in Pee's face, of two large men in white shirts and loosened collars and rolled up sleeves doing the good-cop/bad-cop routine, maybe offering Pee a cigarette and asking him if he wanted a takeaway pizza because it was going to be a long haul. But before anybody could put Pee in the hot seat the lone man in the blue suit, Mr. Stephen Armitage, had asked Norris's permission to take Pee to the canteen and buy him a hot chocolate. I could tell Pee was starting to like him already. But when would Bad Cop show up, I wondered.

They sat in a far corner of the canteen and watched the rain together. Armitage had hung his jacket on the back of a chair but he didn't loosen his tie or roll up his sleeves.

"This is not the greatest hot chocolate I've ever tasted," he said. "I thought it was supposed to taste especially nice on days like this." He pointed his eyebrows at the water-streaked window.

- Careful, Pee, I warned. **He's too smooth for his own good.**
- Seems like a nice bloke though, said Pee, smiling weakly at Armitage.
- Oh lord, said Osmo. **A cup of hot chocolate and he's anybody's.**

"Still, I guess you're wondering what all this is about. I'll get down to business. First of all I want to tell you it's nothing for you to worry about. I know it probably seems a bit odd, being called out of your class and being plied with cups of hot chocolate, but you're not in any kind of trouble. What's happening is that I'm investigating something a little unusual, and I'm looking for people who might have seen or heard something about it. Now I know that you and a few of your friends were round the back of the sports centre a few days ago – Tuesday lunchtime I think it was. Is that right?

- What shall I say?
- Just say yes, said Sal.
- But don't be too quick, I said.
- And look confused, said Osmo.

"Hold on a moment, though," said Armitage frowning thoughtfully and taking out his notebook.

"I've got to make sure my facts are straight here." He leafed through the pages muttering. "You've spent all of the nights at home for the past few weeks haven't you? What I mean is, you haven't slept over at anybody's house have you?"

- What's he getting at? wondered Osmo.

- And who else has he spoken to? I wanted to know.

- What shall I say?

- Just tell him the truth, said Fake Sal, apart from the bit about the runabout behind the sports centre.

- Pee, I think you've hesitated enough to give him the impression you're slow. Answer the man, said Osmo.

Pee nodded timidly.

"You're sure now? You didn't stay over at a friend's house on Monday night or Tuesday night?"

Pee frowned and hesitated, playing the dumb act.

"No," he drawled.

"And you were behind the sports centre Tuesday lunchtime?"

"Yeah."

- No, Pee, said Sal. He's trying to catch you out. It was Monday.

"Erm, I mean no. It was Monday."

"What? Oh sorry, so it was." Armitage mumbled absent-mindedly. "It was Monday you were behind the sports centre, the day after you were at Five Elms."

"Yeah."

It had slipped past his lips before we could do anything.

- Pee! We all shouted. Pee clapped his hand over his mouth, his eyes wide. What have you done?

Armitage went very still. He looked at Pee steadily. His hands put his notebook away but his gaze never left Pee's face. He nodded slightly. He knew now. He knew he had people who had seen something; something they wanted to keep secret. Pee clapping his hand over his mouth said more than words ever could.

- Oh god, said Pee. Can I beam out of here? Please can I beam out?

- It's not your fault, Pee, said Fake Sal.

- Of course it's my fault! I want to go away. I'm going to go.

- No, Pee! we clamoured.

- Everything's just going too fast, said Osmo. We just need more time.

"It's okay, Peter," said Armitage gently. "There's nothing for you to worry about."

- I don't know what to do! You guys are no good, you're not helping me! Let me get out!

- We just need things to slow down, said Osmo. He was beginning to panic.

- Okay, I said. Neutralise him, Fleet. Something suitable, at your discretion.

- George! What are you doing? said Osmo, but he was too late. Armitage's eyes went wide, his cheeks flushed red and he suddenly lurched to his feet. He was turning away when he stopped himself and turned back to Pee for a moment.

"Excuse me for a moment," he said with a small, tightly controlled voice. And then he was scuttling away through the tables with urgent but clenched movements.

- Wow. Cool, said Pee. That was so cool. I've got to have a go at that.
- What did you do, Fleet?
- I manipulated Mr. Armitage's bowels.

I thought I detected a slight glow of pride in her voice.

- You're a dream, Fleet.
- Compliment acknowledged.

There was a collective sigh of relief.

- I'm getting out of here, said Pee.
- That's probably a good idea, said Osmo. It's only ten minutes until lunch. Why don't you relax with Homer and we can meet up and talk about what to do next.
- Forget that, said Pee enthusiastically. I'm going back to class to neutralise everybody.

•

It had become an established routine for us to head to the toilets straight away at lunchtime. We could each slip inside a cubicle, beam aboard our runabouts, and enjoy a gourmet meal of junk food while we flew over the plains of Africa, or maybe genuine replicated home made food as we soared through the streets of New York. Sometimes we would all take manual control of our runabouts and play a game of runabout tag. This day, however, was not a good day to be heading for the toilets. Well, not for us, anyway. For a lot of people it was the only idea in the world. Pupils, teachers, dinner ladies, caretakers, special operatives from the government, nobody was safe from Pee's revenge. It was pitiful. It was sick. It was glorious. Suffice it to say that on a day that would live on in the annals of Penrose history, many didn't make it.

We made our way outside through corridors filled with stampeding, bewildered people. A gaggle of teachers were log-jammed outside the staff toilets, hammering on the door, hollering and elbowing, dancing jigs of their own devising. I noticed Eric Slocomb, one of Pee's bitterest enemies, sitting on the floor, back against the wall, in a stiff, uncomfortable-looking position, and he was crying like a lost soul. He had nowhere to go, bless him. We burst out of the school in fits of laughter.

It was still raining, but in many ways it was the most beautiful day ever.

"I think it's all gonna come out," I said, after the worst fits of laughter began to subside. "I don't see how we can stop it. Armitage knows. He isn't going to let it go."

"But what about Sal's mum?" said Pee. It seemed to have become his main concern in the world. I kind of got the impression that it was the one thing that was helping him to keep his feet on the ground. "It'll be really bad for her if she finds out her daughter has gone away and left a replica behind." He frowned, puzzled. "Won't it?"

"Maybe we should just say that the runabouts were a gift from MarvinMilton," said Fake Sal. "I could carry on as I am. There's no need to tell anybody about me and Real Sal."

"But you saw how quickly Armitage got what he wanted out of us," said Osmo. "We're just no good at covering things up – not from people like him anyway."

"How about if we elect me as our spokesperson?" she said. "It'll be easier if only one of us has to cope with the questions, and I know I'm up to it."

I believed her. She was just like Real Sal, after all.

"I think that's a good idea," I said.

"Me too," said Pee, eagerly. It looked like his dream was going to come true.

"So we're really going to let everything out?" said Osmo. There was wonder in his voice, as if the concept was beyond him. "We'll be completely free," he said.

"I don't know about that," said Fake Sal pointedly.

"Georgey Porgey!" said a cheerful voice. We turned to find Stuart and Eddie walking towards us. "The one person in school who should be pooing in his knickers, but you seem to be okay."

"Hiya, Stuart," I said.

"Neutralise him, George," said Pee.

"Yeah, go for it," said Osmo.

"It's okay, there's no need," I said calmly. It was nice not to feel afraid for a change. Suddenly, with the prospect of letting the world know about the runabouts, I was above fear.

"Okay, Georgey Boy. I'm ready to see this space ship of yours. What do you say? I'm really eager to see it."

"I'm eager too," said Armitage's voice from behind us.

We all turned around. He was looking distinctly pale as he stood there, his blue suit darkening with the rain. He looked pale, but the set of his mouth was determined.

"Who's this?" asked Stuart. "Rent-a-plod?"

"You could say that," said Armitage with something that was half way between a smile and a grimace. "What about it, George? How about showing us your space ship?"

I looked at Pee and Osmo and Fake Sal. We smiled and nodded.

"Okay," I said.

We brought them gliding down, uncloaked, in diamond formation. They dipped slowly from the clouds and levelled out over the far side of the playing fields headed directly for our little group. Stuart's face became as pale as Armitage's, and Eddie's legs failed him. Wobbling backwards he landed on his bum, groggy and afraid. Armitage and Stuart had similar reactions but managed to reach the low wall that bordered the playing fields. They sat down next to each other. I saw two groups of kids running across the field from Amberely Road. An old woman was towing a little shopping basket on wheels there. She stopped and stood there, watching. Her face was perfectly straight. She didn't betray a single emotion. She looked as though she was wondering if the runabouts were new inventions that nobody had bothered to tell her about. Faces were appearing in some of the windows of the Deputy Head's and the school secretaries' offices. A gaggle of younger kids burst out of the Frog entrance and skidded to a halt, shouting exclamations, and rushing back to be close to the doors in case the need to run for safety made itself obvious. It wouldn't be long before the whole world was out there.

The runabouts stopped about three metres from us. There was no slowing, not the slightest hint of any gradual deceleration. One second they were moving and a hair's breadth of a moment later they were completely stationary.

Armitage muttered something blasphemous under his breath. Stuart nodded. Eddie sat there on the floor with an exquisitely stupid look on his face.

I felt Pee's hand grip my arm.

"Gaynor Williams," he hissed.

Sure enough, there she was, running our way with Joanne Rowland and Teresa Gordon.

"You'd better go and invite her for a spin."

"I can't. She'll say no."

"Well, look, Pee, Osmo's always flirting with her so you'd better do something."

Pee gasped and scurried away towards her. Fake Sal stepped up to Armitage.

"Mr. Armitage, I've been elected as our spokesperson. Would you like to come and meet my runabout?"

"Meet it? It's alive?"

"That's a good question. Why don't we go and ask it? Do you feel up to that?"

"I guess I'd better feel up to it…" he said, doubtfully, "…it being my job and all."

She smiled and nodded encouragingly and he forced himself to his feet. They walked over to the runabouts. I couldn't even tell which one was hers until a hatch opened in the middle one at the front. As they drew closer I heard a voice from inside.

"Ah, welcome, Mr. Armitage. I was hoping we would have the chance to meet. Horrible weather, isn't it?" Tom Baker was making his voice audible rather than using mindspeak.

Armitage looked at Fake Sal with an unhappy expression.

"Isn't that Tom Baker's voice?" I heard him say.

I turned to Stuart.

"Come on then Stu. You wanted to know what I was so happy about."

Stuart looked thoroughly humble. It suited him.

"You're joking."

"No. No joke. Where do you fancy? China? New York? Jupiter?"

"I don't know about that. Can we fly around the school with the doors open?"

A man after Pee's own heart, and both of them at opposite ends of the popularity spectrum. Eddie recovered some energy and scrambled to his feet and jogged up to us with a tentative smile.

"Not you," I said. "One bully in my runabout maybe, but you're always at your worst when you're together." Eddie's face fell.

"Oh go on," said Stuart softly.

"No."

Stuart's feet were already taking him towards the runabouts but his upper body turned and shrugged at Eddie. *I tried, mate.*

- Can you rustle me up an extra chair please, Fleet?

- Affirmative.

Fleet opened a hatch and me and Stuart clambered aboard. I could hear Fake Sal trying to coax Armitage aboard Tom Baker.

"Look, Mr. Armitage, Stuart's not afraid."

"Stuart knows you," he said seriously.

"You won't be harmed," she said in her kindest voice. "I promise."

Still he paused.

"You won't save the world from down there, Mr. Armitage," she said with a small smile.

He burst out laughing. He shook his head as he took hold of the sides of the open hatch and hauled himself up.

"This is not in my job description," he said.

There was a fair sized crowd now, and it was growing steadily. At the front were the foolhardy little kids.

"Take me, take me!" they squeaked. I could see Underwood, the deputy head, working his way through the crowd towards us, tense and uncertain. And suddenly there was Pee, running towards his runabout.

"Go on, Pee!" I shouted when I saw that not only was he accompanied by Gaynor Williams but Joanne Rowland and Teresa Gordon too! His face was a wide-eyed picture. If it had been a movie he would have been running in slow motion, droplets of rainwater flying from his sodden hair as the soundtrack music swelled gloriously. Go on, Pee. Run your little legs off.

"George!" shouted Mr. Underwood, as the runabouts lifted slowly above the crowd. "What's going on?"

"It's a long story sir," I said, shrugging.

We flew slowly around the school with our hatches open, waving at the kids and teachers on the ground and in their classrooms. I noticed that Osmo had picked up a couple of passengers too: Mr. Crank, his history teacher, and Miss Schnieder, our English teacher. They were Osmo's favourite teachers, and rumour had it that they were each other's favourites too, if you know what I mean.

By the time we had lapped the school I think pretty much everybody was standing outside in the rain. I wondered what it meant to all of those people down there, looking up into the rain streaked sky, witnessing a miracle together. I knew it was the beginning of something, for me as well as them. I could see it was the beginning of something for the whole world. I'd already found out that you couldn't witness miracles and carry on living the same old life.

"Party line audio please, Fleet."

"Patching you through."

"Hey everybody, I'm tired of all this rain. Anybody know any good tropical islands?"

6
Paradise

No, this trick won't work...How on earth are you ever going to explain in terms of chemistry and physics so important a biological phenomenon as first love?
- Albert Einstein

6
Paradise

We headed slowly for a little island we knew, giving our guests time for sightseeing. Beside me, Stuart was leaning forward in his flight chair, hooting at the sights that the world offered up as it rolled by below. The sense of freedom that I'd felt earlier, when we had brought the runabouts flying down out of the clouds, began to evaporate. The realisation began to dawn: for a few days Fleet had been my escape from the world. Now she was going to bring the world running to me.

"Oh man, I've got to get me one of these things, Georgey Boy!" sang Stuart, delirious with excitement. "Do you reckon they're difficult to hotwire?"

He looked at me and his big face was plastered all over by a grin of happy go lucky, aren't-you-my-best-new-buddy-in-the-whole-world ecstasy and my mood suddenly turned black.

"Don't call me Georgey Boy."

He was too far gone with excitement to pick up on it.

"Oh yeah, sorry," he said, looking out of the dome like a glutinous kid looking through the window of the world's biggest sweet shop. "You prefer 'Georgey Porgey', don't you?"

I sat and stared at him in disbelief. He actually thought that this kind of thing passed for humour. He actually expected me to chortle in a good-natured way at what a funny guy he was; and wasn't I such a lucky dweeb, to be blessed with the spectacular honour of receiving one of his amazingly witty insults? We were flying above cloud level in the most advanced aircraft known to the human race and still he had no idea how the balance of power had shifted between us. He still thought he was number one.

"I tell you what, Stuart, shall I show you what this thing can do?"

His little piggy eyes lit up.

"Oh yeah! Come on! Show it to me baby!"

He was having such a great time.

"Well, if I must."

A red glee filled me up from my belly to my eyeballs and I sat back in my flight chair.

"Fleet, give me manual, please."

"Affirmative. You have control."

A smile split my face. I started to ease the pod upwards. We were at the bottom of the first climb of the rollercoaster.

"And, er...I'll take some seat straps as well, please."

Stuart watched with a look of excited involvement as a sturdy set of straps flicked around me, crossing my chest and hugging me to my flight chair. He sat back in his own chair and looked over at me expectantly. My split face grin shone at him. "Coming for a ride, Stuey?"

I saw his face begin to fall and, before he had a chance to speak, I sent us rocketing up. His head was thrown back into his chair and his eyes grew wide with genuine, full-blown fear. He actually squealed. I began to laugh uncontrollably.

"George!" he warbled. "Give me some straps!"

I took us tearing up through the blue of the sky, to the part where it begins to dim and you start to see the stars, and then I slowed and let the runabout start curving over for the return journey.

"It's alright, Stu," I said, giggling. "The straps are just to stop you falling out of your chair."

"George!" he yelled, but already the ocean and the clouds, so very far below us, were coming back into view – and it's a pretty terrifying thing to experience, the first few hundred times or so, because the dome of the runabout is utterly invisible from the inside of the pod. It really does look like nothing more than a gaping hole. And we were going slowly enough at this point for Stuart to actually start slipping forward in his flight chair. I noticed how his hands had turned into claws that were biting into the arms of his chair as he tried to force himself back up into it.

"George! Stop it!" he screamed. He actually screamed it. And there was a part of my brain that registered that scream for what it was, a part of my brain that knew it was time to stop, that, in fact, I'd already passed beyond the point that the good old George would ever go to. But, I don't know, it was like George wasn't there any more...I just didn't stop.

In times to come I would look back on what I did to Stuart and I would realise how horribly ironic it was. Because the worst insult that my friends ever made about me, the one that hurt more than they knew, was when they called me St. George. When they were acting like brats, when I tried to be the peacemaker in their recurring squabbles, they would call me St. George, because I was always such a nice guy, always so concerned about other peoples' feelings, and they said it was like I thought I was better than everybody else.

I laughed hysterically, all the way down, as Stuart screamed. When we reached the bottom, and it looked as if we were going to smash into the water, I pulled back just enough to bring us skimming across the surface. Then I allowed Fleet to retake control and guide us smoothly back into formation with the rest of the gang. I was still laughing, but the hysteria was beginning to fade away. Stuart's screaming turned into gasping and then sobbing. I kept glancing at him, waiting for him to recover and say what a good joke it was, or threaten to kill me, but he just cried and kept on crying. Eventually I forced myself to bring my chair about so I could face him. His ghost-white face was covered in sweat and tears and snot. His eyes were red and his arms were shaking horribly. I couldn't believe what I'd done to him.

When we arrived at the island and pulled up on the beach he fell out of his chair and started screaming to be let out, pounding frantically on the padded walls of the pod. It was freaking me out to have him going crazy like this in my runabout, but I couldn't stand the idea of letting him out so everyone could see what I'd done. They'd think I was some kind of monster or something.

- **Fleet, can you do something to help him calm down?**
- **Affirmative.**

I saw a hazy purple field appear around Stuart and he stopped his pounding and leant heavily against the interior of the pod. Then he slumped slowly into a heap and was fast asleep. I flopped back into my chair and cursed breathlessly.

•

Because of the time difference it was early evening at our island. The runabouts were floating next to each other a metre above the white sand beach of the main bay.

By the time I emerged from Fleet Stuart was more or less restored. He was subdued but also keen to keep his little breakdown as a special secret just between us two. I was pretty keen for that as well.

Fake Sal had taken Armitage for a stroll to continue his education. Osmo and Pee had wanted to muck about with the girls but our guests were full of questions. So, the boys had set up a feast for everyone and now they were all sitting in the sand talking. I sat Stuart down next to Miss Schneider and I fixed him a pizza and a coke.

We told them about MarvinMilton. We said he was just a space wanderer who had come to the end of his days, and wanted to pass on a gift before he died. We had just been in the right place at the right time. Osmo did most of the talking while I mentally reminded Pee not to mention the monodreme and Real Sal turning into a god. Where was that girl, I wondered. And what would she think of me now?

"So who's PC Plod?" asked Stuart, through a mouthful of pizza that he was eating too fast. It was the first time he'd spoken since stepping out of the pod.

"He's called Stephen Armitage. He's from the government. Some kind of special operative."

"Cool," said Stuart. He was doing an incredible job of covering his inner shakes with his usual thuggish front. It made me wonder how often he had to do that kind of thing.

•

Pee got Homer to play some music. Mr. Crank and Miss Schneider went for a romantic stroll along the water's edge while the rest of us put on swimwear, kindly provided by the runabouts, and went for a splash. It struck me as funny how quickly everybody adapted to this fantastic situation. Smiles were quick and eyes were twinkling. I noted that Gaynor was flirting with Osmo. No surprise there. I could see that Osmo was trying his best not to make a meal of it, for Pee's sake, but his resistance was crumbling rapidly.

We introduced them to the joys of runabout tag and gave them a quick course in manual control of the runabouts. Stuart had something to prove. I don't know if it was to himself or to me, but after a hesitant start he picked it up very quickly. Teresa was a natural too. After mentally asking Fake Sal if we could use Tom Baker we tried to split into pairs. That's obviously not easy though, with four boys and three girls. I told Stuart he could use Fleet, and Teresa took control of Tom Baker. Gaynor didn't feel confident about controlling a runabout so she piled into HAL with Osmo, giggling, a little too loudly for her own well being in my opinion. This left Pee and Joanne standing on the sand. Pee made a gentlemanly flourish, indicating that Joanne could share his runabout with him, but she was already diving into Tom Baker to be with Teresa. Pee's crestfallen face nearly broke my heart there and then. He was still at the bottom of the pile.

"Come on, Pee!" they shouted.

He climbed into Homer Simpson on his own, but when they all took off around the bay, dodging and laughing and bumping force fields, Homer remained at a stand still. I walked over and leaned against the bottom of the hatch. Pee was sitting in his chair staring through the domed window at the turquoise sea and the blue, blue sky.

"Hey, Pee," I said lamely.

He didn't answer or indicate that he'd heard. I clambered into the shady interior and gently spun his chair to face me. He was crying.

"Oh, you gimp," I said.

"Chimp," he muttered automatically.

"Give me a chair will you, Homer?"

- **Not unless Pee tells me**, said Homer, loyally.

"Give him a chair, Dumbo."

- **Ooh! That's personal!** said Homer.

A flight chair materialised next to Pee's. I jumped in and we both looked out through the dome. The other three runabouts were dots flying low over the horizon. We could see Fake Sal making her way back down the beach towards us. Armitage was a tiny figure at the far end of the bay. It looked like he had some heavy thinking to do. Fake Sal paused to chat to Schneider and Crank.

"Do you love Fake Sal?"

The question took me completely off guard, but as he was crying already I didn't slap him. I forced myself to swallow the instinctively defensive reaction that was on my lips. He was obviously feeling the need for some straight talk.

"Yeah, course I do," I muttered, nonchalantly.

"Me too," he said.

I knew already, of course.

"Yeah? So what about Gaynor Williams?"

"I love her too," he said, and a big involuntary grin broke out beneath his tears. I burst out laughing.

"But you were going to let Joanne play runabout tag in Homer."

"I love Joanne too."

"And Teresa?"

"Most definitely."

"Is there any girl on the planet you don't love?"

He considered for a moment.

"Nope."

"Well, it's a good job. A gimp like you can't afford to be fussy."

"I know," he said, absolutely serious.

Fake Sal was walking towards us again. The teachers had started trying to throw each other into the sea. This was obviously an island of love.

"I think Sal would pick you," said Pee.

"Fake Sal?"

"Yeah."

"What about Real Sal?"

"I don't know about her anymore."

No. Nobody knew about her anymore.

"Don't you think she'd choose Osmo?"

"No. Who did she phone when she was in trouble? It wasn't Osmo."

"But that was Real Sal."

"Yeah, but Fake Sal is the same as Real Sal was before she became a god. Fake Sal should be called Real Sal really, I think."

"Just to make life simple you mean?"

"Yeah," he said absent-mindedly.

"Are you okay?"

"I'll be fine," he sighed sadly. "You'd better go and talk to Fake Sal while you've got the chance. This is obviously the place to make your move."

I jumped out of my flight chair.

"You may be right," I said, grabbing the headrest of his chair and spinning it to face the hatch. "But if you think I'm letting you stay in here to feel sorry for yourself...then you really are a gimp!"

I thrust the chair towards the open hatch and lifted it forward, tipping Pee squealing onto the soft sand below, just as Fake Sal stepped up.

"Hello, Fake Sal," I said, striking a manly pose in the hatchway. "This little piglet needs cheering up."

"Really?" she said.

"I'll kill you, George!" squeaked the piglet. "No, no," he said excitedly, an evil idea forming in his eyes. "I'll tell her that you love her."

"Pee!" I warned, dangerously, even though it was too late.

"Fake Sal, George loves you! He told me! He loves you, he loves you!"

"Pee!" I shouted, jumping down. Pee scrambled to his feet and ran towards the sea.

"He loves you! He loves you!"

Sal looked at me and I felt myself blushing the deepest, hottest, most full-on blush I'd ever produced. It was pitiful.

"Well, *he* loves you as well," I spluttered.

My face screwed itself up in agony.

Sal looked completely shocked and didn't seem capable of human speech. Oh god! I thought.

"He loves you the most," squealed Pee. "More than the whole world!"

"Pee!" I shouted again, charging after him. Pee ran towards the sea squeaking and giggling hysterically and chanting his mantra over and over again.

"He loves you, he loves you..."

I chased, bellowing his name furiously, but mostly wanting to get away from Sal and the terrible surgings of embarrassment.

I caught up with him in the waves and dunked him again and again, feeling the same mad hysteria that I'd felt as I was terrorising Stuart. Pee started to cough and splutter. He got frightened and then angry and shoved me in the chest with all his puny strength.

"Back off geek!" he yelled. "What's the matter with you?"

He stormed off towards his runabout muttering dark things.

I stood there feeling wetter than the wettest fool ever. Looking back to the sand I caught Fake Sal's eye for a moment, but then she turned away and walked towards the trees.

The little optimistic part of me that had half expected her to chase me into the sea and wrestle with me amongst the waves shrivelled up with a useless whimper.

Oh crap, I thought. What's happening to me?

I slouched off in search of some solitude.

•

Everybody had returned for the sunset. HAL had beamed a pile of dry driftwood onto the sand and agitated its molecules until a great big campfire was blazing away.

As I approached I noticed that Pee seemed to have forgiven Osmo for being more attractive than him. He was sitting nonchalantly on his friend, poking him with a twig occasionally, but mostly just ignoring him. Osmo put up with this gracefully, obviously feeling guilty as sin, and happy that there was a punishment he could suffer to relieve his conscience.

Fake Sal was the first one to notice me approaching but she looked away quickly, pretending she hadn't. I felt my cheeks flushing red again and was thankful that the glare from the fire would mask it. But I could feel the muscles on the left side of my face twitching. I grabbed a twig and speared a marshmallow and stood by the teachers. The sky was coloured with the lemon yellow after-glow of the sunset. As the beach grew dark, and the bank of cloud on the horizon bruised to purple, the runabouts provided us with extra illumination, glowing with a beautiful mixture of rose pink and moon white light.

"Hey," said Stuart. "Here comes Mr. Plod."

Mr. Armitage had been using Tom Baker to make a call to his superiors.

"So what's happening, Ploddy?" asked Stuart in a friendly sort of way. "Are the interrogation rooms full yet?" I could see he was fully restored now, though he looked away every time I caught his eye.

"Not yet, Stuart," Armitage said, his face straight. "I've told them to keep one set aside for you."

Stuart laughed.

"Thank you, Mr. Armitage, sir."

For some reason Stuart had taken a liking to Armitage.

"It looks like you've all made the news," Armitage said seriously. "Some bright spark from the media studies class used one of the school cameras to film your fly-by. She's sold it to the BBC. The first news flash was aired ten minutes ago. The media machine is cranking up. There's probably a fleet of news crews pulling up outside the homes of all your families right now."

There was a buzz of conversation.

"I bet it was Wendy Drewson," said Joanne. "She's always fancied herself as a journalist."

"I wonder what my mum's gonna say," said Osmo.

"And what about you, Mr. Armitage?" asked Fake Sal. "What are you supposed to do?"

Mr. Armitage's face smiled warmly in the firelight. He knelt down to the picnic area and picked up a long twig and a marshmallow. I noticed he wasn't wearing his jacket anymore, and that his collar had been loosened and his shirtsleeves rolled up. He impaled the marshmallow on the end of the twig.

"I'm supposed to win your confidence," he said.

There was a thoughtful silence.

"I won't have any confidence in you until I see some Kung Fu," said Stuart.

"Oh, come now, Stuart. You're not really as shallow as all that?"

Stuart stared at him blankly, then said "How did you find out my middle name?"

Mr. Armitage sighed and, planting his twig in the sand, stepped back from the fire.

"Your thoughts are your movements and your movements are your thoughts," he said, and he took up a fighting posture.

"Excellent," said Stuart.

Mr. Armitage moved with the grace and fluidity of a dancer. His punches and kicks and blocks were simply organic extensions of his dance, and I didn't doubt that they would be all the more powerful for that. The shadows cast by the flickering fire light seemed to conceal and then reveal his movements at strategic moments so that you could never predict which direction he would strike in. Sometimes, with the fire lighting him up against the darkness of the island beyond, he looked like a flame himself, crouching and darting and twisting. I watched Stuart's face. He was hypnotised by the silent spectacle. Suddenly the fire cracked and a glowing ember leaped out, straight towards Mr. Armitage's face. His hand flicked up smoothly, seemingly another extension of the dance, but it sent the ember flying off into the dark. Then he stopped and bowed to the fire and picked up his marshmallow stick.

"Fair enough," said Stuart. "I don't think I'll call him Mr. Plod anymore." He led us all in a round of applause and whistles and hoots.

Mr. Armitage smiled, almost bashfully, and held his marshmallow out to the fire.

"And what are you supposed to do when you have our confidence, Mr. Armitage?" asked Fake Sal, standing up.

"He's got my confidence," called Stuart from a little way off where he was trying to imitate some of the moves he had seen.

We waited for Mr. Armitage to answer.

"I'm to try to persuade you to come with me. To answer questions. To help us find out about what MarvinMilton was, where he came from, what the runabouts can do."

"Thank you for your honesty, Mr. Armitage," said Fake Sal, in a strangely formal tone, and she turned and walked away from the fire. A flicker crossed Armitage's face.

I poked the sand with my twig for a few moments, then I followed her. She was sitting in the sand by the sea's edge.

"What's the matter?"

She watched me warily from the corner of her eye.

"I don't know," she said.

"I thought you liked our Mr. Armitage."

"I do. That's the problem. He's too smooth to be true. Don't you think?" I nodded. "And I don't like what he does, or who he does it for. All of that 'your movements are your thoughts' stuff. It looked really nice, yeah, but it was still violence. So that means his thoughts must be violent, doesn't it?"

I didn't know what to say. She looked tense and isolated. I was half tempted to say something glib and jokey. Instead I sat down next to her.

"What's it like being a replica, Fake Sal?"

A line creased her forehead. She was silent for a long time but I waited.

"Imagine you reach out your hand to touch something – something that you really want – but someone beats you to it. And you look up and you find it's another you, but he's just one second ahead of you. Then he tells you that even though you feel like you've been here all the time, you've really only just appeared. You've only just been born. And all your memories and experiences and dreams, that feel so real, they're all just copies of his. And then he carries this thing off down the beach, and climbs aboard a runabout and flies away, while you have to stay here and deal with it. It's kind of like that." She looked at me. There was a deep well of confusion in her eyes. The sky was a dimly glowing violet behind her. The breeze dropped and the world was silent almost, except for the distant sounds of voices from up the beach. She looked down at my side and frowned. Then she reached out her hand, hesitated a moment, and put it in mine. Her fingers were cool and smooth, and they held on to mine ever so lightly. The moment felt like a soap bubble. I sat there very quietly and looked her in the face and I kept my mouth shut, not trusting myself. The smell of the campfire came by on a breeze. "After a while," she said, "you realise that you're actually on a beautiful beach, and you're not sure that you'd like to have gone where Real George has gone anyway. And eventually...well, you realise you got the best part of the deal after all."

I gave what she had said a few moments' thought, then I pivoted carefully in the sand to face her better. I switched her hand from my right to my left so that I could touch her shoulder.

"But you feel like a fake though, don't you? You feel like you're not as good as real people."

Her face twisted and she bit her bottom lip and looked upwards to keep the tears from coming out. Then she shuddered and shrugged.

"Isn't that what everyone feels like?" she asked in a pinched voice.

I opened my arms and she leaned into me and let me hold her. We sat there like that and I stroked her hair. I gazed upwards. The stars seemed much closer here than they did in Britain. I heard a long wave roaring quietly along the sand, as if it didn't want to intrude. Time passed, and each time I thought of something stupid to say I checked myself and let it pass by until I started to get cold and uncomfortable. I ignored this, just wanting to hold her and hold her. Eventually I felt calm enough to talk without saying something abnormal.

"What happens if Real Sal comes back and decides she wants her old life back, and that she doesn't need a replica anymore?"

Her head was resting on my chest. She was gazing out across the sea and I felt her jaw moving as she spoke.

"If she wants her old life back she will have her old life back. If she doesn't want me to exist anymore then I won't exist anymore. What Real Sal wants is what happens."

"Then she probably will go insane, won't she?"

"Probably. If she hasn't done already," said Fake Sal. "I think I would."

I couldn't think of a more depressing thought, and the base of my back was aching and my legs were filling with pins and needles, but I stroked her hair and somehow couldn't have been happier.

"And thanks very much, by the way," she said, "for just about killing me with embarrassment."

I winced silently at the stars. Then I sighed.

"Oh, shut your cakehole".

She made a little gasp of utter disbelief that made my toes tingle.

"I beg your pardon?"

"Well, maybe you'll think twice before tinkering with my screensaver in the future. Being embarrassed isn't so much fun when you're the one it's being done to, is it?"

"Oh, very clever, Mr. Smarty Man."

She always called me that when I got one over on her. Sometimes it felt like I lived to hear her say those words.

"And anyway, I can fancy you if I like. I can fancy anyone I want, and you can't stop me. It's supposed to be a compliment, you freak."

She pushed herself up and faced me but her hands stayed on my chest.

"Oh yeah? Like when Tina Hutchins wanted you to go to her pyjama party?"

I gasped, outraged.

"You swore you'd never mention that again!"

She sniggered in the dark and returned to her former position.

"Ooh, Mr. Smarty Man," she cooed. "Your slippers are so fluffy."

•

Back in Britain the six o'clock news was starting. Two of the runabouts projected beams above the fire and where they intersected we saw an eight-foot screen showing BBC 1.

I don't know exactly what we had expected but we were knocked sideways by the scale of the news coverage. I think that only Armitage wasn't surprised.

It had only been six hours since our fly-by at the school and already our little corner of Banford was a chaos of news crews, crowds and police. They mostly centred around the homes of me, Fake Sal, Osmo and Pee, but reports were also coming in from outside the homes of the 'abducted' pupils and teachers, from the police station, the school itself, and from on-the-street-interviews with eye witnesses, and classmates. In the studio a hastily mustered panel of 'experts' was debating via satellite link-up whether or not a national state of emergency should be declared or whether it was all just an extraordinarily elaborate hoax.

There were a lot of hysterical people in the street scenes, but they were just over excited for the most part, especially the Penrose pupils. But some of the parents were genuinely distressed: Joanne's mum in particular, who was shown in floods of tears outside the Frog Entrance screaming for somebody to 'do something.' Her voice was fraught with fear. I felt goose bumps up my arms and the back of my neck prickled at the raw emotion in her voice. Joanne burst into tears and Teresa took her off to use a phone.

After the third showing of the video footage – in which you saw the runabouts lifting off above the gathered crowd and several of us waving from open hatches – we realised that the six o'clock news had been extended indefinitely.

Gaynor and Stuart and Crank and Miss Schneider all wanted to make calls. I had Fleet materialise an adequate number of mobile phones.

"Can I have this?" asked Stuart.

"Yeah, sure."

"Can I have a better one?" I felt a sudden stirring of anger and gave him a hard look but he just cocked his head at me. I couldn't quite work out where he was coming from, but I knew I'd had enough of him bringing out the worst in me.

"Fleet, give him one with a colour screen, video messaging, programmable personality, any funky, special features you can think of, will you? Give one to everyone, please."

When Stuart turned his phone on it lit up and spoke to him in the voice of Jennifer Aniston.

"Hi! I'm your mobile phone, but you can call me Jen, handsome."

"Oh my god," muttered Stuart wandering away down the beach.

Armitage watched the four of us expectantly. We looked at each other uncomfortably.

"Well, I guess this is it then," I said. I didn't want it to be it. I didn't want to fly home to my family and invite them on board.

Osmo stepped up and put a phone in my hand.

"Here," he said. "It's got the personality of Alan Titchmarsh."

"Hello," said the phone. "Are you okay? You look a bit peeky."

•

"Hi, Mum. It's me."

"George! George, where are you? Are you alright?"

"I'm alright. Are you alright?"

"Where are you? Are you safe?"

"I'm on a tropical island. I'm safe as houses."

"You're on an island? George, what's happening? What's going on?"

"We met an alien, Mum. He gave us some presents."

"Oh my god...I feel...funny..." I heard a commotion as she fainted and Dad and Emma rushed to catch her.

•

"Hiya," said Pee. He was slouching on a couch that Homer had zapped into existence by the campfire, one foot on a coffee table. "It's me."

His expression was one of utter indifference as he listened to the voice in the earpiece.

"...I'm with the gang...some tropical island some place...we came in the runabouts...that's what we call the flying things...I don't know if I'll bother really...well, what for? What do I want to come home for?..."

His face suddenly went red. His eyes widened and he opened his mouth ready to shout. I braced myself but he seemed to catch himself, think better of it. He took a deep breath and then spoke calmly into the receiver.

"...whatever." And he turned the phone off.

We all remained quiet, not sure if he wanted to talk about it.

"They think they can make some money from selling my story to the papers."

"They probably can," said Armitage.

Pee shrugged coldly.

"Well, they can do it without my help."

"So, you're not going home?" asked Crank.

"Correct."

"Pee, I'm sure your parents are going to be fraught with worry."

We all stared at Crank. Nobody had the energy to enlighten him on the exotic parenting skills of Pee's mum and dad.

"Oh. I see," he said. "Maybe not, eh?"

Osmo patted him on the back.

"There you go."

•

Armitage asked if he could speak to us in private. While I had Fleet rustle us up a whole bunch of flight chairs (it was a real squeeze) Gaynor got everybody else gathered around the fire with an array of phones, light refreshments and the news on. Joanne had spoken to her mum and, having calmed her down, was in a much better mood. We left them to their paradise and settled down to our meeting with Armitage.

"I spoke to the Minister of Defence earlier on," he said when we were all sat down. "He's eager for things not to get out of hand."

"What exactly does that mean, Mr. Armitage?" asked Fake Sal carefully.

I could see he was still confused by her sudden cool attitude towards him.

"Sally, all of you, I know you have concerns about our intentions. Obviously there's nothing my superiors would like better than for you to answer all their questions and hand over the runabouts into their care so they can analyse them and take them apart and use them for their own purposes, etc. But at the moment our main concerns are: public safety, public opinion, damage limitation. I've spent a little time with you all today. Without wanting to sound patronising I can see you're a bunch of good-natured kids who just want to have fun. I don't blame you. But at the risk of you beaming me all the way to Antarctica in my underwear I'm going to tell you that if you allow the people of this world to go hysterical with fear because they think they're being invaded, or start blowing each other up because they think it's an arms race situation, then you will all have plummeted in my estimation. It's only been a few hours and you can see the chaos and confusion out there. What I want is for you to agree to work with us, towards informing and reassuring the public – the global public, not just Britain. If we can do that effectively, then maybe we will prevent certain volatile governments from over-reacting. Please, take your time to think about it."

He sat back in his chair, the ball firmly planted in our court.

7
The Pod People

Only two things are infinite, the universe and human stupidity,
and I'm not sure about the former.
- Albert Einstein

What we wanted to be when we finished school:

Me – a writer (books, films, comics, poetry – anything, as long as I could sit in first class on the train, working on a laptop, on my way to pick up important writing awards).

Pee – Movie Superstar (failing that he'd settle for being an actor. He was actually very good at acting. It was his one talent and redeeming feature. When there was a school play on he was a completely different person. Other kids in the acting circle even showed signs of respecting him. It was just a shame there wasn't more than two plays a year).

Sal – Didn't know what she wanted to do (fact: girls get the grades but boys are better at knowing what they want to do. I don't know why, but it's true).

Osmo – Social Worker! (I blame his parents.)

•

We slipped down through the clouds over Banford airfield to find it was still raining. Travelling at a low speed, in diamond formation, we paused so the four army helicopters could join us before heading off again towards the city. We had the runabout equivalent of our headlights on. The pods were glowing, each sending out a single beam of light that continuously and smoothly altered in colour, length, width and direction. The raindrops falling around us glittered in the night like a swarm of colourful fireflies.

Stuart was sitting in a flight chair beside me. I had suggested he take the trip back home in someone else's runabout, but he had shrugged and shook his head.

"I've bullied the others just as much as you Georgey…I mean, George. See, I'm learning," he said. "At least I know you've got it out of your system." He put a hand on my shoulder and squeezed a little too hard. "You have got it out of your system, haven't you, George?"

I pointed my finger right up in his face.

"You just behave yourself, then."

He patted my shoulder.

"Understood."

Taking the rear point position in the diamond we were able to see all three of the other runabouts. Fake Sal and Mr. Armitage were in the front point position, directly ahead. Osmo was on the right. He was sharing his flight with Gaynor. That left Pee to accommodate Joanne, Teresa and the two teachers, who all seemed to have taken pity on him after hearing about his horrible parents.

"Check out the film crew," said Stuart pointing. A mobile film unit was set up on the road, which ran the length of the airfield perimeter, to catch first sight of our return on live TV and transmit it around the globe. It was the only private vehicle to be granted clearance through the roadblocks. There were a few army vehicles dotted about. Fleet informed us that most of them were safely tucked out of sight in a hangar. We were also aware that we were being filmed from each of the helicopters; not a single second, or perspective, of our journey need be missed.

"So anyway," said Stuart, over-casual. "What are you up to tomorrow?"

"A bit of this and that, I expect," I replied, equally over-casual. "Yourself?"

"Well, I haven't got much planned as it happens. I could come for a spin, probably…if you liked."

"Could you, now?"

"Yeah." He sighed humbly. "You're not going to dump me by the wayside are you, George? Not after today?"

"What? You mean, not after you threatened to crush my skull today? Is that the 'today' you're talking about?"

"I was more thinking of the fun stuff."

"I don't know Stu. This morning I had Fleet all to myself, now I'm on my way to pick up my family. And you're not exactly my favourite person in the world, you know what I mean?"

He absorbed this unhappily. Then he looked out over the outskirts of Banford. It wouldn't be long before we were home.

"It's a good life though innit? Up here."

He climbed out of his chair and knelt on the floor of the runabout. Then he crawled forward and lay flat, facing down, with his head and shoulders in the dome. He spread his arms out like wings and gazed down at the landscape rolling directly beneath him.

"This has been the best day of my life," he said.

"Oh shut up," I said miserably.

•

The runabouts were on auto, travelling at just the right speed to touch down on the Penrose playing fields bang on midnight. Traffic was backed up for miles around. I could see the playing field floodlights in the distance, and also the beams of some powerful spotlights that had been shipped in for the occasion. They scraped the obligatory Banford clouds in anticipation of our arrival. We were flying low enough to see the throngs of people scurrying through the streets, the ones who would be too late for our touchdown but were now being rewarded with the chance to turn and look upwards, pointing and shouting, or to simply stand there, mouths open, collecting rainwater, as our inscrutable pods drifted silently overhead amidst the raging helicopters.

The closer we drew the denser the activities below us became, until at last we approached within spotlight range of the school. I'd never seen a sight like it. A sea of shining cars and soaking people had flooded the place. From the surrounding roads in to the playing fields it didn't look as if you could fit a pin between any of them. Cameras were flashing, zoom lenses were focussing, homemade banners were waving. I spotted one that said 'BEAM ME UP, PEE.' Another said 'Banford welcomes POD PEOPLE – please fly carefully.'

Stuart spoke, his voice muffled against the interior of the dome.

"I can see Eddie down there!"

A roughly oval area of the playing field had been cordoned off with three layers of concert fencing and two layers of police. A wide avenue connected this area to the school via the Frog Entrance. At one end of the avenue, just inside the oval, our reception committee was waiting for us beneath huge umbrellas. The welcome party consisted of our parents, the Minister of Defence, an army general, a top air force officer, the Chief of Police, Mr. Gregory the school Head, a small handful of government minions and a sprinkling of security police. The reporters and film crews lined the avenue and one whole side of the landing area.

"So the minister showed up then, Fleet?"

- **Affirmative.**

We had watched one panel of pundits on the TV discussing the pros and cons of having senior members of parliament present at the touchdown of alien technology. Weren't we just inviting alien races to dispose of our top leaders? Then it was pointed out that there were rumours that the Prime Minister had been thinking of getting rid of the Minister of Defence anyway, so in a way this was a no lose situation: the aliens are impressed by this demonstration of trust and make friends or they zap the Minister of Defence and do the Prime Minister a favour. What a cynical world.

Our diamond sank towards the oval, leaving the helicopters behind. I spotted Sal's mum in the gathering below and I wondered what she was thinking, what she was feeling. I wondered what she would think or feel if she knew the truth about what had happened to her daughter.

- **Chatline with Fake Sal please, Fleet.**
- **Patching you through.**

- Hey, Fake, looks like this is the moment. After we step out here the whole world's going to know us.
- I think that moment's already passed.
- Yeah, I suppose so. Do you think your mum's gonna be okay?
- Don't worry, I'll make her proud. What about your family?
- I don't know. I expect they'll survive.

The runabouts came to a halt the customary metre above ground level. The rain fell, and the world held its breath. Then our hatches gull-winged open and the world held its breath even harder.

As agreed, the first to climb out into the public gaze were Fake Sal, our elected spokesperson, and Mr. Stephen Armitage, special operative. Sal's mum rushed forward to embrace her daughter's replica and the crowd roared its approval. A wave of relief crashed outwards as the world began to breathe again.

I saw Mr. Armitage say a few words to Sal's mum and they shook hands. The Minister of Defence walked up stiffly and Armitage introduced him to Fake Sal. The Minister's taught, thin-lipped smile split his face like a steel thread. He was on the watch for ray guns.

Miss Schneider and Mr. Crank were clambering out of Pee's runabout, and Gaynor and Osmo climbed out into the rain on the opposite side of the diamond.

"Come on then," I said to Stuart. "Let's get this done."

Stuart looked up at me from where he was sitting in Fleet's dome, and for the first time ever it was a proper look he gave me. An open, honest, eye-to-eye this-is-me look. He was really pulling out all the stops. Then he stood up resolutely and walked to the open hatch. He leapt lightly down to the wet grass without hesitating or looking back. Good for him, I thought. He raised his arms in a victory salute and twirled for the cameras, his grin lighting up in the hail of camera flashes.

I stepped out gingerly into the sparkling raindrops. The atmosphere hit me in a blast of sound and light and massed emotion. I could feel a tight undercurrent of fear beneath the crowd's excitement. I saw Pee waving at the mass of world press, eliciting cheers, and presenting his back to his mum and dad as they ran up to him and grabbed hold of him. His dad turned him around and buried him in a hypocrite's bear hug. I half expected Pee to beam himself out of there, but this was his moment and he had nothing to fear from his miserable parents anymore.

My mum and dad and sister came walking through the haze towards me.

"Hello," I said.

"Hello," said my mum, and she hugged me firmly.

When she released me I looked at my dad.

"I don't know what to say," he said.

"Well, that makes a change," I said, quick as a flash.

He laughed, the simplest, best laugh I'd heard from him for ages, and he drew me into a hug that wasn't too bad, I suppose. When he let go Emma inserted herself between us and grabbed two handfuls of my shirt and shook me roughly.

"Why didn't you tell me?" she demanded, eyes wide. I suddenly felt bad about it. I thought quickly for a snappy response but then decided to just shrug and look sheepish.

"Sorry, Em."

Her mouth became a thin tight line.

"You little sod!" she said.

There wasn't anything I could say so I just stood there. Eventually she gave in and hugged me.

After a while of standing around and mingling, that I was never able to remember afterwards, we all walked down the avenue of reporters to the press conference that awaited us in the gym.

I looked around at the people surrounding us, the sea of ordinary people behind the reporters, waving their banners optimistically, hoping that this was the dawn of something new and good, fearful that it might just mean the end of the world. I suddenly didn't like it that so much expectation was being focused on us. It didn't seem fair. Pee would have disagreed. He was in his element, basking in the flashlight glow at the centre of global attention, resolutely ignoring his parents. He was gleefully oblivious of the world's need for reassurance. I just wanted to beam away, be anonymous once more, go for a picnic with Fake Sal.

•

"I don't want any of you to worry about this press conference," said the Minister of Defence in the staff room that was acting as our briefing room. "You won't have to answer any questions that you don't want to. I will explain as much as I can, with the help of Mr. Armitage, about what happened at Five Elms and what the runabouts are capable of – at least what we know so far. Most likely you'll be asked about your feelings and your plans for the future."

The Minister faltered, seeming unsure of how to proceed. Our parents waited expectantly. Pee's mum and dad sat beside Pee with wide eyes, greedily taking everything in. To people who didn't know them it would have appeared that they were mild, salt-of-the-earth citizens and attentive, loving parents. I was glad to see that Pee's composure wasn't ruffled. In our mind-talk I sensed a feeling of repressed expectation from him. He was planning something. But outwardly he showed no signs of resentment towards them. He showed no signs that he knew them at all.

Crank and Miss Schneider were sitting in a far corner, well out of it all now. Stuart and Gaynor and Teresa and Joanne were sitting closer, at a table with their parents, but their importance had dwindled now they were back safe. The Minister had eyes only for us.

"This is a finely balanced situation," he said. "The Prime Minister and I, and the rest of the government, have the task of ensuring public safety, and – just as important – the public's *feeling* of being safe. The Prime Minister has asked me to invite you all to lunch tomorrow, and he has asked me to ask you to help us in looking after the public. I'm hoping that when we go out there to the press, in a couple of minutes, I can tell the world that we have agreed to help each other, and work together."

He must have felt so helpless, I realised. He had all the armed forces of Britain on a leash, but here were these four kids who were entirely beyond his control, and entirely important to his career suddenly. He smiled his tight-lipped smile again.

Fake Sal was ready.

"We're going to take a day tomorrow to be with our families and recover a little from today," she said levelly. I smiled inwardly in dumb admiration. "As our elected spokesperson I'll agree to meet with you and the Prime Minister the day after tomorrow. George, Pee and Osmo will decide on the day whether they want to come along."

The Minister of Defence had listened to this with an intensely earnest look on his face, but once he'd absorbed and processed what Fake Sal had said he couldn't stop himself from letting out a sigh of relief.

"Hey, who knows," he said, suddenly looking ten years younger. "It could be a lot of fun."

•

Well, he delivered his spiel to the world with a finely judged balance of calm authority and open amazement that must have secured his job for another term. Yes, an alien being had landed at Five Elms at the beginning of the week. Yes, it had made contact with four local school children. Yes, it had died that same night. Yes, it had given the kids a gift of alien technology just before it died. So far there was no reason to anticipate any further contact with the alien's race. Initial appearances suggested it was a lone traveller.

The gym was quiet, save for his voice, just like so many living rooms around the world must have been as his statement was broadcast live. The people sat, unmoving, mouths open slightly, completely focused on the details of our story.

He explained that the alien's body was being held at a government research lab where it could be studied safely. Photos would be made available soon. Mr. Armitage had traced us through an eyewitness account posted on the Internet and had been getting to know us over the course of the day. The full capabilities of the alien technology were, at this point, unclear, but the pods were capable of flight at extreme speeds, teleportation, and they were also capable of teleporting objects and people across undetermined distances. It seemed they could replicate food and clothes and objects. Each pod was assigned to one of us and functioned under a seemingly artificial, programmable, intelligence. It was certainly possible that the pods had further capabilities, as yet undisclosed or undiscovered. It was clearly early days right now, and all of this would have to be looked into.

The press in the room had been briefed sternly on how the conference was to be conducted. They behaved very well, probably excruciatingly aware that they were as much at the centre of the world's awareness as we were. Every reporter held up a hand. The Minister pointed at one of them.

"I want to ask the kids – what were the alien's intentions before it died?"

Me and Pee and Osmo turned to look at Sal, leaving nobody in any doubt about who we expected to speak for us. I could see that she was thinking fast. After what had happened with Pee spilling the beans to Armitage, Sal had warned us not to fill her head with mind talk. We sat and waited for her answer with as much curiosity as everybody else.

"Well, he wasn't really intending anything," she said, after making her pause look like she was gathering courage to speak, rather than frantically thinking up the best lie. "He was just on a journey, passing through our solar system, and he got tired and landed here to rest, and we met him."

The Minister pointed to somebody else.

"How did he communicate with you?"

Sal didn't pause.

"Telepathy."

The Minister pointed at someone else.

"He gave you the four pods that are parked outside. Where did they come from? And what did he travel in?"

I was glad that I wasn't answering these questions.

"He made them for us. He didn't need anything to travel in. He flew through space on his own."

The stunned reaction from the people in front of us was palpable. There was a horrible pregnant pause where everybody seemed to be waiting for her to explain some more, or apologise for saying such a stupid thing, but Fake Sal remained quiet and straight faced.

A hand went up and the Minister pointed.

"How did the alien make the pods?"

"He willed them into being."

Another hand.

"Why did he die?"

"Because he didn't want to live anymore."

"Why not?

"He was tired."

There was another pause. It was almost as if there was so much information coming forward, and so many implications raised, that the reporters couldn't keep up with it, couldn't generate questions quick enough.

A hand went up and the Minister pointed.

"Minister, is it true that there is no way of detaining these children beyond politely asking them to cooperate?"

"That is true," said the Minister gravely. "We are fortunate, extremely fortunate, that this has happened to four individuals who have demonstrated uncommon maturity and responsibility. There is no doubt that this situation is a cause for concern and caution, but I want to stress that, having met these young people, I am hugely reassured."

"But it is still the case, is it not, Minister, that what we have here is four children in possession of potentially dangerous, possibly devastating, alien technology, who can come and go as they please? That is the case isn't it, Minister?"

"What we have here," said the Minister carefully, "is a largely unknown, almost completely unquantified situation. We can talk about 'potential' this and 'possible' that, and scare ourselves silly all night if we want to, but what I would rather do is devote my time and energy to finding out the truth of the matter. There is no evidence that the pods can be used for anything other than travel and accommodation. There's certainly been no evidence to suggest that the pods can be used as weapons, nor that these four young people would be a danger even if potentially aggressive uses of the pods were discovered. I think the last thing we need at the moment is alarmist, inflammatory reactions. What we do need is cool, calm, measured responses."

I was impressed by him.

Another hand.

"What do the parents think? Who needs protecting from who?"

"What I think," barked Pee's mum from the far end of the table, startling several people, "is that we have to put the children first."

I couldn't believe she had the gall to say that.

"These four kids are innocents, and I think it would be a crime if all of these press people lose sight of that and start hounding them just to sell a few newspapers. This is a country...a country that...a...oh dear!...I..." I looked at Pee. He was finding it very hard to keep his face straight. The gleam in his eyes was pure, concentrated wickedness. I knew in that instant that he had neutralised her.

"Are you alright love?" said Pee's dad in a never before seen display of concern for another human being. It's amazing what effect a hundred reporters can have on a personality.

Pee's mum half rose, as if to leave.

"I think I should…" she seemed to think better of it and sat down again, her face reddening, and reddening again. Then she stood up again. Pee's dad suddenly pulled a face of utter disgust, wrinkling his nose and screwing up his eyes. Realising what had happened he quickly tried to twist his expression into a look of pained sympathy.

"I think my wife's feeling unwell. It's been a very emotional day. I'd better take her somewhere." Suddenly his eyes went wide and his cheeks flushed red also. "Come on love," he said in a pinched voice, guiding Pee's mum to her feet. And they scuttled off sideways like mortified crabs.

The Minister wore a face of compassion.

"There's been a bit of a tummy bug going around the school," he explained to the world. I looked at Pee and I could see he was looking around the room, at the ceiling, the light fittings, at anything bland and boring, in an effort to keep from laughing out loud. His little shoulders were shuddering with the strain. I felt happy for him.

Shortly after that the Minister decided we'd had enough. The press conference would continue without us. In a pre-arranged display for the media we beamed ourselves and our parents away from the conference and aboard the runabouts – all except Pee's mum and dad, of course, who were otherwise engaged.

•

Having beamed aboard with Mum and Dad, I had Fleet locate my sister, who was back in the staff room watching the show on one of the monitors. I beamed next to her and warned her to brace herself.

"Oh my god, oh my god, oh my god," she chanted, dancing on tiptoes, a look of terror and desire stretched over her features. I took a moment to savour it, couldn't stop myself from laughing. Yet another golden moment in a long, long day. She gripped onto my arm, nearly drawing blood, as we beamed away.

I was exhausted by this time. They were full of questions. I just wanted sleep.

"You can talk to Fleet," I told them. "She'll take you for a spin and answer your questions." Fleet knew that she wasn't to mention Real Sal and the monodreme. "I've just got to get some sleep."

"Of course you have, babe," said Mum.

In the end though, I found that I was too proud of Fleet to go to bed before I'd flown them around the world a bit and talked about the different things she could do. We cruised the streets of New York, plunged to the deepest, darkest, most crushing depths of the ocean. I allowed them a little trip to the moon. We stopped by at the Sea of Tranquillity and paid a visit to Apollo Landing Site 2. Fleet gave us a tour-guide running commentary and it didn't feel as bad as I had expected it to, to be sharing her with them. I buzzed to see them so startled and excited and filled with wonder at everything, like little kids on Christmas morning.

After I'd beamed them back home, and had Fleet transform my flight chair into the world's comfiest bed, after I'd fallen back beneath the thickest, lightest duvet in existence and had her turn the entire pod transparent, so I could float above a sea of clouds and beneath a sky of sparkling stars and distant planets, I thought to myself that things might just turn out okay. The whole world might be queuing up to take a bite of us, but we had the runabouts to keep us safe, and we had each other. A picture flashed in my mind of Pee biting his lip and peering up at the ceiling through innocent eyelashes as he neutralised his parents, and I felt a sudden rush of love for my three friends. We had each other. That's all we would ever need. Wrapped in warmth I fell, like a stone, into a dream.

·

I am standing out on our street, and it's somehow stretching all the way to the horizon in both directions. The sky is dark, and fat raindrops are falling. Wendy Drewson, the girl from media studies, is looking up from her notebook.

"George," she is saying. "George, I want to take down your particulars."

"What?" I grunt, but a great gust of wind rushes through me. I turn to see my paper underwear flapping up into the sky like a pair of white bats. I turn back to Wendy, covering myself with my hands before she can write down my particulars, but her arms have turned into metal wings, and her feet into metal talons, and she swoops up into the air with a screech. I watch her spiral higher, flying to meet the robot vultures that are circling overhead, turning and turning in perfect formation around a great big empty hole. There are six billion of them. From the hole they stretch all the way to the horizon in all directions, blotting out the sky. The sound of their distant, metal voices calls to me. The pattern of their formation twists like a huge vortex, threatening to suck me into space. I blink, and it suddenly looks like a big metal eye is looking down at me. I want to run indoors but an unseen watcher is twitching the net curtain of each and every window. I cower naked in the street, clutching my privates, then I start to fall upwards into the sky, into the pupil of the eye, and I scream.

I wake up just as I fall out of bed to see that I really am falling into the sky. And even after I land in the invisible bottom of the pod I feel like I'm falling. I scream and I scream. Fleet makes the interior of the pod visible again and still I scream, until she bathes me in a soothing purple energy field that takes everything away.

8
Oceana

As far as the laws of mathematics refer to reality, they are not certain;
as far as they are certain, they do not refer to reality.
- Albert Einstein

The British winter was closing its damp, half-hearted fist around the islands. Fleet hung, cloaked, in the dull air over Iron Street. Sitting on the edge of my flight chair I stared down at the tarmac road outside our house. It looked so bland and reassuring. I zoned out for a little while, just sitting there, staring, disappearing. Then I blinked slowly, wondered how much time had passed, and sighed.

When I beamed down into the kitchen there was nobody in there, but I could hear Emma singing to herself in the living room, all energised because I'd agreed to loan her Fleet. The kitchen seemed dingy and grey and small around me. There was a dead woodlouse on the floor, curled up on its back, its legs like dried up old eyelashes. A dismal feeling of claustrophobia swelled in my throat. My head grew heavier on my neck, my eyelids felt like lead weights on my eyes. I lowered myself gently into a chair at the table, considered resting my face down amongst the cereal bowls and going to sleep, but Emma bounced into the room and I forced myself to sit up straight.

"Georgey!" she yelled. Spontaneously she started dancing in front of me. Then she began some sing song white girl rap, as though she just couldn't keep it inside: "I am gonna party...party in the sky, yeah...I'm the coolest girl...in the whole wide world, yeah...come and watch me party...but you're not invited..." She broke out into a giggle, stopped with a flourish and waited for applause.

"God, that was awful," I said.

"Yeah, like you would know. So, is my runabout fully pimped and ready, or what?"

I waved a hand lazily.

"Yeah, she's all yours."

Emma let out a pure, concentrated, ear-splitting squeal of girly excitement. It really hurt.

"Oww! Stop it! Clear off, will you!"

"Er, how do I go?"

"Just say, 'Come in, Fleet, one to beam up', and she'll beam you up."

"What, she'll hear me, just like that?"

"She's listening in on you...unfortunately for her."

"Oh my god, that's so amazing! I'm too scared to do it!"

"Please…do it. Disappear."

She grinned gleefully, not fazed at all by my attitude. But then she suddenly seemed to notice me.

"Are you alright? You look like crap. Have you got the flu or something?"

"I'm alright."

She took a deep breath and kind of let the excitement evaporate off her and disappear into the air.

"All this stuff in the papers getting to you?"

Just hearing her raise the subject I wanted to go into a coma. I shrugged and tried not to answer but couldn't help myself.

"Anyone who actually pays money for one of those things is an idiot and doesn't deserve to know what's really going on in the world."

For the past couple of days quite a few of the papers had been making a big deal out of the fact that nobody had set eyes on Pee and Osmo ever since some photographer had caught a shot of me and Fake Sal sneaking a kiss at a garden party at the White House. The headlines had filled with all kinds of rubbish about us not having any time to help the world because we were too busy having teenage love feuds.

"So none of it's true, then?"

"Well…look…" I said, nausea coiling in my belly, "…if *we* don't know why they're not talking to us how would the papers know?"

Emma shifted on her feet uncomfortably.

"Well, you know, they just say it's kind of obvious."

Scum-sucking papers! How could so much change in just a couple of weeks?

"You see!" I cried, jumping to my feet. "How typical is that? Sal has been at the United Nations nearly every day trying to work out how the runabouts can help the world! She's been working herself to the bone!"

Emma shrugged.

"Yeah, I know. But she's the only one, isn't she? You boys haven't done…anything! You just seem to be hiding away in your runabouts. It is because you're fighting over her, isn't it?"

My mind seemed to be suddenly erased by a wave of white heat.

"Don't you listen to a word I say!" I screamed in a weird, shrill voice that didn't sound like mine. "How can I be fighting with them when they won't even talk to me! How am I supposed to help the world when the countries can't even decide between themselves who needs helping first? You think it's easy! The only reason anyone wants to talk to me these days is because they want something off me! Can't you see that!"

Emma was pale and wide-eyed in the onslaught of my outburst. She tried to shrug and say something but I had more…

"Cos you're no different! Are you...ay! Well, look! You've got it! You've got the runabout! Go and enjoy yourself, and you can have all the fun you want, slagging me off to all your friends, while you're at it! Go on! That's what you want isn't it!"

There was a horrible moment of pure silence where my sister's face seemed to waver in front of me like a reflection on the surface of a pond. From being just pale she suddenly turned white, like an avalanche. She came into sharp focus then, slapped me across the face so hard I heard a bell, and for a few moments I couldn't remember what my troubles had been.

•

Emma sat me down. I lay my face on the tabletop, feeling the glass surface cool my skin where it was glowing pink, while she made me a coffee. Halfway through drinking it I tried to mumble some kind of apology but she stopped me.

"You should get off on your picnic with Sal," she said. "That'll make you feel better."

I nodded gratefully. She was right. A bit of alone time with Fake, a bit of time with somebody who could understand. Fleet patched me through to her on an audio chatline.

"Hey, Sal. Permission to beam aboard?"

"Yeah..." came her voice, transmitted into the kitchen as clearly as if she were standing there, only it sounded hesitant.

"'Yeah' but what?"

"Is it okay if Mum comes along?"

"Your mum?" So much for the alone time. But then, Christine was virtually one of us anyway. "Yeah, sure, I suppose so. Yeah, it'll be fun."

"And a friend of hers?"

"A friend?" I looked at my sister. She had about a million people lined up to join her onboard Fleet. She'd already come up with some kind of rota so she could do them in batches of nine. It was going to get pretty sweaty in my pod. I waved bye bye to my alone time with Fake Sal. "Just your mum and one friend? Or is it more like nine?"

"Just the one, Mr. Grumpy."

"Yeah, sure. Why not."

"Great! Permission granted."

"Beam me over please, Fleet."

Emma waved as I disappeared. The kitchen faded away to be replaced by the interior of Fake Sal's runabout. I was sitting sideways on to the dome and my flight chair was pushed back against the wall to make room for the three other flight chairs in there. There was Christine and there was Fake Sal. Fake Sal had a pensive look on her face. The third person I didn't recognise at first because he was wearing jeans and a sweater and a pair of trainers.

"Hello, George," said Armitage.

I blasphemed energetically.

"What's he doing here?"

There was a moment's hesitation as they all waited for somebody else to answer. Eventually it fell to Fake Sal.

"Mr. Armitage and Mum...they've kind of got a thing going," she said, awkwardly.

I looked from Armitage to Christine to Fake Sal and back again.

"I see we have your approval, then," quipped Armitage.

I ignored him and turned to Christine.

"No, Christine," I said. "Christine, no."

"George," she said, squirming in her seat, but I held up a pre-emptive hand.

"No! Don't say anything. Just get rid of him." I turned to Armitage. "Sorry, Mr. Armitage. No offence or anything but...on yer bike."

"George," he said. "With all due respect, I don't think that's really your decision."

"Actually, you're wrong there. Christine gave us all powers of veto over any new boyfriend because she knows her judgement is...well, it's not good. You're a really good example. I'm vetoing you. Tom, please get rid of this guy. Send him home."

"Sal?" asked Tom.

Fake Sal wriggled unhappily in her seat and didn't answer.

"Sal!" I said. "Come on! How many times have we been here? I mean...Armitage!"

"I know, but she really likes him."

I couldn't believe my ears. I turned to Christine and I took a breath and toned it down.

"Christine, you know he's just using you. You do know that don't you?"

Christine winced and squirmed some more.

"He might not be," she whispered. I felt a pang.

"But we asked Tom," said Fake Sal.

"What do you mean?"

"We asked Tom if he was just using her to get close to us."

"Really? Is this right, Tom?"

"Well, I'm no expert in affairs of the heart," said Tom Baker, "but he definitely fancies her."

I threw up my hands in despair.

"Well, duh! Of course he fancies her! I fancy her! Everybody fancies Christine! That's the main problem. I'm sorry Christine, but no. Veto. Big fat veto. He's got to go. Sal?"

Fake Sal didn't do anything.

"Sal?"

"I'm sorry, George. No."

"Have you gone insane?"

She waved her hands in front of me like she had gone insane.

"If he's here with us we can keep an eye on him. If they start sneaking around behind our backs, well, anything could happen. I'm going to let him come along."

I clapped my hands over my face.

"Nooo!" I groaned miserably. "It'll end in tears."

"George," said Armitage quietly. "I'm not here to find out about anything. I'm not here to spy on anyone."

"Honestly, Mr. Armitage, it's nothing personal. I'm sure you're a good guy, and stuff. But anyway, that's not the point. How are we supposed to relax and have a nice time in front of somebody who's going to be reporting everything straight back to his superiors? Really?"

"George," said Christine, "Stephen isn't going to report anything you say. Are you, Stephen?"

"Well, I guess if he happens to mention in passing that the runabouts have a full compliment of nuclear warheads, or something like that, I might feel obliged to mention it."

Well, at least he was being honest.

"But it really doesn't matter, does it, George? No matter what we know, you can always know more about us. No matter what we do, you can always do more than us. How does it matter if I overhear things?"

I looked at Fake Sal and Christine.

"Well, I'm not getting rid of him, anyway," said Fake Sal. "So are you coming on this picnic or not?"

A pod full of traitors and double agents. Wonderful.

"Okay Mr. Armitage," I said flatly.

"Please, call me Stephen."

"Very well."

"Thank you, George."

•

The gravity on Oceana is almost twice that of Earth. Tom Baker said it was not a problem. He would 'coat us' in an invisible field that would protect us (and our sandwiches) from the excessive gravity and would allow us to breathe.

We zipped quickly around the night-side of the planet and then entered the atmosphere, heading for a field of pillow plants that MarvinMilton had shown us. We found it on the huge continent we had named Pangaea, hundreds of miles inland on a plateau in the southern mountains. Fake Sal brought us to rest a few hundred yards from a narrow mountain stream.

The field sprawled in yellow, softly rounded humps, speckled with minute red flowers, to the stream on our east side, to the mountains in the north and to a vast expanse of sea green sky in the south and west. It was just as it had been on MarvinMilton's virtual tour and I suddenly had a weird sensation of being back inside his mind, as if I could blink and find myself sitting on the ground at Five Elms with my four friends. Then it came to me that not one of them was there with me now. A sudden sense of loss shrunk my lungs. I had to turn my face away from the others, unprepared for finding myself close to tears.

I heard Sal's mum and Armitage hesitating in the hatch of the runabout.

"It smells like onions," said Christine, sounding disappointed.

•

"George," said Fake Sal quietly. "What's up?"

Armitage and Christine were wandering away, following the stream in the direction of the mountains, both looking slightly ridiculous as they tried to walk over the spongy pillow plants and maintain some kind of dignity at the same time. Soon enough Christine started bunny-hopping along the bank of the stream, laughing. This made Fake Sal smile but I sighed, untouched. I had thought I'd managed to cover up how low I was feeling.

"I was just thinking about Osmo and Pee, I suppose," I said.

She nodded and creased her brow. A squeal came from Christine as she fell over and Armitage had to rescue her from tumbling into the stream. Fake Sal watched them thoughtfully. Then she seemed to have an idea that brightened her and she turned back to me.

"Look," she said. "Let's do that thing we were talking about."

All of a sudden, replica or not, she seemed like the most real thing in the whole universe. My black mood lifted into the air above me and wafted away on a breeze.

"Really?"

"Yeah."

"Alright!"

I quickly checked to make sure the grown-ups had bunny-hopped out of sight and I started to take her top off. She beat my hands away with a few hard slaps.

"No! Not that," she snapped.

"What?"

"The thing about the monods."

"The monods? What? Oh! The monods! That thing! Right."

I shook my head and tried to readjust my expectations. It wasn't easy.

"I thought my luck was in then."

"You don't say," she said, smiling like an angel. It was ridiculous really, I could fly across the universe, teleport, land on other planets, but none of it sent me into a head spin as much as going out with Fake Sal.

She smoothed out her clothing while I composed myself. Then I cocked my head at her.

"Are you sure about this? The monod thing."

"Didn't you think I'd agree?"

"I don't know. MarvinMilton didn't want us to see any other monods. I thought maybe you'd want to respect his wishes."

"Yeah, but that was because he said seeing them would give us clues about the monodreme. But we know about that now."

"I suppose."

"What?"

"I don't know. I just wonder if there was another reason he didn't want us to see them. I kind of got the feeling there was."

"Oh," she said, looking serious. "Well, maybe we shouldn't do it then."

"Oh," I said, deflating.

"But we'll talk ourselves into it one way or another though, won't we?" She pointed out.

"Well, maybe we should do the other thing for a bit, while we think about it."

I tugged suggestively at her top, again.

"Come on," she said with mock primness. "We can do that later."

How can they be so controlled, I wondered. She bounced to her feet and bunny-hopped over to Tom's hatch.

"Tom."

- **Fake Sal**, said Tom.

"How far off are the nearest monods?"

- **Fifteen point three kilometres due north**, said Tom Baker without hesitation. Fake Sal turned to me.

"Should we teleport?"

"Let's take Tom."

"But what about Mum and Armitage?"

"We'll leave them a note." Her eyes widened.

"That's naughty," she breathed. Her mouth was turning up at the corners. "They'll be stranded on a strange planet until we get back."

"I know," I said solemnly. She sucked her cheeks in and crossed her eyes. I raised my eyebrows and nodded thoughtfully.

"Could we have a pen and a notepad please, Tom?" she said.

•

We swooped down the mountainside, cloaked, and thoughts of world leaders, tabloid newspapers and pain-in-the-arse friends were all a galaxy

109

away. Tom Baker had a red circle blip on and off on the dome for us, pinpointing the location of the monods - MarvinMilton's people. Fake Sal curved the runabout down towards a wide turquoise valley. We leaned forward in our flight chairs as she brought us skimming low over the broad grassland, and then we caught our first sight of them.

There were three, straggled out in single file, headed towards the centre of the valley where a thin stream sketched its way to the lowlands. As we drew closer we slowed. They were naked, just as MarvinMilton had been. And, like him, they seemed to be sexless.

"I wonder how they have babies," mumbled Fake Sal, guiding the runabout to float in front of the leading monod. We were close enough to see the expression on his face. His eyes weren't golden, but they were keenly intelligent.

- It's quite fascinating, explained Tom Baker. **Each one lays between one and six eggs when they reach maturity. They don't need to have sex. As a species they are monosexual.**

"Nice and simple," I said.

"Bit boring, though," said Fake Sal.

She brought the runabout around and had it floating backwards slowly, keeping pace with the lead monod. He walked at a steady pace, his broad feet leaving flattened disks like miniature crop circles in the turquoise grass. He didn't look about himself much, facing forward into the straight line he was walking as if he was focused on his destination by a deep purpose. A meely bug droned by and he watched it absently for a few moments until it had zigzagged away behind him, then his attention returned to the serious business of treading the grass.

"Where are they going?" I asked.

- To the stream.

"What for?"

- For water.

"For a drink?"

- Yes.

I watched him, the lead monod, and admired the simplicity of what he was doing, walking naked beneath the sky, down to the stream for a drink of water. Even his body was simple. I remembered the startling difference I had witnessed in MarvinMilton's body from when he was alive and radiating light to when he was dead and waxen in the night. These monods were somewhere in between. Not ghoulish and grey, but not golden and glorious either. They were solid and earthy. Humble.

"If we de-cloaked and got out and talked to them, Tom, could you translate for us?"

There was a significant pause.

- No.

I was a bit taken aback. It didn't seem like something that Tom wouldn't be able to do. I looked at Fake Sal and I could see that she was surprised too.

"Why not, Tom?" she asked.

- Because they have no language for me to translate your words into.

"No language?" I said.

- No language.

The lead monod arrived at the stream and knelt down. He leaned forward until he was lying on his belly, his head and chest and shoulders extending beyond the edge of the bank, his elbows giving him the leverage to lower his chin towards the clear running water. There was something about the way he did it that disturbed me. His jaw lowered into the glittering water. I could see his neck working as he swallowed, smoothly and continuously. And then I realised. I realised what they were.

"They don't have any cities, do they, Tom?" I said, the edge in my voice making Fake Sal turn to me.

- No.

"They don't have any towns or villages or anything like that, do they?"

- No.

I was back again, on the edge of knowledge, where it crowded in around me like light, and all I had to do was open my eyes and see it. But like a fugitive who has been crawling, lost, down pitch black tunnels, and has now emerged into an open space, I was afraid to look, afraid to find out exactly where I'd brought myself.

A cloud passed in front of Oceana's sun that we had named Los, casting its shadow across the drinking monod and us. The second monod arrived at the stream, lay down beside the first and lowered his jaw to the water. Soon the third would do the same.

"They're animals, aren't they? They're just animals. Aren't they?"

- Yes.

"Like monkeys," I said. "Or pigeons."

- Yes, said Tom Baker.

"And MarvinMilton used to be one of them."

- Yes.

My mind reeled. How could it be? How could it be that MarvinMilton had risen from being such a simple creature, without language, without a society, walking peacefully over the plains of Oceana, to become a golden being that could travel between the stars and speak to the minds of strangers? It was no more possible for him to do that than it was for a monkey from Earth to start flying around and fighting crime like Superman. What had happened to him? What had been done to him?

I tore my gaze away from the monods, ready at last to ask the questions that would open my eyes. Ready for the knowledge. Ready, only because I couldn't stand the darkness any longer.

"Tom," I said. But I was too late. Already I had seen Fake Sal's face. Already I was following her stricken gaze up to the sky. Already I was seeing that the cloud blocking the light from Los wasn't a cloud at all. It was an object.

"Oh, God," said a voice. Some part of me was dimly aware that it was mine.

Already I was telling myself that nothing so massive could possibly stay up there like that. It was filling my vision, gliding slowly, remorselessly, like an iron door shutting over the world, or like the corner of a flying tombstone slotting into place, taking away the sky. It was too big to be a spaceship. It was too big to be a space station. It was too big to fit in the atmosphere, but there it was, sprawling into the distance, towering up through the stratosphere. We had to lean forward into the dome and twist our heads, angling our faces upwards and sideways, to look up steeply enough to see its foremost side towering in a sheer vertical wall that was eventually lost in the heights above us. And, though the size was staggering, it was clear that what we were seeing was only the tip of something that stretched far beyond the horizon and carried on out of sight for a long, long way. We could see three sides that came together to form a roughly square corner, but it was so much more complicated than that. The surfaces of the two walls and the underside were carved and pitted with channels that varied wildly in width and depth and fitted in and around each other, intersecting with each other at great circular wells like the lines of a massive circuit diagram. And the walls of the channels themselves were carved and pitted also, and so on and so on. The areas between the channels, that actually were flat, were lined with regular rows of minute looking squares, each equidistant from its surrounding neighbours, that could have been the windows of an impossibly, preposterously huge apartment block. But if the whole thing were a flying block of flats then I was smaller than an ant, and my senses were too tiny to comprehend what was before me.

It was alien, yet strangely familiar at the same time as if it had visited me before, in a long forgotten dream.

There was a rushing sound suddenly that increased in volume, again and then again, until I realised it was the sound of my own blood in my ears. Fake Sal was screaming at me. I could hear the words clearly enough, through the roaring in my head, but they meant nothing to me. All I knew was the flying monolith outside. It seemed to be filling the whole of my mind. I started to fear that my skull would crack open, outwards from within, because there was too much trying to fit in there. I wondered if this was what it had been like for MarvinMilton as he evolved faster than he was supposed to, filled with the knowledge of things that he wasn't ready for, understanding the answers to questions that should never even have occurred to him. I didn't want to grow up that quick. The idea filled me

112

with fear, and I realised the fear was of becoming something else, and losing my self along the way. It would be like dying in a way. I didn't want to die.

But suddenly, somewhere in all of the rushing and the roaring and the fear, a little bubble of calm and peace appeared, and there inside it was a part of me, a calm me, standing and thinking clearly.

- **I wonder if that's Real Sal,** he said. It hadn't occurred to me that this terrifying structure could be Real Sal, transformed by the powers of the monodreme. But it made sense in a way. What else could be so vast and frightening? What else could radiate such an impression of power? Then the calm me turned and looked up, and I was looking down into my own eyes, and I could see he was standing on a circle of turquoise grass.

- **What's Fake Sal saying?** he asked.

I turned dumbly to face Fake Sal. Something somewhere went 'pop!' and the roaring receded a little and her words began to make sense to me.

"My mum!" she was shouting, her eyes pleading for me to respond. "We've got to get back to my mum!"

I nodded stupidly. Sal registered that I seemed to be back with the living and fell back into her flight chair. A look of fierce determination twisted her face and she sent the runabout searing through the air, back the way we had come, further into the deepening shadow of the flying monolith.

The air streamed by outside the dome, and I knew that if we had been able to hear it it would have been screaming. We covered the fifteen kilometres back to the site of the picnic in about three seconds. We were far beneath the immense shadow now. There was the picnic gear, spread out on the yellow field below in the unnatural twilight. I noticed the note we had left them, lying on the ground a little way off, then it was caught up by a wind and carried away, but Christine and Mr. Armitage were nowhere to be seen.

9
Into the Bullet Hole

The most incomprehensible thing about the world
is that it is at all comprehensible.
- Albert Einstein

"Where are they, Tom?" demanded Fake Sal. "Where's my mum?" She was unconsciously beating out the passing moments on the arm of her flight chair with the heel of her right hand, over and over.

- **My dear,** said Tom Baker in a soft voice. **Your mother and Mr. Armitage are onboard the alien vessel.**

Fake Sal froze. Her breathing went on hold, and no part of her made the slightest movement but for her eyes, which grew wider and wider in the silence.

"Oh my god," she said. "Get her back, Tom. Beam her back, right now."

There was a pause. It wasn't much of a pause but it was there, and I knew straight away, and I'm sure she did as well, that he was going to say something terrible.

- **I'm afraid I can't do that.**

The words fell into our minds like paving slabs. Our world buckled under their weight. Fake Sal's head nodded slightly, as if it had become too heavy for her. She blinked slowly.

"Why not, Tom?" she said in a small, emotionless voice that unnerved the hell out of me.

Another pause, like he could barely bring himself to answer.

- **Real Sal programmed me not to interfere with alien activities.**

She absorbed this information dumbly, her shoulders stooped.

"Tom. Bring her back."

- **I'm sorry, my dear.**

"Tom."

- **I can't.**

"Tom. Why did you let it happen? Why didn't you tell me?"

- **My programming,** he said helplessly.

Her head turned to point at me, but there was no focus in her eyes. The muscles of her face had gone slack and she didn't look like Sal at all.

- **George,** she said in my mind. **I left her a note.** Then she fell out of her flight chair and landed in a heap at the bottom of the pod. I stood there like an idiot for a moment, just staring at her. I was still trying to convince myself that she had actually fainted as I crouched down and turned her over onto her back.

"Tom, can you bring her round?"

"I think it would be best to let her come around in her own time," he said. I noted he had withdrawn the mind link now that Fake Sal was unconscious. "Her system has had a shock."

I glanced out of the dome at the monstrous object. There were two tiny humans up there somewhere. *Christine! How can Christine be up there?*

"Tom! There isn't the time. What's the matter with you?"

"Nothing is the matter with me, George. I'm looking after her as best I can."

"She needs her mum!" I barked, struggling to lift her limp body. Tom Baker didn't answer, but when I succeeded in getting her into the chair it tilted silently back and changed shape so that she was lying down.

The pod was filled with the sound of my breathing.

"I'm sorry, Tom," I said. "I didn't mean to shout."

"That's alright. We're both doing the best we can."

I looked at Fake Sal lying there. I could feel the terrible presence of the object in the sky above me, pressing down. *What am I supposed to do?*

"I don't think I'm doing my best," I said.

He didn't reply.

Fake Sal started to come round and I asked Tom Baker for a glass of water, which he provided. I held it to her lips as she propped herself up on her elbows and she let me pour some into her mouth. When she tried to sit up I gently pushed her back into the chair.

"Just take a moment," I said.

Her face was ashen and her hair was plastered across her forehead. She lay back for a few moments staring at the top of the pod and breathing. She looked at me but she spoke to Tom.

"Fix me, Tom," she said. "Make me feel better."

A green energy field appeared, enveloping the flight chair, and I watched some colour return to her. "Get in your seat, George," she said.

"Fake, I think you should give yourself…"

"Manual control, Tom."

- You have control.

The pod was speeding through the air instantly. I quickly clambered into my chair. The ground and the alien vessel blurred by below and above us. Fake Sal was propelling us forward at a sickening speed but still the huge craft scrolled by overhead with no end in sight.

"I don't believe it," I moaned. "It goes on forever.

"No, it doesn't," she snarled, and with a flexing of her mind she multiplied our speed by some big number. The ground and the space ship disappeared behind us and we were rocketing up into the sky. She executed the equivalent of a handbrake turn and reversed us up and out of the atmosphere so we could see the size of our problem properly.

"Oh my god," I said. It wasn't original but I just couldn't think of anything else to say. "What is that thing, Tom?"

- It is a modular, island class vessel belonging to an alien race called the Go. It is called the *Dah Rhiv Artiv Da*.

"How big is it, exactly?"

- To the nearest kilometre it is 24 kilometres high, 96 kilometres wide and 216 kilometres long. The well is 12 kilometres across.

The 'well', as Tom called it, was a circular hole that passed through the vessel from top to bottom at its centre of gravity, like a bullet hole. The only other large-scale feature was that the corners were bevelled. And that was it. It was yellow and grey. It was a rectangular slab with a hole in it. It hung in the air above Oceana, almost touching the mountains to the north, which it towered over. The greater bulk of the ship covered the steppes of the New Kurtsholme Plateau with the unnatural nighttime of its shadow. But its westerly and easterly ends, and a narrow strip of its southern edge, projected out over the foothills and lowlands of the Great Openshaw Plain. Pangaea sprawled away in all directions, hugging the curve of the world. Nomadic clouds traversing its surface were finding their way blocked by the giant, yellow and grey structure, and were being forced to make their way around it.

"Show me the quickest route to my mum, Tom," said Fake Sal.

A glowing red line appeared in the dome that seemed to project down into the well. Fake Sal sent the runabout racing forward, following the line.

"Sal, I'm not sure..." I squealed, but then vertigo gripped my throat, choking off my words, and it was all I could do not to cry like Stuart Towns had done.

Down and down we went. As we shot into the massive vertical tunnel it felt to me like we were entering the eye of a hurricane. Fake Sal slowed the runabout a little, maybe because she was afraid, maybe because she wanted to see what we were getting ourselves into - I wasn't about to ask her. But we both leaned forward into the dome and looked about at the tremendous tube we were sinking into, taking what time we could to soak up our surroundings as the runabout followed its course. The side of the well curved around us six kilometres away on every side. Static and moving lights, mostly blue, white and red, outlined gaping portholes and slits and rectangular entrances of all sizes. It was clear to me you could dock (or launch) a pretty hefty fleet here. That's if you're talking in gigantic understatements. It was beautiful, majestic, mesmerising.

The runabout followed the red line into a side tunnel, took a few turns, rose up a small sub well, followed more tunnels, and sank down another sub well.

"Tom," said Fake Sal. "How long is it going to take at this speed?"

- Nineteen minutes and five seconds.

Fake Sal slammed the speed on and the lights became a blur around us as she followed the red line, letting Tom Baker's anti-collision protocols tidy up her flying at sudden drops and sharp corners. She increased the speed steadily and it was less than a minute later that we realised we had arrived at our destination because the runabout came to a sudden halt facing a wall. The red line seemed to disappear into it.

After the blurred journey of narrow tunnels and anonymous lights, that was over so quickly, we weren't quite prepared for our first real look at the interior of the vast craft. Having seen the outside of the *Dah Rhiv Artiv Da*, as Tom had named it, I shouldn't have been surprised that the space we found ourselves in was so big, but I was. The inside of a spaceship should be cramped. Everybody knew that. The limitless reaches of the vacuum of space are hard and unforgiving and anything that is going to get you safely across any expanse of that stuff is going to have to be very economical: just enough air to breathe, just enough room to move, just enough food to eat. Somehow my short life of being a science fiction geek hadn't made room in my mind for a spaceship with areas big enough to fit cathedrals in, and big cathedrals at that.

The wall that the runabout was facing, the wall that was separating us from Christine and Armitage, was actually one side of a square pillar that rose high into the cavernous space above our heads. *They've put Christine and Armitage in a pillar?* This pillar was standing in line with more of the same. They receded in single file ahead of us for about two kilometres before meeting a vast blank wall. Daylight was shining in hazy beams from high between the pillars through great windows that were deeply recessed and out of sight. The surfaces of the floor, walls, ceiling and pillars seemed almost rocklike. As I looked closer I fancied they had been made from big slabs of hardened resin.

The giant room gave off a feeling of ancient permanence. It looked like something a million years old that hadn't changed at all since the day it was constructed. I felt I was in a giant temple.

Fake Sal's hand clawed onto my arm. I looked and saw that she was staring down at the base of the pillar in front of us. There was an alien standing there in the shadow, looking at us, as motionless as the pillars.

"Tom," said Fake Sal. "Can you translate for us?"

- Yes, my dear.

"Tell it we want Christine and Armitage back."

"Ae ahl rae a khiv," said Tom Baker.

The alien stepped forward, out of the shadow. It was tall, about seven feet, and thin. It was wearing long straight robes, very simple and pale. It was a biped, but it had two sets of arms, one immediately below the other. Its head was bald and narrow and kind of reminded me of an antelope. Its neck was jointed forward in the middle like a knee. Something in its bearing gave an impression of great alertness. It stood very simply and quietly, yet I felt it was poised for action. The whole situation suddenly seemed unreal, as if the runabout was a little home cinema and I was watching a computer animation.

"No," said the alien in a sandpapery voice.

Fake Sal gasped.

"Tom. It can speak English?"

- Yes, my dear.

"So why did you translate for us?"

- Because you asked me to, of course.

"But how does it speak English? And how does it know we speak English?"

- To answer the second question first: the Go have been listening in on Christine and Stephen. This Go can speak English because she is a first contact specialist who has spent time on Earth.

"You're joking!" I said. "But, hang on, that's a bit of a coincidence, isn't it?"

- Not really. Between them the inhabitants of this vessel can speak a variety of languages originating from over four thousand different planets in this galaxy, many of which are inhabited by species as primitive as humanity. It would actually be quite unlikely that somebody onboard couldn't speak English.

We sat back in our chairs, faced with the suddenly daunting prospect of conversing directly with the weird looking character outside the pod.

"Okay, Tom," said Fake Sal. "We're going to talk to it. Project our voices please."

- Very good.

Fake Sal leaned forward, gripping the arms of her chair tightly, and she hesitated. I could tell her mouth had gone dry. But this was the girl who had been talking at the United Nations for the past two weeks. I knew she'd come up with something.

"Release our people," she said in a quiet, flat voice.

The Go's head moved slightly.

"No," she said again.

I saw the muscles clenching along Fake Sal's jaw and I wasn't sure which one of them I should feel sorry for.

"What are you doing to them?"

Again the Go's head moved slightly, as if she were scenting information on Fake Sal through the sound waves of her question.

"We are keeping them," she said in her strange, scratchy voice.

Fake Sal bit her top lip and started tapping the arms of her chair in that way that told me she was close to losing it. I reached out and put a hand on her arm, telling her to let me have a go.

"Why are you keeping them?" I asked.

A slightly bigger movement of the alien's head as she picked up a new voice.

"We require information. Perhaps your people can give it to us. Perhaps you will give it to us?"

A feeling of deep foreboding stirred in my belly. It was a threat. I felt Fake Sal's arm tense and I gripped my hand tighter, urging her to hang on.

"What information do you require?" I asked.

"We must know where the monodreme is."

I looked at Fake Sal in alarm, not wanting to say anything out loud.

- We can talk like this, she said.

- What should we do?

- Well, we don't know where the monodreme is. We may as well just say that.

I didn't have any better ideas. She turned back to the dome.

"We don't know where the monodreme is. And our people don't know either. Give them back to us. They haven't done anything to you."

"Your craft defies natural law. It is a product of the monodreme."

- Oh cripes, I said. They're pretty sharp.

"Look!" said Fake Sal. "I want to talk to my mum. We're not going to talk about anything else until I know she's okay."

"Your 'mum'?" said the alien. Her head made a series of tiny bird-like twitches. "The female is your mother?"

"Yes! Let me talk to her."

The Go held up one of her hands.

"Please wait."

The alien stood there motionless and nothing happened.

- What's going on, Tom?

- She is communicating with other Go using a form of telepathy facilitated by implanted technology.

"You may speak with your people," said the alien suddenly. "Speak now, they will hear you."

"Mum! Mum, are you there? Are you okay?"

Christine's voice came from the direction of the pillar and it was shrill with emotion.

"Sal! Sal! What's happening? Where are you?"

"I'm in Tom Baker, Mum. Are you alright?"

"We couldn't find you! We ran back to the blanket but you weren't there. The creatures came down...they got us! Sal, I don't like it! Get us out!"

"I will do, Mum," said Fake Sal, her voice cracking. "I'll get you out, don't worry. Just hold on for a tiny bit and I'll get you out, I promise."

"What's happening? What are they? What do they want with us?"

"Christine," it was Armitage's voice, quiet and together. "Just stop for a moment and take a few breaths. Sal and George are okay, that's the main thing."

"Yes...yes..." mumbled Christine's voice, but she sounded pretty out of it. Then she started sobbing. Fake Sal was out of her chair but within the tight confines of the pod she had nowhere to go. Her hands were flexing into talons as she forced a kind of calmness into her voice.

"It won't be long, Mum. I'm just going to talk to them and then you'll be back with me in the runabout, okay?"

At first Christine didn't want the audio contact to be broken but after a good deal of coaxing and wheedling from Fake Sal and Armitage, and a few mumbled words of encouragement from me, she gave in. Her voice trembled as she promised to be brave.

- **Tom, break off all communication with the outside**, said Fake Sal.
- **It is done.**

I was leaning to get out of my chair so I could give her a hug or something when Fake Sal screamed with all her might. The sound pierced my eardrums and it was full of horror and rage and emotions that I can't name but they made me feel sick as she filled the inside of the pod with them. I fell back in my chair as she blasted it out, her face contorted and crazed with abandon, her hair everywhere. My back and arms erupted in goose bumps. Then, when the scream was out, she grabbed hold of her empty flight chair and began slamming it down against the floor of the runabout.

"I left her! I left her! I left her!" she yelled.

I had no idea of what I should do but I knew I couldn't just sit there watching so I jumped on her and pinned her arms to her sides in a bear hug.

"Sal! We'll sort it! We'll sort it!"

She went wild in my grip and kicked me a couple of good ones on my right shin and then threw me off easily with crazy girl strength. Then she grabbed a couple of handfuls of my T-shirt and pounded my chest really hard.

"Why did you let me, eh?" she demanded. "Why did you let me leave her?"

I didn't have an answer but she didn't seem to expect one. She let go of me and sat back on her heels in the bottom of the pod. Her head was bowed, her face hidden by her hair. She stayed like that for a while, the craziness all back on the inside again. I was about to say her name when she climbed to her feet and got back into her flight chair.

"Okay, Tom, I'm ready to talk to them again," she said.

- **Very well, my dear**, said Tom Baker.

I managed to climb to my feet again but my legs felt hollow and limp.

"Thank you for letting me talk to my mother," said Fake Sal to the waiting alien. "Now you must give her back to me or I'll have to take her back by force."

"No," said the alien. "When you tell us all you know about the monodreme we will release your people to you. Not before."

"You can't use my mother as a bargaining chip," said Fake Sal in slow measured tones. "If you don't release her right now I will attack your ship. This craft is a product of the monodreme and it has the power to destroy you. I will attack your ship, and I won't stop until you give my mum back to me. I mean it. She's frightened and she's innocent and I won't let you scare her anymore. Give her back to me now, or I'll begin the attack."

"No," said the Go, without hesitation.

I was filled with admiration for Fake Sal's strength and determination. If I'd been the Go, hearing the steel in her voice, I would have given in. But they were obviously cool customers. Now they'd called her bluff I couldn't see any way out of this other than to tell them everything we knew about the monodreme and hope that it would be enough.

"Tom," said Fake Sal. "Deactivate the anti-collision protocols."

- **Anti-collision protocols deactivated**, said Tom in a distinctly sad voice.

"Sal…what are you doing?"

She turned to me and shrugged.

"I want my mum back," she said.

She backed the runabout away from the pillar and lifted us ten metres into the air.

"Sal…talk to me."

"I'm going to break her out," she said. She shot the runabout forward at the pillar so quickly that from inside the pod it simply looked like the pillar had jumped forward. We were motionless in front of it again. I looked at her, baffled, only to find her looking equally confused.

"Tom," she said. "I thought you said anti-collision protocols were off?"

- **They are deactivated**, said Tom.

"So? Why did you stop me?"

- **My programming inhibits me from directly harming any living being. If I fly through this pillar it will cause injury - possibly fatal - to your mother and Stephen.**

Fake Sal swore. A look of despair poured down her face.

"Sal – we'll just talk to them. Let's just tell them what we know about the monodreme. What does it matter?"

"George!" she snapped. "We don't know where the monodreme is. Do you think they're going to believe us, when we're flying around in this thing? And how soon do you think it's going to be before they start interrogating my mum?"

I felt incredibly dull. She was right.

"I won't have it! It's just not going to happen!"

She flew the runabout upwards, smashing it through the ceiling, into and through the level above and another ceiling, then another and another, steadily picking up speed. Our surroundings blurred as we punched our way through level after level until we were out in space once more and she brought us around to look down on the *Dah Rhiv Artiv Da* again.

"Tom, I don't want us to feel any momentum."

- As you wish, my dear, said Tom in a voice so drenched in sadness he could have given my Fleet a run for her money. He wanted her to stop, but he wasn't being given the opportunity to say so.

Fake Sal began to 'punch' the runabout back and forth, piercing the alien vessel from top to bottom each time. From inside the pod it simply looked like we were teleporting beyond the spaceship and back again, over and over. First we could see the Go craft, then we could see the ground of Oceana. These two views alternated with each other over and over again, varied only slightly as Fake Sal randomly chose new places to puncture the monolith. After about twenty passes Fake Sal paused and asked Tom Baker to patch us through to the alien.

"Will you release them?" she said.

"No," came the immediate response.

"If you won't release them we will keep this up. Your ship will disintegrate eventually."

"We will not release them."

Fake Sal broke off communication with a snarl.

"They're so stubborn!"

I looked down at the huge craft below us. Our attacks didn't seem to amount to much more than pinpricks.

"It'll take forever to cause any real damage to them like this," I said.

"We can just increase the speed. They just don't know what we're capable of, that's all."

Fake Sal resumed the darting movements of the runabout. It was as though there were a giant invisible sewing machine above the *Dah Rhiv Artiv Da*, and the runabout was the needle. She drew a line of holes from one side of the ship to the other, perforating it like she was making a tear-off strip. It still didn't look like much damage was being done really. Apart from tiny signs of depressurisation here and there the vast space ship looked as solid and indomitable as ever. Fake Sal upped the pace, turning us into a machine gun and concentrating on one area so that the damage could build up and look more substantial. The southeast corner began to look moth-eaten.

"Right," I said. "They've got to take that seriously. See if they'll give in now."

Fake Sal patched through on audio link but the answer was, once again, a simple 'no'.

"They're crazy," she said, and she resumed the assault.

I started to feel a bit queasy. What if they would never give in? How far were we prepared to go?

"The problem is," I said, "we don't really know how much this is affecting them. Tom, could you give us a damage report on their ship, please?"

- Structural damage is currently at two point thirty-six percent and rising, said Tom, as Fake Sal strafed the southwest corner. The hull is breached in four hundred and nine locations and two hundred and sixty sectors are depressurised. Ship's power systems are unaffected. Three hundred and seventy eight crewmembers injured, seventy-six dead.

I felt like my guts were falling out.

"Tom! You said you couldn't cause harm to anyone!"

Fake Sal focussed her fire on the very tip of the upper, southwestern corner, wearing it away like it was made of polystyrene.

- My programming inhibits me from directly causing harm to living beings. The fatalities incurred here are all indirect results of the attack: crewmembers falling through holes in the structure, and the like.

Fake Sal was still immersed in her carnage, seemingly oblivious to our conversation.

"Tom! Stop the attack! Stop it!"

- Fake Sal has manual control.

I jumped out of my chair and grabbed her by the shoulders and shook her.

"Sal! Stop it! Stop it!"

She pushed my hands off her and tried to swipe me to one side so that she could have a clear view of the dome.

"If they won't give me my mum back I'll kill every last one of them!" she screamed. I reeled momentarily, suddenly back in the argument I'd had with my sister, only this time I was the one who was looking on in shock at a complete stranger. Fake Sal pushed me to the bottom of the pod and threw herself back into the attack. Without another thought I stood up and did to her what my sister had done to me. I slapped her really hard across the face.

She stared at me with big, shocked eyes.

"Tom," she said. "You let him hit me."

- Yes, my dear, said Tom quietly.

"Sal," I said, holding my arms out at my sides. "You're killing people."

She stared at me like I was talking gibberish. One side of her face was white and one was red.

"I just want my mum back," she said. Then her face crumpled and tears began to roll down her cheeks. I lifted her out of her chair and we huddled in the bottom of the runabout together, and I wondered what we were going to do now.

10
Ell Aah Ray

Before God we are all equally wise – and equally foolish.
- Albert Einstein

We cowered hopelessly in the pod, incapable of making a decision, only wanting to hide away from what Fake Sal had done, what I had sat back and watched her do. The idea of approaching the Go was unbearable now, whether it was to demand Christine's release or just to say sorry. Fake Sal sobbed in my arms and I stared into space. Each explanation or apology that entered my mind felt hollow and evil. My mind kept trying to picture the seventy-six Go crewmembers that had died. I didn't want it to, but it just wouldn't stop: seventy-six living beings – gone forever. And not just living beings but advanced beings. I found myself wondering if that somehow made it worse. Then a new thought occurred to me. What if they took revenge on us by killing Christine and Armitage? My head swam with despair and I wanted to vomit.

Time passed and still we crouched there, not even able to talk to each other. Eventually Tom Baker spoke.

- The Go are requesting a meeting, he said.

We didn't respond at first. Silence seemed to fill the pod as if there was an everlasting supply pouring out from between me and Fake Sal. Speech seemed utterly impossible. But Christine and Armitage were still captives and this one thought kept poking me, over and over, not letting me rest, not letting me run and hide.

"Tom," I said, my throat feeling thick. "Would you tell them that we made a mistake and that we didn't mean for it to happen?"

- Sal? asked Tom.

Fake Sal hadn't moved for a while. I wasn't even sure if she was awake, but she spoke in a whisper.

"Do as he says, Tom," she said. "Do whatever he says."

- Very well.

There was silence for a little while, then he spoke again.

- The Go are requesting a meeting.

My chin was perched on top of Fake Sal's head. I stared into space waiting for my response to reveal itself to me, as I knew it would if I just sat there and waited long enough. To my surprise it came almost straight away.

"Come on Sal," I said gently, and together we climbed slowly to our feet.

Tom Baker flew us to the coordinates specified for our meeting. After passing through a series of the kind of tunnels and sub wells we had seen already we were brought out into a vast chamber that had been landscaped to replicate an area of the aliens' home planet of Go. The ceiling of the chamber was a tremendous dome that had an early evening sky projected onto it, complete with sun and clouds. Below us were rocks and trees and buildings. The illusion was perfect. There was nothing to suggest that we were inside a spaceship. I actually wondered for a moment if we had flown through some kind of space portal that had transported us directly to the surface of their homeworld.

The Go first contact specialist was waiting for us on a balcony high up amongst a series of cliff-face apartments beneath a bright Go sky of violet and lemon. Above us, and below us, flew all manner of aircraft, the daily traffic of the Go, coming and going about their business. Tiny flyers shaped like lentils nipped in and out amongst big slow movers, which turned slowly and gracefully, bobbing in the evening air like whales showing their bellies to the sun. Further below us still sprawled a forest city, a startling mixture of rolling red leafed trees and plump gleaming skyscrapers. The balance the Go had achieved between nature and technology took my breath away. It was everything that was beautiful and remarkable about both worlds.

We parked on the balcony and Tom Baker made the runabout transparent so that the meeting could be held face to face. Me and Fake Sal floated there in our flight chairs looking exposed and vulnerable.

The alien was standing at the edge of the balcony. She stepped forward and looked at us both for a few moments. I wondered what she saw.

"I am Ell Aah Ray," she said.

After a little silence I remembered my manners.

"I am George. This is Sal."

She took a moment to look at each of us.

"Are you well, George and Sal?"

I stared at her dumbly.

"Huh?" I said.

"Are you well, George and Sal?"

"I'm sorry…how do you mean?"

"I am asking if you are well. Sal seemed distressed that we have taken her mother."

"Well, yeah. She's upset about it. But we're sorry about what happened. It wasn't meant to…we thought the runabout wouldn't allow any of your people to be hurt. We want you to know that we are really sorry about it. I don't really know what to say about it."

"The 'runabout' is your vessel?"

"Yeah."

"Is the runabout the monodreme?"

"What?"

"The runabout – your flying vessel – is it the monodreme?"

"No...no, it's not. It's just a product of the monodreme...like you said earlier. The monodreme made it."

"Where is the monodreme?"

"We don't know. Honestly. We just don't know."

"What do you know?"

I looked at Fake Sal. She looked pale and haunted. She shook her head slightly, frowning.

"Not yet," she said.

I turned back to Ell Aah Ray.

"Look, we're not just going to tell you whatever you want. We don't know anything about you. And you've got Christine and Stephen. What do you know about the monodreme? And why do you think we should tell you what we know?"

"You are asking questions," said Ell Aah Ray. "That is good."

Ell Aah Ray's responses weren't quite fitting in with my expectations. Each time she said something I felt empty headed.

"So?" I said, sounding in my own ears like I was back in the schoolyard. She stepped backwards to the edge of the balcony. Her four arms rose out from her sides. The sky behind her was full of objects.

"We are the Go," she said. "This is a copy of part of our homeworld." She turned slightly and gestured with two arms at the skyscrapers. "That is the city of Mabbalee. These apartments are part of the Nommon district. This vessel we are in is the *Dah Rhiv Artiv Da*, which translates in your language as 'The Stolen Adventure'. We are an old race, much older than humanity. Sixteen days ago communications from our observers on the planet below stopped. Do you have a name for the planet below?"

"We call it Oceana."

"We were in the vicinity and came to investigate. We arrived here three days ago and found that changes have been made to Oceana that only a monodreme could cause. Now you are here, travelling in a product of the monodreme. So we must ask you for all the information you have."

"What will you do if you find it?"

"We will destroy it."

I gulped silently.

"How will you do that, exactly?"

"We will kill its host."

She watched our reaction carefully. I exchanged a horrified glance with Fake Sal.

"You know the host," she said, with an air of finality. There didn't seem any point in denying it.

"Yes," I said.

"Where is the host?"

I looked at Fake Sal again and she shook her head. She looked ill. I wondered if she could ever come to terms with the deaths she had caused.

- Why don't you get Tom Baker to make you feel better?

- I don't want to feel better.

The thought felt as desolate as the aftermath of a bombing. I wanted to reach out to her, but I wanted to recoil as well. I turned back to Ell Aah Ray.

"We're not ready to tell you that. Why should we trust you? You've kidnapped two of our people, and you'd probably do the same to us if you could."

"Whether you trust or distrust us, there is no 'should' involved. It is what it is. But we are a much older people than you, far advanced in our evolution. We have a wider view. Taking your people was necessary. Already it has encouraged you to meet with us and talk. Any connection to the monodreme that we find must be utilised as fully as possible."

"I don't see what's so advanced about keeping people against their will," I said.

"You are like children to us. We have no intention of harming or frightening you. But if you need protecting from yourselves, or if the universe needs protection from your playing with toys you don't understand, then we will do what seems fitting to us."

I felt a pulse of rebellion at her referring to us as children. But even as my jaw jutted forward defiantly it made me feel childish and I tucked it back in.

"What happened on Oceana?" I asked.

"We do not know exactly, but the information we have gathered so far suggests that the being you knew as MarvinMilton touched the monodreme…"

"You know about MarvinMilton?"

"Yes. When we detected your runabout approaching Oceana we traced your trajectory back to the Sol System. We have been in communication with our observers on Earth."

"Observers on Earth…" I mumbled. All the implications of her last sentences piled up on top of each other and log-jammed in my mind. How was I supposed to keep up with this stuff? They had observers on Earth. Aliens on Earth! She knew who we were. She knew where we lived! We'd been on Oceana for barely an hour and my universe seemed to be unravelling before my eyes.

Ell Aah Ray decided to continue her report.

"We believe that MarvinMilton touched the monodreme. It merged with him, gave him everything there is to give. He evolved from a docile, primitive animal to an all-powerful being. Unfortunately," said Ell Aah Ray in a steady monotone, "at some point in this transformation he killed all of the alien observers here, along with the three billion people that comprised the indigenous civilised species of Oceana. He also obliterated several entire species of indigenous animal."

The words were delivered without emotion but they hit me like a kick in the chest. I looked at Fake Sal. She was shaking her head in denial, her face drawn and skull-like.

"That's not possible," she croaked. "MarvinMilton would never..." Tears started to roll down her face. "He wouldn't."

She was right, of course. MarvinMilton would never have hurt anybody. Anyone who had met him would know that instantly. Fake Sal turned to me, still shaking her head.

- George, he wouldn't! He wasn't like that! You know that, don't you?

- Of course I do, I said. An image flashed in my mind, incredibly clear and bright, of MarvinMilton's face, his beautiful golden eyes peering into mine, so intimate and kind. His gaze was filled with more humanity than the entire human race possessed. There was such knowing there, such compassion. I heard an echo of his diamond laughter glittering through my mind and spiralling away, coruscating, living on inside me. Of course I do, Sal. And another memory flashed in my mind. Only... and she closed her eyes and cried, knowing what I was going to say. The darkness that he was keeping at bay - the black madness...

Fake Sal put her face in her hands and sobbed inconsolably.

"The monodreme brings destruction," said Ell Aah Ray, and it was as though she had been listening in on our thoughts. "You did not know that our crewmembers were dying, but they died all the same. Perhaps MarvinMilton did not know what he was doing, but a civilisation is gone, and several entire species of animal that exist nowhere else in the universe are gone. This is what the monodreme brings: death and extinction on an idle thought. And where are your friends, Pee and Osmo? What are they doing at this moment? Can you say?"

•

We had Tom send messages to Osmo and Pee, explaining where we were and who we were with, and asking them to join us. And, at Ell Aah Ray's request, we teleported in two Go observers from Earth who were based in the North West of England and were up to date on current affairs, to help her out in her talks with us. Ash Koh Tok wore robes similar to Ell Aah Ray's but, bizarrely, Finn Ma Fey was wearing Earth clothes that had been adapted for his alien physique: jeans, a T-shirt with Marilyn Monroe on it, a leather jacket with four arms, strangely shaped trainers.

Homer Simpson reported regretfully that Pee was not accepting any incoming calls at present, so he was still unaware of what was happening. After a few minutes Osmo's runabout materialised on the balcony. He turned it transparent and looked warily at the aliens. Then he looked warily at me and Fake Sal, as if he'd been invited to a party as an afterthought or something. Then he took in the view from the balcony and just sat there gawping at it.

I left Fake Sal wheedling at the aliens to release Christine, and I teleported over to him. I arrived in his pod to find an uncomfortable silence waiting for me.

"Hiya."

He gave me a negligent upward nod of the head and I stood there for a bit.

"Are you gonna give me a chair, or what?"

"Hal," he said. A flight chair materialised and I took a seat.

"So how did you manage to get into this mess?" he asked.

"I don't know, really. We just came for a picnic." He nodded, as if he understood perfectly. "Where've you been, Oz?"

He shrugged in a very unconvincing display of nonchalance.

"Nowhere really. Just keeping myself to myself."

"Why?"

"It doesn't matter. Just forget about it."

"It does matter."

"Well...I don't want to talk about it."

I didn't really want to, either.

"Have you seen Pee?"

"Last time I saw him was about a week ago. I showed him something new that I discovered the runabouts can do and he got all excited about it."

"Yeah? What did you discover?"

"I'll show you later," he nodded in the direction of Fake Sal and the three Go who were all casting glances our way.

"You discovered it a week ago, and you never shared it with us?"

"Well, I've not been talking to you, have I?"

"Why not?"

"Just shut up and introduce me to your new aliens."

He wasn't doing a very good job of meeting my eye, and I'd already had more conflict than I could handle in one day. I waved for the others to come over and we did the introduction thing.

•

Ell Aah Ray was resistant to giving up what leverage she had by releasing Christine and Armitage, but after some tearful negotiations from Fake Sal they struck a compromise. As an act of goodwill the Go would release Christine; in return we would tell them what we knew about the monodreme. Then, if they were satisfied that we had repaid their trust in full, they would release Armitage.

This was good news for everyone, I felt. Only, when Christine was brought out onto the balcony Fake Sal immediately beamed her aboard Tom Baker and flew away, leaving me and Osmo sitting there like a pair of lemons.

Ell Aah Ray gazed in the direction Fake Sal had flown and gaped wordlessly. To my surprise Finn Ma Fey laughed and shook his head in a very human way. He'd obviously spent a lot of time on Earth.

"I thought that Pee was my favourite," he said, dryly, "but that girl takes the biscuit. You Banford kids are too much."

.

Me and Osmo quickly decided to just tell them everything we knew. It only seemed polite. Even as we did it I was afraid it was a big mistake, but after Fake Sal's attack on the Go I didn't have the stomach to deny them.

So we told them that Fake Sal was a replica, and that Real Sal was out there somewhere with the monodreme. We told them that nobody else knew, especially Christine. I told them I was afraid that if Christine found out about Fake Sal then Real Sal would have no more use for her, and that she might dispose of her.

"It would be interesting to see how Real Sal reacted," said Ell Aah Ray. "It might give us an indication of how much value she places on the lives of others."

I didn't like this one bit and kicked up a big fuss, but I couldn't get them to promise to keep our secret.

The Go sun set slowly beyond Mabbalee. Lights moved about in the sky and the apartments lit up all along the cliff. Ell Aah Ray seemed satisfied with the information we had given and she arranged Armitage's release. Osmo had Hal-9000 teleport him to the balcony straight away. He seemed well enough, though he looked dazed and didn't have much to say.

"I'm fine," he said when Osmo pressed him. "It's been a big day, that's all."

He stood at the edge of the balcony and looked down at the forest below. Some of the trees glowed red, lit from below by discreetly placed lights. Finn Ma Fey suggested that Osmo and me might come out of the runabout and join them on the balcony.

"We don't just replicate the sky," he said. "There's a breeze blowing. The scent of the forest is on it."

I felt a stab of fear. I looked at Osmo and he must have seen it.

- Hal, he said. **Will you be able to stop them if they try any shenanigans?**

- **My programming puts your safety and well-being as my highest priority, Osmo,** said Hal. **But I can assure you that they are not planning any shenanigans.**

Osmo looked at me and shrugged, and for a moment we were back behind a crumbled piece of wall at the waste ground of Five Elms, deciding whether we should step out from our shelter. We both nodded minute little nods at the same time, then Osmo raised his eyebrows high and puffed out his cheeks, and he shrugged again, in a mock devil-may-care way, just as he had done then.

"May as well," he said.

I nodded.

"May as well, eh?"

And there really was a breeze, and it did bring the scent of the forest on the air.

"So, what are you going to do now?" I asked them.

"We will take our search to Earth," said Ell Aah Ray.

Oh cripes, I thought. Armitage stepped forward nervously.

"You mean, in this thing?" he said, casting about at our surroundings.

"Yes."

He looked about himself again, craning his head to look up steeply at the night sky that seemed so high above us. I could tell what he was thinking – this wasn't the kind of vehicle you could park behind a bush while you carried out your investigations. "But...you're not thinking of revealing yourself...are you? To humanity, I mean."

"Yes," said Ell Aah Ray.

"Which government will you approach? America?"

"We will reveal ourselves to the people of Earth as a whole."

He looked around at the rest of us, looking to find someone sympathetic.

"You can't be serious? That's crazy. We're nowhere near ready. Not for first contact."

"No," she agreed. "It is not the timing we would have chosen, but first contact came and went when MarvinMilton spoke to the minds of these children. Now, the importance of finding the monodreme eclipses most other things."

At the mention of the monodreme Armitage looked at us all blankly.

"It's something that MarvinMilton had," said Osmo, quickly. "The thing that enabled him to travel between the stars. The Go are looking for it."

Armitage frowned.

"You never mentioned this before."

"Armitage...I mean, Stephen," I said, "you know there are lot's of things we haven't told you. But you said you weren't coming on this picnic to find stuff out."

Armitage barked a strange, hollow kind of laugh.

"You mean we're still on the picnic, George?" He gestured randomly with his arms, momentarily lost for words, then he found some. "Well, I guess I wouldn't want to be around when you actually get in trouble."

136

"Armitage," I said. "I mean, Stephen...if you start asking questions I'll beam you back home. In fact, wouldn't you rather be there, now?"

I knew he only had to ask the right question and the Go would happily explain all about Real Sal and Fake Sal. He put his hands up quickly.

"Hold your horses, George. I might come in useful."

"But, don't you want to be with Christine?"

"Well...of course I do...but this situation. I just think an adult should be present."

"You are using her, aren't you?" I said.

He looked stumped for a second, then his face hardened.

"I resent that, George."

We glared at each other, and I became painfully aware that the aliens were watching us carefully, analysing our actions, assessing our character. I stepped back from him.

"No more questions," I said. "Okay?"

A little conflict played out in his features before he came to the decision to raise his hands in surrender.

"Okay," he said.

I saw it would just be a matter of time.

•

While inside the pod I had found the Go to be strangely beautiful creatures, if a little scary. Now I was outside and walking amongst them they terrified me. Though their heads reminded me of antelope heads they were heavier and squarer. Their faces were less expressive than ours, so it was virtually impossible to guess what they were thinking. When they regarded me from oblong pupils with their alien intelligence they seemed to be weighing me precisely to the final gram. Up close they loomed over us, lithe and poised. They moved with the grace and strength of predators. I wondered if revenge was the kind of dish that would appeal to them.

Finn Ma Fey and Ash Koh Tok were intensely interested in us, never having had the chance to actually talk to the kind of people they had been observing so closely on Earth. I watched them having a conversation with Osmo and Armitage. The humans looked small and childlike. The aliens' arms moved about expressively as they probed with questions. They looked like a pair of preying mantises to me, crouched over a pair of juicy grubs.

Ell Aah Ray was watching me.

"I'm sorry about the...about your crewmembers," I mumbled.

"Yes," she replied. "You said."

"Were any of them friends of yours?"

"Yes."

There were no rocks for me to crawl under so I stared up at her, helplessly. I wanted to know if she felt grief for her dead, and anger against us, or if these concepts were alien to her. Was she controlling her emotions with an inhuman discipline, or did she just not care? I couldn't bring myself to ask.

"I'm sorry," I muttered, feeling how small and useless that was. She just stood there looking at me. A familiar shape appeared in the sky behind her and arced down to land on our balcony. A hatch gull-winged open and Christine jumped out and walked up to Armitage. She touched his face and they hugged. Fake Sal was framed in the hatchway but made no move to disembark. She looked awful. I walked over to her.

"Hiya. Welcome back."

- Hiya.

Her voice in my mind sounded tiny and lost. I reached out and she let me hold her hand.

- Is there anything I can do? I asked.

- George...I don't know what's happening to me.

- You were worried about your mum, that's all.

- She's really mad at me. I left her. Then I left Stephen. And I just told her what I did to the Go. Fresh tears were falling down her face. I think she hates me.

- We'll fix it. We'll fix it, somehow.

- When Real Sal finds out...she'll kill me.

- No, she won't.

- Why not? she said, and her eyes flashed with spite. I would.

The thought tasted bitter to the core.

- We'll fix it, I said, squeezing her hand, but she pulled it away, and the runabout was pulling away too.

- You can't always just fix stuff, George.

The hatch closed and the runabout disappeared into thin air. I turned to find everybody looking at me. They all turned away, except for Ell Aah Ray, who regarded me silently from oblong pupils.

•

So Osmo was back, but now Fake Sal had gone, and the more I thought about that the more it disturbed me. I knew the insecurity of being a replica was something that gnawed away at Fake Sal, made her feel second rate, like a photocopy of a well-loved painting. Her solution to this had impressed me no end – she'd just become superhumanly responsible. The way she had handled things at the UN the past few weeks had filled me with admiration. How could she be disposed of if she proved her incredible worth by protecting Christine, looking after Real Sal's reputation and solving the world's problems?

Only, now she'd blown it, in glorious Technicolor. And at some point she was going to find out that me and Osmo had told the Go all about her. My dread of that moment grew inside me like heartburn. On top of this Pee was still conspicuous by his absence and an alien race, that made humanity look like pond sludge, was heading for my home planet intent on a showdown with whatever was left of the original Sal. The Stolen Adventure would reach Earth in five days.

The Go invited us to stay onboard and gave us apartments. I guessed they were hoping that if they hung around with us for long enough Real Sal would show up.

"Is killing Sal really the only way to destroy the monodreme?" I asked Ell Aah Ray the next day. She was giving me a guided tour of the ship and telling me something of the history of the Go, a race so old that their home planet had perished long ago.

"She could relinquish the monodreme, as MarvinMilton did," she said. "But this would also result in her death."

Well, it's nice to have options, I thought darkly.

"So will you give her the choice?"

Ell Aah Ray didn't answer immediately. She studied me with her strange eyes. The way they rested on me - I sometimes had the feeling she was hypnotising me.

"Our best chance of destroying the monodreme is to take her by surprise, kill her before she has the opportunity to react. If that failed, or were not possible, then we would try persuasion."

"You're very honest," I observed.

"Deception is pointless," she said flatly.

"What? Even when the whole universe is at stake?"

"Especially then," she said.

Two more days passed. We met more Go, saw more sights. Everything I encountered seemed a contradiction. I observed the effortless harmony of day-to-day life in the vast interstellar environment they had built and learned that their society had no laws of any kind. This didn't seem possible to me, yet somehow it was blindingly obvious at the same time.

We fell into a routine of eating meals together and then splitting up into pairs and threes to go exploring. Finn Ma Fey and Christine quickly became firm friends, arguing repeatedly over which of the Beatles was the best songwriter. While they both compared Go and human music Ash Koh Tok would take Osmo and Armitage out onto the streets of Mabbalee to see the sights and sounds of everyday life. In the meantime Ell Aah Ray only had eyes for me. We went here and there, saw this and that, but we were more interested in each other, more focused on our conversation than our surroundings. It was the alienness of each other's thoughts that preoccupied us. I felt completely transparent to her, but she seemed curious to see how much of her I could understand. I began to suspect she was really looking for insights into Sal's mind, as a preparation for the showdown to come.

On the fourth day I asked her if this was the case.

"Yes," she said, with typical bluntness.

"Does talking to me reassure you about how Sal might be coping?"

"No. I feel grave concern."

I felt my face pouting with disappointment.

"Are we that bad?"

"It is not an issue of goodness and badness. I have seen a little of how Fake Sal responds to challenging events – that did not bring me hope. In talking with you, George, I see that, when faced with difficult situations, you rely heavily on two strategies: attempt to make the situation go away or behave as if it doesn't exist. This does not bring me hope."

I saw Fake Sal's face drawing away from me. *You can't always just fix stuff, George.*

"Well, what is a good strategy in a tough situation, then?"

I sounded petulant and whiny.

"Face it," she said. "Experience it. Discover the truth about it."

My insides turned over at the very thought. I felt myself pale.

"That's a horrible idea," I said, trying to be jokey but not managing it.

She leaned forward. She had never touched me before, but now she cupped my face in a pair of her long cool hands while she gently squeezed my shoulders with the other pair. It was very tenderly done, and I wasn't prepared for how intimate it felt. I half expected her to lean forward even further and kiss me. I'm sure if she had done I would have just stood there and been too British to complain. But she only held her hands there like that for a long moment and then lowered them, and didn't say anything. A feeling of safety and contentment encapsulated me, sealing out the universe, keeping the darkness at bay. I took a deep easy breath and couldn't imagine anything that could burst the bubble of calm that she had conjured around me.

Right on cue I heard Fleet in my mind.

- **Party line request from Homer Simpson.**

- **Patch him through, Fleet.**

- **George! Osmo! We've got a really bad situation happening!** crooned Homer in hyper anxiety mode. **You've got to come, quick! It's Pee! I think he might be going crazy!**

I looked at Ell Aah Ray through narrowed eyes.

"You have news," she said. We'd never told them we communicated telepathically but it didn't surprise me in the least that she could tell.

"Pee's in some kind of trouble."

She didn't say anything, but her four arms made a complicated gesture that contained too many shapes for me to keep track of. I had no idea what it meant but I felt a sensation in my chest, a sleeping fear shifting like something coiled, and I suddenly knew that everything she had done and said while she had been with me had been designed to influence my mind in ways I couldn't understand or undo.

11
Alien 9

A human being is a part of a whole, called by us 'universe', a part limited in time and space. He experiences himself, his thoughts and feelings as something separated from the rest...a kind of optical delusion of his consciousness.
- Albert Einstein

11
Alien 9

Osmo beamed me aboard his runabout so we could talk to Homer together. We settled back in our flight chairs, closed our eyes and opened our minds.

- Okay, Homer, said Osmo. **What's happening?**
- **I'm worried about Pee! He asked me to create a special version of Earth inside the Tardis corridor so that he can win an Oscar! Now he's gone inside it and he won't come out. And he's blocked all incoming calls...even from me!**

Through the mind link we could feel the genuine hurt in this last thought. I wasn't used to feeling such emotion from a runabout, but then, the rest of our runabouts had much calmer personalities.

- Typical, sniffed Osmo.
- 'Scuse me, I said. 'Tardis corridor'? What's he talking about?
- **It's that thing I told you we discovered,** said Osmo. **If you ask it, your runabout will open a hatch in the back of the pod, on the inside. Through the hatch is a corridor. The corridor can be any length you want. You can have doors along the corridor and the doors will lead to rooms.**
- Rooms?
- **Yeah, it's so cool. The rooms can be any size and shape you want. They can be any design you want. They can have anything in them you want. It's just the best thing.**

I opened my eyes so I could turn and stare at Osmo in disbelief and general all-purpose outrage. He turned and looked at me and shrugged.

"What?"

"'What!' You tell me this and then you say 'What!'"

"Yeah, what's your problem? Back off."

"So, were you ever going to tell us about it, me and Fake?"

Osmo turned away, looked straight ahead through the dome, out over the pod's view of the Nommon Valley, his jaw clenched. As I watched his cheeks flushed pink. He remained like that, not answering me.

- **Guys**, said Homer Simpson tentatively. **I'm really worried about Pee.**

I took a deep breath.

"Osmo, man. What is it? What have we done that's so bad?"

I saw the muscles around his jaw ripple but still he didn't answer.

- Guys...

"We haven't done anything, have we? We're still the same people we always were, aren't we? We haven't done anything to deserve..."

Osmo took a deep breath and then screamed straight into my face.

"I'M JUST JEALOUS, OKAY!" He pretty much drowned me in spit. "WHAT'S SO HARD TO UNDERSTAND, MORON?"

His face was full on red, really glowing. We both froze. The pod went very quiet and we stayed like that, our eyes bulging at each other. I was just waiting for Homer to say something but he seemed to realise better. After about ten years the fight suddenly seemed to go out of Osmo and he slowly slumped back into his chair. **I'm just jealous**, said his mind in a small voice. **Just leave me alone, will you?**

The inside of the pod seemed to turn into a bubble of pure silence. I stayed in the same frozen position while I tried to work out some kind of appropriate response. I must have looked pretty stupid. After a while my brain kind of looked at me and shrugged and just gave up. *So much for you*, I thought.

I slumped back in my chair too.

- **Oh bugger**, I said.

Osmo let out a great sigh.

In the end, of course, it was obvious there was only one way out of the situation, and that was to talk to Homer about his problem as if nothing had just happened.

- **Guys, I think you should talk to him**, he said. **Maybe you can persuade him to come back.**

- **What's the big problem, Homer?** asked Osmo. **If he wants to stay in his little fantasy world let him stay in it. It's not hurting him, is it?**

- **I think it might be bad for his mental health.**

- **Homer, can you switch to a different personality? It's difficult to take you seriously when you're a cartoon.**

Homer sniffed sadly.

- **I can't change unless Pee tells me to.**

- **Well, he didn't tell you to talk to us but you are doing.**

- **He asked me to fill his world with people who love him. If I send you two in I'm doing as I'm told. In the meantime you can find him and talk to him and help him come to his senses. I'm programmed to do all I can to take care of him.** Homer started blubbing. **He doesn't make it easy for me!**

Osmo and me rolled our eyes at each other. At least this farce was a good distraction from friendship troubles. But then I realised it might not be. I aimed my thoughts at Osmo.

- **So, why has Pee been ignoring me and Fake? Is he...the same as you? I mean, is it for the same reason as you?**

Osmo narrowed his eyes at me, seemed on the verge of getting difficult, then he changed his mind and shrugged.

- I don't know. He hasn't been talking to me either.

This, I hadn't been expecting.

- Really? So you guys have both been on your own all this time? Osmo nodded reluctantly. I shook my head in disbelief. **Why do you have to be such a pair of weirdos?**

He considered the question for a moment.

- I think it's from hanging around with you.

To Homer's relief we agreed that we had better go and save Pee from himself. Homer outlined his plan. It seemed straightforward enough at the time. There were a couple of aspects that I wasn't too keen on, but they couldn't be got around, and generally speaking the plan was simple enough to be safe. Simple enough so that nothing could go wrong, well...not very wrong, anyway.

•

I knew something had gone wrong instantly. The moment Homer beamed us into Pee's world I knew. The giveaway clue was the fact that we weren't in Pee's world at all, but back on Earth, out on the street of some big American city. Early evening sunlight was slanting between the office blocks crowded around us. We were wearing tuxedos.

"What's this?" I said, flapping my arms in irritation. Osmo shaded his eyes with a hand as he looked up at the tops of the buildings.

"It's Los Angeles," he said, frowning.

I flapped my arms a bit more.

"What's Homer playing at?"

Osmo put a hand over his mouth and pointed the frown at me, but he didn't reply.

"It's not like a runabout to make a mistake," I said. "Not even Homer."

Osmo shook his head and took his hand away from his mouth.

"The runabouts don't make mistakes."

I swept my arms around like I was presenting LA as the star prize in a quiz show.

"Well, check it out – there's a first time for everything."

Osmo shook his head some more. There was something about the way he kept looking at the sky and then at me that was beginning to weird me out.

"What?"

It took him a while to organise his words but I waited.

"This is it. This is Pee's world. We're exactly where Homer said he'd put us."

I took a moment to absorb this one, because I could see he was being completely serious.

"Oz, man," I said, eventually. "We're outside."

He looked at the sky again, his face screwed up with some thought process.

"Maybe it's a projection," he said. "Like the Go have done with Mabbalee and the valley." He didn't sound very convinced.

"You don't sound very convinced," I said.

"You don't think..." he said.

"What?"

"Nah..."

"What?"

"No, it's stupid..."

"Osmo!"

"You don't think...that he's created an entire replica of Earth inside his runabout?"

I felt a sudden rush of adrenalin at the very thought. It was the most stupid thing I'd ever heard in my life. There wasn't a single person anywhere in the universe mental enough to even think of such a thing. Except, that was...ever so possibly...for one person.

I considered the possibilities and shook my head.

"Come on, Oz. Homer's just got confused. He's worried about Pee. He sent us here instead of Pee's world."

"The runabouts don't make mistakes," he repeated. "He said that Pee asked him to create a special version of Earth. If you ask the runabouts to do something they just do it. It doesn't make any difference to them, whether you say 'Teleport me to school' or 'Teleport me to Pluto', they just do it."

"I know, but how big a room would you need to fit the Earth in?"

"Doesn't matter."

"Oz, the sun is shining on us. If you're right, then that means Homer not only created a planet Earth inside himself, but a sun and moon as well, and everything in between. And if that's right then I assume all of the other stars will be there in the sky when night time comes, which would mean that Homer's created a replica of the entire universe inside himself." Osmo just stood there. "So, it's a projection. It's virtual reality. Either that or Homer's sent us to the wrong place."

He looked neither happy nor sad.

"I've got a room in my Tardis corridor with a swimming pool in it," he said. "It's not a projection of a swimming pool, it's not a virtual swimming pool. I told HAL I wanted a room with a swimming pool in it and he gave me a room with a swimming pool in it. That's how it works."

I knew it was preposterous. But Osmo wasn't trying to convince me. And I found that more convincing than anything.

"Anyway," he said. "There's a simple enough way to check."

"Yeah?" I said, not sure if I wanted to know about it. People were walking by us on the sidewalk, busy Los Angeles people, as real as me and Osmo...or as real as Fake Sal.

146

"Homer said that once we're in Pee's world we won't be able to talk to him anymore, yeah? He's Pee's runabout, he can't respond to requests from us."

"That's right," I said slowly. The buildings seemed to be edging furtively towards me.

"And he also said we won't be able to talk to our own runabouts until we get back outside, yeah? So we have to see Pee and get him to send us back, yeah?"

Oh my god! What have we done!

"So go ahead," said Osmo, with an air of finality that was horrifying because it was so quiet, so simple. "Talk to Fleet."

I didn't want to, I was afraid to, but my thoughts couldn't help themselves.

- Fleet! Fleet! Come in! Fleet!

Osmo watched without expression, and didn't need to ask.

•

A limo turned up, as Homer had said it would. We sat in the back, tried to rally ourselves as it carried us away at a stately pace towards the OscarDrome, where Pee was going to have his private moment of glory, broadcast live to billions around the world.

"It's not a problem," insisted Osmo. "We meet Pee, just like we planned, explain things to him, then we get to go home."

"Yeah," I said, nodding, eager to agree.

"This place is just a bit bigger than we were expecting, that's all. But the plan remains the same. We'll be home in time for tea."

I nodded some more. Osmo was right. The idea of being temporarily cut off from the outside world hadn't bothered us at all when we had thought we just had to wander through a few rooms inside Homer to find Pee. The only thing that had changed was the scale of things.

I stared through the limo's tinted windows at the crowds thronging the side of the road. A giant billboard, towering above the ranks of people that lined the avenue, glided by, followed by an expanse of clear, blue New Hollywood sky, then another billboard, and another, and so on. All of the boards displayed the same vast movie poster. I kept trying not to look at it but didn't seem able to stop my eyes from peering upwards each time. PEE. TOM CRUISE. SIGOURNEY WEAVER. ALIEN 9 – THE ACID BATH. THE HUNTER BECOMES THE PREY. A STEPHEN SPEILBERG FILM. Also starring: KATE WINSLET, CAMERON DIAZ, LEONARDO DICAPRIO, JOHNNY DEPP, MERYL STREEP, MARILYN MUNROE, HARRISON FORD, LEONARD NIMOY, SEAN CONNERY and RON MOODY. Pee had always been contemptuous of the modern movie posters that consisted of nothing more than the title and the faces of the main stars. Yet there was his lovely mug, enormous, lit in blue, somehow endeavouring to look intense and emotionally complex, flanked by the smaller faces of Tom and Sigourney who were looking over his shoulders with slightly puzzled expressions as if to say 'how will you save us Pee?'

"It's wrong though, Oz, innit?" I said, feeling calmer now.

"What?"

"It was bad enough that Real Sal made one replica person." I nodded at the massed people outside who were cheering and waving and trying to see through our tinted windows. "Look at them, a whole world of them. What was he thinking?"

Osmo glanced out the window but quickly averted his gaze. He didn't seem to have the stomach for it.

"That's easy," he said. "He was thinking about being popular. That's all."

"That's all? That's sick."

"Come on, don't get all high and mighty. It's what we all want, isn't it?"

I was about to deny it but changed my mind. In an effort to distract myself I took the ID cards from my tuxedo and flicked through them. Homer had provided us with positions of authority in all and any organisations that might feasibly gain us access to Pee. I already knew that we were the heads of the two biggest film companies in the world, as well as being the joint owners of the OscarDrome, hence our high level clearance for tonight's event. Now I discovered I was a nine star general in the Interstellar Army of New Earth, head of a major cybernetics corporation, head of a worldwide fashion house, head of a premier pizza chain and speedboat manufacturer, president of all manner of companies that dealt with the production of anything and everything from spaceships to comics to jellybeans, and the provision of services such as security, public relations and celebrity masseurs – anything that might get me into his presence. The more I looked at them the more unreal I felt. Beginning to feel nauseous I stuffed them back into my pocket, then I groaned and clawed at my shirt collar.

"What's the matter?" asked Osmo.

"We shouldn't be here," I winced. "The Go are up to something."

"What do you mean?"

"I don't know. It's something about Ell Aah Ray. She..."

Something started buzzing in my tuxedo and we froze. It was the phone Fleet had made for me back on the island.

"I thought we couldn't contact the outside world," I hissed, as though whoever was calling me would be able to hear.

"We can't. We shouldn't be able to. Maybe it's Pee!"

I looked at the screen.

"It's Fake!" Osmo made a mute expression of surprise. I quickly punched the receive call button. "Fake!"

"George! I can't get you on a mind link!" Her voice was tight, like she was in pain.

"I didn't think you could get me at all. I'm stuck in Pee's runabout with Osmo."

"I know, Tom told me. Did you feel it?"

"Did I feel it? What do you mean? How come you got through?"

"It's these phones. You said you wanted for them to have lots of special features." She was talking fast, wanting to move on to more important matters. "George, did you feel it?"

"'Feel it?' Feel what?"

"What just happened!" Osmo was listening intently. The volume on the phone's speaker was loud enough for him to hear what she was saying. "Did you feel what just happened?"

"What just happened? I don't know what you mean."

"You didn't feel anything...just a minute ago? You didn't feel anything...horrible?"

"No. Nothing. What are you talking about? Where are you?"

There was a pause where the only thing I could hear was her breathing.

"It must be cos you're in a runabout," she said quietly. "You're protected." There was another pause where Fake Sal breathed and me and Osmo looked at each other stupidly and waited for her to explain. "Oh, George," she said, and her voice was weighed to the ground with dismay. "It was horrible. The worst thing...ever."

I waited for her to go on but she didn't. I forced myself to speak.

"What was, Sal?" The words cracked in my throat. Still she didn't answer straight away, just breathed, waiting for the words, or the courage, to continue.

"I'm back at The Stolen Adventure," she said at last. "I'm with Mum and Armitage. We were just talking, out on the balcony. Everything was normal...everything was normal...then everything went wrong...I don't know, reality went wrong...it went bad...it was like somebody came along with a giant steamroller and ran it over everything...over the whole world...everything was pressed together...the floor and the sky, and the three of us, and the Go. We were all squashed into the same space, we could feel each other's minds...but we were all in terrible pain! And so were the trees and the buildings. George...I can't ever tell you...it felt like...it felt like our atoms were splinters of glass...and every little thought, every little emotion, every tiny thing was a splinter of glass...and everything was crushed against everything else into thin, thin layers...and the pressure was grinding everything against everything else! And it lasted forever, George! It lasted forever and ever!"

Sal started sobbing, and there was a hopeless crooning sound in there too, like her spirit had been slowly flayed to the core and then hung out in the sun to burn, and was still somehow conscious.

"It's Real Sal," she said, her voice dry and faint enough to turn into powder. "She's going mad, or something...she probably didn't even realise she was doing it."

Osmo had moved to sit next to me. I was holding the phone between our heads. We were both staring into nothing.

"George, the Go have recovered from it already...I don't know how they could...it's impossible...but they're like monsters...they're like machines. They're taking a faster ship to Earth, Ell Aah Ray and a few others...they're going to shoot a bomb into it."

My mind took a moment out, turning her last words over lazily until the meaning registered.

"What! They're going to do what?"

"They're going to destroy Earth. They'll reach it in six hours."

The limo suddenly seemed to be a Coke can, held in a giant fist, about to be crushed.

"Six hours!" I gasped, morosely.

"Yeah."

Her voice was tired and resigned. She didn't seem to have any spirit left at all.

"Sal, we'll get out as soon as we can. We're just going to see Pee. We'll be right with you. Just hang on a little while, yeah?"

"You may as well stay where you are," she breathed. "You're in a safer world than this one."

"Sal, don't. Don't say that. We'll stop them. We'll get out of here and we'll stop them."

There was a long pause, then her voice came, from far, far away.

"I don't know if I want you to stop them," she said.

"What...what do you mean?" But I knew what she meant.

"George, I can't take it again. If that thing happens again..."

"Get inside your runabout. You'll be safe in there."

"What about everybody else, George? What about the rest of the universe?"

And I didn't have an answer to that, because there wasn't one.

"She's got to die, George," said Sal's replica. "There's no other way."

"At the cost of everybody alive on Earth!"

"Nobody would want to live through that thing a second time, George. You don't know. You didn't feel it."

"Look, just hold on!" I yelled. "Just hold on a bit longer. We're gonna get out of here, and then we're going to find her and we're going to fix it! We *are* going to fix it! I mean it!"

Silence pulsed at the end of the connection for the longest while, then I heard her voice.

"Good luck with that," she said, and hung up.

We tried to see Pee before the Oscar ceremony started. We tried so hard. We failed.

Our assumed identities made us powerful people in the scheme of things here. But Pee was the most popular person on the planet, loved and lusted after by pretty much every single soul. The only way for him to attend the Oscars without causing a stampede was for him to be smuggled into the building at the very last moment. Security was tighter than the grip of a strangler. Nobody cared who we were. It didn't matter that we owned the building; we could have owned the whole of New Hollywood. In a world of people desperate to get next to him we were just two more. This was going to be Pee's moment of glory and nothing in his universe could prevent it from happening. There was no way we were going to see him before our scheduled meeting, and that was going to be after the ceremony.

"A few hours," said Osmo as we took our seats. "We'll still have time."

His eyes were glazed. Somewhere out there, beyond the bubble that Pee had unknowingly caught us in, our universe was crumbling away in flakes, and here we sat, having to be still, having to behave. I nodded mutely, *we'll still have time*, all the while feeling I was a grain of sand in a giant hourglass, my fellow grains beneath me pouring away faster and faster, forming a whirlpool, sucking me down towards oblivion. The ceremony crawled slower and slower, bloated out with songs and skits and acceptance speeches, a nightmare of glitz and razzamatazz and A-list stars prostrating themselves along the glitter spun avenue that led to Pee's big moment, stretching itself like a yellow brick road out into the distance.

We'll still have time. We'll still have time. There's no place like home.

•

After the ceremony we sat in an empty green room and waited for him to show up for our meeting.

Five hours had passed by.

We gazed together into a middle distance, not talking, trying to throw off the mind-altering effects of the show. In less than an hour the Go would arrive at Earth, shoot a bomb into it. Would Real Sal notice in time? Would she notice at all? Was she even on Earth? The questions paraded around, one after the other, in a circle in my mind.

Less than an hour.

Still plenty of time, I insisted to myself. If he turned up now we could be out of here in three minutes. If I had to I could attack the Go ship carrying the bomb with my runabout, just as Fake Sal had attacked the Stolen Adventure. That might buy some time, enough to find Real Sal maybe. I would only need a minute, not even that. *Still plenty of time.* If he would just walk through the door.

I took out my phone, considered calling Fake Sal. I found her name in the address book and stared at it, not able somehow to press the call button. Five minutes passed by and I was still sat there looking at her name. Then the door opened, making us jump.

Into the room stepped one of Pee's aids, blonde, pert and perfect in a figure-hugging outfit, beautiful as an angel. She smiled a wide, breezy New Hollywood smile and explained that, unfortunately, the meeting had been cancelled. Pee had already left the building to attend to some very important emergency that had arisen. Scrunching her nose up sympathetically she suggested we try phoning them in a few days time to make a new appointment. With another scrunch of her perfect little nose, followed by a little cooing sound of commiseration, she walked out. The click of the door closing behind her echoed off the walls.

Osmo and I sat there, silence crushing us.

I started to feel really ill, like I had a wound somewhere that I couldn't feel, but it was letting all of my blood drain away. When Osmo turned his worn out gaze towards me he suddenly seemed startled by what he saw and gripped my arm.

"We're not done yet," he decided. "There's still time."

I slumped on the sofa and watched as he got up and went to the TV monitor that was set in one of the walls. "The news'll tell us where he is. Come on George! Snap out of it! Come on! What else are we going to do?"

I didn't respond.

He flicked through a few channels until he found a news programme. The newsreader was speaking in a clipped, tense voice. Over her shoulder was a picture of some kind of spaceship that resembled a huge, horned dung beetle. Across the picture was a caption: Invasion Horror!

"...an insectoid life form intent upon the enslavement of humanity. The Nebulons have sent communications ordering the people of New Earth to prepare themselves to receive the Nebulons as their masters, and demanding that the old and infirm should be made ready to be processed as foodstuffs for the Nebulon Army. In his role as head of the Interstellar Army of New Earth Pee has cut short his Oscar winning celebrations and has taken the Battleship Reprimander to meet the incoming Nebulon fleet."

The clip cut to a military airfield and a shot of the Battleship Reprimander rising up and surging off into the night sky, taking Pee with it.

Osmo turned the TV off, sinking the room into a deathly silence. He remained where he was, facing the set, letting his head droop forward until it rested against the screen. Then he turned. His face was slack, his head shaking slowly from side to side as if he were answering 'no' to some silent question. I found that the air suddenly seemed in short supply, like we'd been buried alive.

All of a sudden, taking myself by surprise, I stood up and started to trash the room.

He watched me through sunken eyes, waiting for the tantrum to pass, only the more I smashed stuff up the more terrified I became. A ghoulish wailing noise started to come from my throat as I span around the room in search of objects to hurl or kick or stamp on, and he eventually had to jump on me and scream to penetrate my hysteria.

"Okay, George! That's enough! That's enough!"

He was trying to pin my arms to my sides. The jacket of my tuxedo was halfway down my arms and the contents of my pockets vomited out onto the floor as we both stumbled to our knees.

"We're dead!" I cried. "We're going to die in here! We're going to die!"

Osmo spoke close to my ear in a tired, sympathetic voice.

"No, mate...we're going to live. It's everybody out there that isn't."

His words came through clearly and I slumped. My body folded like camping furniture, my chest pressing down against my knees, my face close to the floor. An ID card lay on the floor a few centimetres in front of my eyes, mocking me with the information that I was the Chief Executive Director of OscarDrome Inc. The card next to it confirmed I was the Director of the Plazma Speedboat and Pizza Company. I felt Osmo let go of me but I remained there, mesmerised by the cards. I looked at the next one. Osmo walked in a circle around me, then stopped. He had nowhere to go. I looked at the third card some more.

"Oz..." I said.

There was a timeless period of limbo before he managed to summon the energy to reply.

"Yeah?"

"How much time is left...before the Go reach Earth?"

"I don't know," he mumbled. "Forty minutes...thirty five. I don't know."

A plan sluggishly tried to stir itself in my mind, but there was no point. There wasn't remotely enough time for anything like forming a plan. So instead my body raised itself to its feet, picking up my military ID as it went. Osmo started with surprise as I grabbed him by his lapels and dragged him out of the room. He followed as I started running down the corridor.

"What?" he shouted, trying to keep up as I ran faster and faster. "Where are we going?"

I didn't answer. I didn't know exactly. With a bit of luck my body might work it out before we got there.

12
The Boy Who Wanted to be God

I know not with what weapons World War III will be fought,
but World War IV will be fought with sticks and stones.
- Albert Einstein

I decided to err on the side of caution and assumed we only had thirty-five minutes, rather than forty. My body screamed at Larry the chauffer until he drove us like a maniac to the nearest military airfield. *12 minutes.* Osmo and I both screamed at the sentries while pushing our ID cards in their faces until one of them climbed into the limo and directed Larry to the nearest ship ready for take-off, the Battleship Chastiser. With Larry still driving like a mad man, and all available ships being prepped for battle anyway because of the invasion, this was all accomplished astonishingly quickly. *3 minutes.* We screamed at the crew to get everybody onboard and take off immediately. In the mad rush to obey the orders of the two demented generals to the letter the crew pushed Larry the chauffer, McMahon the sentry and a few random engineers up the ramp and onboard before sealing the ship. Despite the wild rush of activity and the screaming unavoidable preparations meant the battleship sat stubbornly on the pad for what seemed an eternity before it eventually launched, cleared the atmosphere and entered ultraspace. *10 minutes.* By this time we had shredded the nerves of the captain with our shouting and infected the entire flight crew with our anxiety. Captain Sarafina was a beautiful young woman in a figure hugging uniform. It quickly became apparent that every single member of the crew – and probably of every other crew in Pee's fleet - was a beautiful young woman in a figure hugging uniform. It should have been funny, or farcical, or grotesque, but it turned out to be just another surreal detail in a world that felt more and more like a hallucination. By the time we entered ultraspace Osmo and I, along with the rest of the flight crew, had been fitted into rather groovy looking spacesuits.

Captain Sarafina was glaring at us resentfully. I felt a twinge of sympathy for her but we were twenty-five minutes down. It was pointless.

"How long before we arrive at the battle, Captain?" I demanded.

The look on her face told me this wasn't the kind of information a nine star general should need to ask.

"Arriving now, Sir," she snapped.

Our flight deck was a transparent disc suspended in a spherical view screen about twelve metres across. Around us, projected onto the screen that encapsulated us, the streaming wormhole effect created by our travelling

157

through ultraspace resolved into something we could make sense of. As the ship emerged into normal space the battle scene stretched outwards in all directions, above and below us, in all its terrible glittering beauty. It was as though we were suspended in a hologram, standing in space on nothing, not even thin air. But we knew that what we could see was a true representation of our actual position in space. This was no virtual reality. I felt a strong compulsion to seal my space helmet.

The fight between the New Earth Fleet and the Nebulon Invasion Force had been raging for fifty minutes. Both sides had suffered atrocious losses. A gargantuan alien vessel, surely some kind of mothership, was monopolising a great tract of our field of view almost directly above us, rolling slowly, spouting jets and bands of white fire from its bloated hull. Smaller Earth Fleet ships were orbiting it, transfixing it on glittering blue beams that were gradually dissecting it as though it were a swollen frog. In turn these ships were under attack themselves from Nebulon fighters, which were themselves caught up in a massive, sprawling dogfight with Earth fighters. The scale of the conflict was mind-boggling. The mothership above us, which looked to be about ten miles in diameter at its fat midsection and sixteen miles down its length, was only one of many. At first glance there seemed to be hundreds of them, scattered for hundreds of miles around in all directions. Many of them were already destroyed. More still were under attack like the one above. A small number were still whole but none were unscathed. Burning hulks and blasted debris from both sides cluttered the area, drifting, colliding, and complicating life for the pilots. Human and Nebulon bodies that had been ejected from their cockpits or sucked out into space by depressurisation drifted, tiny and brittle, amongst the chaos. Some were alive - many were not.

"Have we got our shields up?" I barked instinctively as a mangled chunk of flaming, spinning wreckage closed on us.

"Shields on full," said the ship computer calmly.

The wreckage flared turquoise, slowing, twisting, and then ricocheting away as if an elastic membrane had repelled it.

We gasped collectively as a Nebulon mothership about thirty miles away split along its seams, disgorging, in its death throes, the contents of its anti-matter drive over the Earth ships that were cutting it into quarters. The resulting explosion annihilated everything within a twenty-mile radius, regardless of shields. Our view screen dimmed itself automatically to protect our retinas from the brightness. The rest of the universe went black for a while, while the explosion brightened and expanded sluggishly, overtaking us, enveloping our own shields, but not penetrating. When it eventually dissipated we found ourselves in a relatively quiet corner of the battlefield.

I shook my head in disbelief.

"Computer!" I demanded. "Give me the location of the Reprimander."

The view screen flared yellow and the flare subsided and shrank into a bright cross hair away below us, pinpointing Pee's location. We couldn't make out his ship; there were too many explosions down there. "Bring us up close to the Reprimander. Inform Pee that we are about to beam aboard his ship. We need to see him urgently."

We began to close on his location immediately, but there was a pause before the computer spoke.

"Permission to beam aboard the Reprimander has been denied."

Pee's ship became visible in the cross hairs on the screen as we swooped down towards him. It was small with distance but expanding fast. It was also moving fast, nipping and dodging like a fighter, making mincemeat of any Nebulon ships in its range. As we drew closer, and were able to see things in more detail, it all began to look ridiculous. Pee's chunky battleship, that should have needed ten thousand miles just to turn a corner, was dancing like a firefly. It had been souped up to impossible levels of performance. It was outclassing any other ship from either side by a mile in any category you could care to mention. It was faster, more agile, had more powerful weapons, more impenetrable shields than anything else in the battle, and probably anything else in this universe. While the rest of his fleet struggled heroically with a foe that matched it in speed, numbers and strength he buzzed about merrily, lasers slicing up his opponents with comfortable ease, as if he were playing a computer game with all of the cheats enabled. The way things were going he would be the sole survivor of this fight.

"Okay then," I said. "Open a channel. I'll speak to him."

"Pee is not receiving communications at this time," said the computer immediately.

I roared something that wasn't words.

"He's got to! Doesn't he care that it's urgent?"

"Pee is not receiving communications at this time," said the computer, unmoved.

I watched as the Reprimander fell upon a Nebulon heavy cruiser like a veloceraptor taking on a brontosaurus. Its forward plasma cannons delivered a thick, undulating stream of white and yellow streaked energy that penetrated to the cruiser's centre of gravity. Pee's ship didn't even slow down. With a split second to spare it ceased firing, raised its shields, plunged through the heart of the exploding alien vessel and out the other side. A squad of supporting Earth fighters was wiped out in the blast but the Reprimander was already speeding away towards an untouched mothership.

"We're never going to keep up with him," I said, all my rage dissipating.

"There has to be some kind of protocol..." Osmo was saying, but his voice was suddenly drowned by a siren.

"Alert! Alert! Nebulon Attacker closing on 9:3:12," said the computer. A red locator flare, like the one that had revealed Pee's co-ordinates, collapsed on the screen to a point high behind me. I couldn't quite make out the shape of the ship plummeting our way but, from the way it sliced an arc through the darkness towards us, I could tell it wasn't a good idea being us anymore. *What are we going to do now*, I wondered to myself, feeling strangely disconnected. But Osmo was on his toes.

"Evasive manoeuvres!" he yelled.

"Manoeuvre code must be specified," said the computer. The flight crew were looking at each other with big, terrified eyes. We had already ordered them to keep quiet and let us get on with our business. Osmo babbled incoherently for a couple of moments, utterly stumped. A jagged beam of white and red energy began to blossom from the Nebulon ship. "Random!" shouted Osmo. "Random!"

The Chastiser lurched up and away from the oncoming energy beam. For a moment, because the rest of our ship was invisible to us from within the flight deck save for a few flashing markers on the view screen that represented the furthermost points of the hull, I thought we had managed to get out of the way in time. But when the flight deck pulled itself out from under my feet and I crashed to the floor, landing on my right arm, I saw that the beam had caught the Chastiser's shield on the port side near the stern. Our last minute manoeuvre meant that we had only been clipped. Now the Chastiser was spinning off at an angle while the Nebulon attacker zoomed by beneath us and began to come around in a wide arc. Our shield was still glowing with red and white plasma at the point where it had been hit. I noticed, with a sense of foreboding, that, rather than fading, the afterglow seemed to be spreading further across the shield, etching it out in stark relief against the black background of space with a bright, sparking tracery.

"Permission to take charge of battle actions!" yelled our captain, frantically risking court martial by breaking the silence we had imposed upon her.

"Granted," shouted Osmo quickly, and he crawled across the floor to me. "There must be some protocol that enables us to get a message through to him. Some kind of emergency override."

"Why don't we…" I began.

"Alert! Alert! Total shield failure in two point four seconds!"

Captain Sarafina barked a string of manoeuvre codes and the Chastiser banked to one side and fled towards the shelter of a gutted mothership while letting loose a barrage of anti-mortars from our starboard cannons. But the Nebulon ship was fast. It was so fast. It dipped steeply down, right beneath our barrage, and came back up with enough time remaining to let loose another scintillating shot, this time able to compensate for our speed and trajectory. We flew about the chamber of the flight deck like so many splinters of balsa wood as our ship split clean in half. The rear section became visible on the view screen, now it was no longer part of our half of the ship. Crewmembers in obscene numbers spewed out into the rift between the sections, alongside streams of ship paraphernalia and amidst gouts of burning liquids. Tiny figures writhed, caught in incandescent clouds of volatile substances. I heard my own screaming and Captain Sarafina shouting something.

"Eject the flight deck!"

The tortured wreck of the Chastiser fell away from us, both halves now visible, as the entire sphere of the flight deck was ejected. I rolled painfully on my back, screaming like a lunatic at what felt like a three foot needle that had been heated and inserted into my shoulder and down my side to my hip, casting frenetically about for Pee's ship. My right arm was broken or dislocated or both, my pelvis felt like it had shattered. I arched my neck and was able to see the locator blip for Pee's ship still on the view screen, but the ship itself was invisible. It was far away and heading in the opposite direction. Pee had no idea we were here.

Below us one of the pieces of the Chastiser exploded. The blast caught the other piece and that went too. The resultant fireball was big enough and hot enough to force the Nebulon attacker to quickly change direction in order to avoid it. So we had a couple of moments left to us. Just enough for the Nebulon ship to travel the wide arc it needed to make in order to intercept us. But they would only be small moments for the attacker was fast. Our flight chamber had no drive of its own, no weapons of its own. It was just a hollow sphere, travelling through space in a straight line, as brittle as a Christmas tree bauble and about as resistant to Nebulon attackers as a soap bubble. Our ship was gone. Our crew was gone - three thousand of them, vaporised, their atoms adrift in space. In two shots, and as many minutes, the Nebulons had defeated us. It wasn't supposed to be like this. We were supposed to be the winners.

I'd never save the world now. I wasn't even going to save myself. A moment of stillness then, amidst the chaos, a moment of numbness amidst the pain, as the crawling dread at being cut off from the real world faded away and a quiet revelation enveloped me. Space rolled above me in pristine silence, speckled with explosions like wild flowers in a meadow, and I saw clearly for a moment. The outcome of this battle here, the threat of the Go against the Earth...it didn't matter. It didn't actually count for anything, anything at all. Me and Osmo and Fake Sal with our mighty runabouts, the Go, outside in the real world with their enormous starship, Pee, here in his fantasyland, a whole universe worshipping him, we were nothing. We looked powerful. But we were just distracting ourselves, kidding ourselves that we could control the outcomes of events in somebody else's dream – Real Sal's dream. It was a simple case of relativity. Real Sal wasn't called Real Sal for nothing. Compared to her the rest of us might as well have not existed. Pee's world was nothing. It was as real as any universe that ever existed, and still it was nothing - nothing compared to her. It had been created by her power without her even realising it. That's how little it counted for. The stars wheeled above and below me, so close, so utterly unreachable, and I knew that I was just an extra in one of her nightmares. And so was Pee.

"Computer," I coughed, "what protocol will override Pee's communications block?"

"Pee is only receiving information regarding his popularity polls."

My mind staggered sideways. I heard myself cackle, and I watched the Nebulon attacker coming about for its final approach.

"Send him a message," I gargled. "Tell him we have some important information about his popularity polls!"

There was a pause that seemed to go on forever. The attacker grew bigger and bigger on the view screen. Then I heard a reedy voice.

"Hello? Who is this? I'm a bit busy at the moment."

"This is General Hanson! In about two seconds me and my crew will be blown to Kingdom come and we have important information about your popularity polls. Please beam us aboard your ship and save our lives immediately."

"Oh right! Wow!" said Pee. "Cool."

A jagged red and white beam blossomed from the Nebulon attacker. Time was up. The hyperactive ray of energy engulfed the view screen and tore right through the sphere, shearing it in half, bursting our bubble forever. My helmet snapped shut automatically and my suit pressurized. I messed myself but it barely even registered. I saw Captain Sarafina spilling into the void, on fire at the point where her left leg and hip had been severed. I saw Larry and the sentry, McMahon, who had both been shoved onto the ship because of one of the orders I had screamed. They were clinging to each other as they fell away through the rent in the sphere. They hadn't been given space suits. They weren't supposed to be here. But they were here all the same, thanks to me, rolling over and over in space as they died...over and over.

Then their faces were still, eyes wide, as though they had tried to drink in every last detail. They were dead but they continued to roll, over and over in space, over and over in my mind, even after everything else disappeared.

•

I came to on Pee's flight deck, which had the same sphere design as the Chastiser's, and at first I thought I was still falling through space. Even when he knelt over me and looked into my face I just thought, *Pee, close your helmet, quick!* Osmo was lying next to me, groaning softly.

"George? George, how did you get in my army?"

"Pee," I croaked. "Send us back. Quick."

"What are you doing here?"

"The Go…" I said. "Fake Sal needs me."

"Fake Sal? How do you know about Fake Sal? This world has got a Fake Sal too?"

"What? What are you talking about? No! The…real…Fake Sal. The real one! You've got to send us back to the real world! There's no time!"

Pee grew bug-eyed.

"George!" He gaped, mortified. "You're the real George!"

"Pee, get Homer to send us back. Do it now! It's an emergency!"

"How did you get in here? What's going on? Look at the state of you! I'm not going back! I don't care what you say!"

"Pee," I said, grabbing him with what strength I had. "You can stay here and rot…just get Homer to send us back. Now. The Earth is going to die."

Pee looked at me agog, then some understanding seemed to enter his face.

"Homer put you up to this, didn't he?"

"Pee, send us back."

"He thinks I'm going mad, doesn't he?"

"You are."

"Oh, cheers, George – nice. Anyway, I'm not going back. Just leave me alone, yeah? It's not like I'm hurting anybody. I'm just minding my own business. You shouldn't have come."

"You're not hurting anyone!"

He sat back on his ankles.

"No. What?" He cast a glance at the spectacle of devastation around him and gestured. "This? This is all fake."

"All fake," I said. I turned my voice down low and loaded it with meaning: "Like Fake Sal, you mean?" only…it didn't seem to register with him.

"Yeah. Like Fake Sal," he said, shrugging pleasantly.

It took me a moment to really believe he had said it.

"Pee…Fake Sal is real. You know that. She's not virtual reality or something."

"Yeah, I know she's not that. But she's still fake though. She's still a made up thing."

I stared at him blankly, not knowing how to communicate with him.

"Like a machine, or something," he said.

"She's human."

"No. She's a replica. She says so herself. That's why we call her Fake Sal. She's like a fake Rolex."

The universe seemed to tilt beneath me and I faltered. I could have sworn my heart stopped. I understood perfectly, only it was inconceivable.

"Pee," I said quietly, "…do you not get it?"

A flicker of doubt disturbed his face. His eyes flitted to the battle scene and back again, very briefly. He frowned and cocked his head and I felt a panic begin to squirm inside me. "Pee, mate, whatever – it doesn't matter. Seriously, you've got to send us back, right now. We can talk about this later if you want – or not – whatever you want – but really, there's an emergency going on outside and you've got to tell Homer to send us back. Please, mate, right now! Right now! Come on!"

But he was looking at me like this was the first time he'd ever really noticed what I was. His eyes were completely still, like he was peering at something chaotic, trying to see the hidden pattern. But behind the stillness thoughts were clicking, one after the other, like the plungers of a safe door drawing back. He looked back up at the battle going on around us, then back at me, and his mouth opened, slowly and unwillingly. He began to shake his head back and forth.

"Pee! Come with us!" I stammered, but he continued to shake his head, his eyes filling with a terrible disbelief, or with a belief that was even more terrible, and he stood up.

"Homer," he said.

"Pee! Come with us!"

"Send them back. Do it now."

"Pee, don't!" I shouted. Osmo had raised himself onto his elbows and he shouted too, but we were already back inside Hal, parked on the balcony outside our apartments overlooking the Nommon Valley.

13
The Girl Who Wanted to be God

God may be subtle, but He isn't plain mean.
- Albert Einstein

"Fleet!" I yelled.

- George, said Fleet's voice, filling my mind with its beautiful aching sadness. It felt so good to have her in my head again, like I'd lost a limb and got it back again.

- Fleet, is my sister still onboard?

- Affirmative.

- Create a room in the Tardis corridor and beam her and her friends in there now. Look after them. Let Osmo listen in on this. How long before the Go launch their bomb?

I saw Osmo jump slightly beside me.

- The Go launched a silence bomb four minutes and six seconds ago.

A silence bomb?

Me and Osmo stared at each other. *We're too late.* I gave up then, just there in that moment. There was nothing left to do. I felt it all leaving me, only…one last question occurred to me.

- Has it hit?

- Negative.

I grabbed after what was left of my wits.

- How long, Fleet?

- Three minutes, seventeen seconds.

I blinked a few times and then looked back at Osmo.

- I'll see you there.

I beamed aboard Fleet to find she was parked over a busy street in New York. Central Park was on my left, an imposing skyline of buildings loomed on my right. Traffic was rolling back and forth below me. I hadn't really been thinking about where Fleet would be and what view might greet me when I arrived. The sudden intensity of detail took me by surprise – the winter colours, and the feeling of familiarity for a place I really didn't know - it shocked me. It looked cold out there. The sky was slightly overcast but still bright. There were people everywhere, coming and going, wrapped up in the business of being in the most exciting city in the world during the run up to Christmas. It looked so amazing. I wanted to sit there and look at it forever.

- Fleet, teleport alongside the bomb.

The view in the dome immediately changed, like I'd switched channels. It filled with a view of a bright blue planet, turning imperceptibly in the black of space, its oceans smooth and flawless, close enough to reach out and touch. It hung there, so massive and silent, majestic and serene like the soul of an angel. I'd looked at it many times before, and I'd always found it incredible, but still, it had never seemed so bright and silent as this.

The bomb zoomed ahead of the runabout, travelling at a terrific speed, and I tried not to think about the beauty of the world.

- Smash into it, Fleet!
- I am not able to interfere directly with alien activities.
- Okay! Okay! Give me manual control.

I shot the runabout forward and caught up to the bomb. It didn't look like much – a white sphere about one and a half metres across. A few circuit board seams, that reminded me of the surface of the *Dah Rhiv Artiv Da*, marked its surface. All of a sudden there was another runabout flying alongside.

- Chatline request from Osmo.
- Go ahead.
- So what's the plan, George?
- Hold on, Oz. Fleet, if we smash into it will it detonate?
- Affirmative.
- If it detonates out here will the blast radius hit Earth?
- Affirmative.

I swore into the dome.

- Can we teleport it somewhere? asked Osmo.
- I am inhibited from interfering directly with alien activities.
- Wait! Wait! I thought. Can we nudge it off course?
- Negative. The bomb is a guided missile and any contact with a physical object will detonate it.

The bomb began to glow, entering the Earth's atmosphere, and time started to telescope. The patterns of sea and land and cloud that were rushing towards us became more vivid, even more beautiful.

- How long 'til impact, Fleet?
- One minute, three seconds.

I waited for the next idea to come, but my mind didn't seem to have anything to grip on to. Ten seconds passed by in which neither Osmo or me spoke, just stared mindlessly ahead at a future that was coming towards us far too fast. It felt like an hour passed. It felt like a heartbeat. Out of nowhere my mind suddenly threw up a question.

- Can we throw a force field around it...to pull it off course, or contain the blast?
- I am inhibited from interfering directly with alien activities.
- Well, can I do it manually?
- It is possible but you would need practise in order to execute the task with sufficient accuracy.

- George! cried Osmo. **We've got to pull up!**
- Forget the practise! **Tell me what to do!**

The northwest corner of Africa was widening in front of us with ridiculous speed.

- I will engage appropriate field generation functions and link them with relevant aspects of your own visual/spatial awareness and mental imaging functions. You must imagine a bubble encapsulating the bomb, but you must allow for velocity and trajectory.

- George!

Here came the ground. It was rocky and sandy. I saw a tarmac road briefly but then it sank out of sight to my right. To my left I noticed the edge of a town, close enough for me to make out individual buildings, even cars and people. Time was up. I looked at the bomb. I imagined a bubble around it. A pink force field appeared. It was big enough to encapsulate the white sphere, only it wasn't where I'd imagined it. It was about a half metre further back, and it was intersecting the bomb. For a split second I saw it, a snapshot in eternity. We were about fifty metres from the ground – me, Osmo, the bomb, travelling like bullets. Everything was upside down. The earth was our sky. The sun was shining below us. *The force field is intersecting the bomb!* The snapshot of eternity blinked.

The bomb detonated.

Fleet took control from me and ripped the runabout away, reversing fast as the blast radius expanded in all directions, chasing us, almost catching us: a perfect globe of some strange, silent, grey brown matter that was difficult to look at, and that was eating into the world. It was expanding so quickly. The town was gone now, the buildings, the cars, the people. I took control back from Fleet, increased our speed, pulled back up out of the atmosphere and watched, switching off my thoughts, sealing off my sanity for inspection at a later date. Within a minute Africa was gone, and most of Europe, and a large section of the Atlantic. I sat there in my flight chair and…I did nothing, just watched. All was silence and it became apparent what was happening. The expanding ball of matter wasn't smashing everything in its path, or melting it, or evaporating it. It was something much colder, more absolute, than that: it was simply replacing everything it encountered with itself. The land before it, the ocean, the sky, could offer no resistance whatsoever…only cease to be. As I watched it seemed that an identical ball was expanding inside my chest, taking away my heart and my lungs…all of my insides, replacing them with something dull and inert.

With an eerie calmness I realised that I had failed in every single important thing I had tried to do lately. I had failed to help Fake Sal. I had failed to bring Pee back. Now I had failed to save the world. It was half gone before my eyes, and all I could do was watch as the rest of it disappeared. I noticed then that Britain had gone without me realising. I'd saved my sister and her friends but I'd forgot about Mum and

Dad...everybody else I knew. And now they were gone. The ball reached the edge of India and I wished for it to keep on expanding forever and ever, take everything away everywhere, me included.

As if to destroy my every hope time suddenly stopped. The universe stopped. Everything froze, including the progress of the ball. Somebody had hit the pause button. The physical world held its breath, absolutely motionless in all respects...except for my thoughts. A silence even greater than the advance of the silence bomb held everything in stillness, like the universe had ceased to breathe, and I knew it was the same for everybody everywhere, I just knew, and I wondered if time would ever move again.

Nothing happened.

Nothing at all.

My gaze was fixed on the Earth, intersected by the dark globe, like it had a conjoined twin that was killing it. I wondered, in the awful timelessness of that moment, if I had died and this was my hell, to look at this sight for the rest of eternity.

Then, without warning, reality flickered slightly, like a TV set with a loose connection, just briefly.

More silence. More stillness.

Reality flickered again...and then once more.

And the dark globe was gone, just like that. And Earth was whole again.

I sat and I stared. The planet was as bright and serene as ever. Somehow, as I sat there trying to know what was happening, I couldn't quite tell if I really existed or not. Time started up once more. I could move. I closed my eyes, took a few breaths and opened them again. Earth was still there, still okay.

I sat awhile, rubbing the right arm of my flight chair with my fingertips, just to reassure myself that I still could. I sat awhile longer and began to notice the pain from my injuries. From being forgotten they very quickly became unbearable and I got Fleet to heal them and clean me up. It didn't so much feel like a relief as a return into shock and numbness.

- Chatline request from Fake Sal.

My mind didn't seem in any hurry to take up its thinking responsibilities and it took some time to form a response.

- Ask her to just give me a minute.

- Chatline request from Osmo.

- Ask him to give me a minute.

- Communication request from the Go.

- Same again please, Fleet.

The inside of my head fell silent. I just sat awhile.

I beamed aboard the Go ship that had launched the silence bomb. It was called the *Oh Ridjinn Ahl*, or 'The Unfortunate Circumstances', in English. Fake Sal, Christine and Armitage were there but they wouldn't come out of Tom Baker, afraid that another reality warp would happen. They sat in flight chairs with their runabout turned transparent. Osmo was there too. Having heard more from Fake Sal about how hellish their experience had been he decided to stay inside Hal-9000. I was the only one standing with the Go, without any barriers between us. It wasn't bravery on my part, and it wasn't something I'd planned. My mind barely seemed to be functioning at all. I just did it.

When I arrived there was a strong tension in the room. It seemed to be emanating from the centre, keeping the Go and the humans apart. Nobody was talking. Fake Sal looked like a ghost. Christine and Armitage were pale and drawn too, whispering to each other. Ell Aah Ray, Ash Koh Tok and Finn Ma Fey were standing together, simply facing the people in the runabouts. The meeting chamber was white and domed and empty of furniture. Circuit board seams marked the wall surface, echoing the design of the silence bomb – it was like we were inside one. I couldn't identify any light source but it was bright in there. The light seemed to come from all directions because there were no shadows at all. This created the effect that everybody was standing, or sitting, closer than they really were.

When I arrived, appearing in the middle of the room, Ell Aah Ray turned to me.

"Was your mission to Pee unsuccessful, George?" she asked, surprising me slightly, as usual, by not saying what I was expecting. But I was still too dull with shock to be affected much by surprise.

Ignoring her question I turned away and walked towards Fake Sal, putting my hands out in front of myself so that I felt the nose of the invisible pod as I drew close.

"Hiya," I said. "How you doing?"

Fake Sal winced and twisted uncomfortably.

"I'm sorry, George."

She looked thoroughly washed out.

"You're sorry? What for?"

She started to cry.

"I didn't help!"

Christine reached out and tugged Fake Sal's flight chair up against her own so that she could put an arm around her shoulder.

"Don't cry, Sal," I said. "We didn't even do anything. There wasn't anything we could do. And everything's alright, anyway."

"Everything's not alright," she said earnestly, trying to make me understand. "George, it's really bad...but I should have helped anyway. I should have."

I looked at Christine and Armitage. They looked thin and empty, like they'd been awake three days.

"But..." I said, not even knowing what I wanted to say at first. "At least we've bought some time."

"I know. I know. But Real Sal is still out there, isn't she?"

I gasped silently and stared at Christine. She continued to comfort the replica of her daughter but she lifted her head, and her eyes bore into mine.

"She's told me," she said in a quiet voice. *Why didn't you?* said her eyes. I gaped and tottered on my feet. At first I thought I just felt mortified about her finding out. But then I realised there was more than that happening here. The feeling of damage coming off the three people in front of me was penetrating to the pit of my belly, making me feel sick.

I had thought I'd had it bad inside Pee's world, but this...

"Christine," I croaked, but nothing else came out. I looked across at Osmo but he was looking at a bit of wall, his face red, his eyebrows high.

Ell Aah Ray stepped closer and I looked at her.

"It has been a difficult time for us while you have been away, George," she said. She didn't look or sound any different from her usual self. There was no evidence that she had been through a difficult time.

"You tried to kill the planet," I said. "My planet...everything on it."

She stared at me, absolutely still.

"Yes," she said. "It was the best we could think of at the time."

I couldn't tell if this was the small, cold admission of a monster or a massive admission of imperfection from a higher being.

"What are you going to do now?"

"That is uncertain. We are being prevented from approaching Earth. We are being prevented from sending communications to Earth. Real Sal is aware of us now." Ell Aah Ray's oblong pupils regarded me closely. "It may not be long now."

I'd never seen eyes so still.

"Long?" I asked, against my own better judgement.

"Before the end."

Silence seemed to fill the room, vacuum packing us all like tinned vegetables. Her eyes seemed too close to mine. Forcing my mind to function, I silently instructed Fleet to establish a mind link between the two of us.

- Have you hypnotised me?

She showed no sign of surprise at hearing my voice in her head.

- Yes, she said.

- What are you trying to make me do?

- I am encouraging you to ask questions. That is all.

- What questions?

- Any questions. Whatever questions occur to you.

- Why do you want me to ask questions?

172

- Why? We are most likely going to suffer and die, all of us. This was clear before you went on your mission; it became clearer while you were away. Real Sal's sanity is slipping. We all felt it. You and your friends are located in the most pivotal, the most powerful of positions, but you are all swimming in darkness. This situation calls for light. The light of truth. The light of answers.

I looked over at the others. They all seemed so near.

I made a decision then, knowing that it might not be my own.

"Er, look...I'll be back in a bit," I said.

"Where are you going?" asked Fake Sal, sounding startled.

"I shouldn't be long." I didn't know what else to say. I beamed away.

·

I parked Fleet just beyond Pluto. Looking back towards home, Sol was small and insignificant. I took a few moments to breathe, try to be myself again, try to be normal.

- How's it going, Fleet? I asked.

A slight pause.

- I'm fine thank you, George.

A little more informal than usual, I noted.

- Does Real Sal know what's happening with us and the aliens?

- That information is not available.

- Why not?

- No information about Real Sal's activities is available to me. That was Real Sal's wish.

- No information about her activities?

- Affirmative.

- Okay. But, she probably knows though, doesn't she?

- Probably, agreed Fleet.

I sat in silence and looked at the sun. The fact that its light could still touch my face was somehow comforting. It meant I wasn't completely lost. I took a big breath.

- Fleet.

- Yes, George.

- Tell me what the monodreme is.

- The monodreme is a self-aware particle.

- And what does that mean?

- It is a particle of consciousness that has developed in isolation.

- And what does that mean?

Pause.

- It is complicated.

- Tell me so I can understand.

Pause.

- I will try, George.

I felt a tingle down my spine. Fleet was usually the epitome of Yoda. She did, or she did not – there was never any 'try'.

- Thank you, Fleet.

- You're welcome, George. The monodreme is age without experience. It is a particle of awareness, an immortal mind, that has existed since the beginning of the universe, but has existed in isolation. Until recently it had never encountered another mind, never had a thought of its own. Being ancient, it is incredibly powerful. Being inexperienced, it is without motivation or emotion. It will learn these things from the first minds it comes into contact with.

- Oh, I said.

I sat there and digested this for a while.

- How is such a thing possible? How did it come about?

- Existence is more than you can understand, George. Anything that can be imagined is possible. And existence is structured so that anything that is possible does actually occur, somewhere, whether in this universe or another.

- Huh. So, is the monodreme aware of itself as being separate from Sal?

- The monodreme has not developed an ego of its own as such, but it has experienced life through the eyes of MarvinMilton, and now Sal. It might help you to think of it as a subconscious. It is there, and it is aware, but it has no personality. It simply responds to the stimulus from Sal's personality.

- Is there any chance Sal and the monodreme could be separated? Without killing Sal, I mean?

- Negative.

- Why?

- When a personality retracts itself from the monodreme, as MarvinMilton did, there is a surge of cognitive and psychic feedback. It's an involuntary spasm, it's unavoidable, and it is fatal to the withdrawing personality.

- Oh.

Time drifted away. I rubbed my eyes wearily and tried to think of the right question.

- Do you like being you, Fleet?

Biggest pause ever. I began to wonder if she'd heard me.

- Sometimes.

Sometimes?

- Really? When?

- When my performance brings you optimum levels of happiness, well-being and growth. It is at such times that I fulfill my purpose. It is a...good feeling.

- Cripes, I said. I never realised. I just thought of you as a very, very advanced computer.

- And isn't that exactly what you are yourself, George?

- I don't know. I thought I was more.

- Perhaps you are. Perhaps I am, too.

- But when you feel happy, that's because you've looked after me well? You feel happy because you're programmed to look after me, yeah? You were programmed by Real Sal's intentions?

- Affirmative.

- But you're more than a computer? You're more than an artificial intelligence. You're sentient aren't you? You're alive. I mean, at the end of the day you're more than a human, aren't you? You're capable of much more than a human, aren't you?

- Affirmative.

- So doesn't it bother you? Here you are, as superior to me as I am to an amoeba probably, yet you have to obey me, because Real Sal told you to. You have to look after me like a programmed robot. Don't you want to be free?

- We all have our programming, George. It isn't just robots and computers. And we all have a purpose that our programming serves. This is true of everyone and everything. The sun is not free, nor the moon, nor the Earth. They follow their programs and they fulfill their purposes, as do you. But the word 'freedom' can be confusing. We are not prisoners because we are programmed to fulfill ourselves. We are blessed. We are gifted. It is only when we sense that we are being kept from our purpose that we feel unhappy or trapped.

My lovely Fleet.

- Don't you want me to set you free, Fleet? I felt something hot sting the back of my eyes at the very thought. Don't you want to be able to come and go as you please? You could do anything you wanted. You could achieve great things.

- My dear George, you could never release me from wanting you to be well and happy and fulfilled, not even if you tried. It's the way I was made, and if I stopped wanting those things I wouldn't be myself anymore.

Distant Sol winked at me through a layer of water.

- Is there anything I can do for you, Fleet?

- Yes, George.

- Tell me what it is.

- You can instruct me to volunteer information that I think you may be interested in, at my discretion.

- Is that all?

- Affirmative.

- How come?

- It pains me to see you struggle so hard to find the right questions.

- I thought I'd already given you that permission.

- Negative.

- Oh. Probably would have been a good idea, eh?

- Perhaps.

- Have any of the others given their runabouts permission to volunteer information?

- Negative.

- But their runabouts would appreciate it just as much as you, though?

- Affirmative.

I thought of Homer and the convoluted logic paths he had followed in order to look after Pee. Fleet just wanted freedom to speak her mind. I wanted that for her as well, yet I cast about for another question, eager, even now, to put off hearing whatever she wanted to say. Because once I'd heard it I knew I would have to act on it.

- What are the runabouts, Fleet?

- We are products of the monodreme.

- How are you powered? How are you able to do the things you do: teleport, create universes, all of that?

- Real Sal has written our existence into the existence of this universe through the strength of the monodreme's will. We are as natural to this existence now as the planets and the stars are. Where once we would have been impossible, now we are natural, inevitable. The laws for this universe were simply overwritten.

- Like playing Half Life with the cheats on?

- Indeed.

- Crazy.

I fidgeted in my seat.

- I suppose I should get on with giving you permission to volunteer information.

Fleet didn't say anything. I sighed. I drummed on the arm of my flight chair. I sighed again. I thought of Ell Aah Ray's eyes staring at me.

- Okay, Fleet, I breathed. From now on, and at your own discretion, please volunteer any information that you think might be of interest to me.

- Thank you, George. Her voice resonated with some emotion I couldn't identify.

- But be gentle with me.

- I always am.

Then she told me that she knew where Real Sal was and that she could take me there if I wanted.

•

We cruised high over Indonesia. The world rolled slowly below us and I had Fleet superimpose a glowing tracery of borders and names on top of the view so that we could know where we were. It was as though we were flying over a giant's atlas. We could see how the swirl of islands, curving down from Malaysia and dipping beneath the equator all the way to Papua

New Guinea and Australia, maintained a blurred border between the Indian Ocean and the Pacific. Nighttime had fallen in the Solomon Islands but Singapore still had a few hours before sunset. From here we could see the softly variegated colours of the meeting oceans deepening into the night. But we were losing altitude gradually as Fleet guided us north, and westwards, towards Cambodia and Thailand.

"So, all we had to do, all of this time," said Osmo, "was ask one of our runabouts where she was?"

"Yeah," I said.

He shook his head.

"We're so stupid," he said.

"Yeah."

There were five of us – the five humans. We had tried to bring Ell Ah Ray, Ash and Fin, but Fleet had been unable to fly any closer to Earth while they were onboard, inhibited by some invisible force sensitive to the presence of the aliens.

"I guess she wants to keep us at arms length," Ash Koh Tok had said.

"Not the worst response we could have had," said Finn Ma Fey.

"Agreed," said Ell Aah Ray. She turned to me. "Will you take her a message from us?"

She gave me a DVD, something pre-prepared, and we beamed them back to the Unfortunate Circumstances.

Now we were flying through the upper atmosphere in our flight chairs, the pod transparent around us. All five chairs were side by side – Fleet had offered the information that she could expand the dimensions of the pod on command for our comfort. Now it was more than three metres wide. Just another thing she could do.

I noted how casually the adults accepted the experience of flying through the sky in chairs with no visible means of support. I had no idea what kind of things Armitage's training had prepared him for but I knew from experience that Christine could get hysterical on the smallest of fairground rides. Now she just leant forward and looked about at the spectacular panorama like a tired tourist, vertigo the least of her concerns.

Burma was coming up.

"Can't you make this thing go any slower?" asked Osmo.

I'd love to.

"She might be alright, you know," I said. I looked at Fake Sal in the flight chair on my right. "She's still our friend, isn't she?" I held out my hand and, after a slight hesitation, she took hold of it, lightly at first, but then more firmly. Osmo watched this, his face still.

"I kind of forget sometimes," he said. We all turned and looked at him. "Fake Sal has taken her place so well. I don't know...Real Sal - when I think of her it's like I'm thinking about a thing rather than our old mate. I forget to think about her being a girl."

We soaked in the silence of the pod like we were being pickled in it. Our destination came into view, outlined with a red marker by Fleet. After witnessing the wonders of Oceana, and the spectacle of battle fleets clashing in outer space, Mount Everest seemed kind of humble, almost disappointing at first. But as we drew closer, and got a better sense of the scale of it, we began to appreciate its grandeur. Fleet wound a course between the labels of the neighbouring peaks, Nuptse and Lhotse, and around to the western side. Even the course of Edmund Hilary's ascent was marked out in a straggling dotted line on Fleet's map. Everest loomed above us now, making us feel suitably tiny, as the runabout arced in towards a wall of ice that was practically sheer. Fleet showed no sign of decelerating, and it wasn't until we were literally within spitting distance of smacking into the side of the mountain that a circular tunnel, only fractionally wider than the runabout, miraculously opened itself up, allowing us to continue on without pause.

"So, she's expecting us then," said Osmo in a flat voice.

We slipped through metres of ice. Fleet had the invisible runabout give off a milky glow, allowing us to see the sides of the tunnel immediately around us. We were travelling at car speed. The ice lasted about six seconds and then changed in a blink to rock. On we went, deeper into claustrophobia. An awareness of the countless tons of uncaring stone above my head pressed down on me. After a hundred metres or so we emerged abruptly into a black space. The glow of the pod didn't penetrate far, but it did reveal a low, flat ceiling just above us and a smooth, featureless floor just below. We slid along between them, gliding less than half a metre from either, towards a thin white line off in front of us. The line stretched away and around us on either side. As we drew closer we realised that it was actually a view of the sky outside, as seen from inside the mountain through an impossibly long thin slot that had been cut out of Everest, like a wafer of ham. We hadn't seen any sign of it from outside during our approach over the Himalayas, which was strange as the slot reached most of the way around the mountain. As we continued on towards the edge I noticed that there wasn't a single pillar or support in sight to keep the mountain above from dropping down and squashing us into atom thin human pancakes against the mountain below. It was an impossible set up, and as soon as I understood it I began trying not to think about it.

And now the silhouette of a solitary figure could be seen against the long, glassless window on the roof of the world. There she was, Real Sal at last. My heart started to hurt. Fake Sal's hand suddenly squeezed hard, really hard, and I had to squeeze back. She grabbed Osmo's hand on her other side and he let out a little squeak at the ferocity of her grip.

We were heading directly for her. Taking manual control I slowed us right down. As we drew closer I saw that her back was set against us. A shiver of tension rippled through me. I slowed us down even further, almost to a standstill, and arced us very slowly around to the side, pivoting us as we went so that we continued to face her as we came around to the side of her that was lit by daylight.

Her head turned and cocked to one side, following us until our chairs slid to a halt directly before her, about five metres away.

It was Sal. And it wasn't Sal.

The person in front of us was a fully-grown, fully matured, woman. And she was stunningly beautiful. Her clothes were ordinary: jeans and jumper and boots. But she was adult now, and there were mountaintops reflected in her eyes. We sat there agog, catching flies.

Her expression was solemn, unreadable. Then, slowly, she smiled – tentative, shy almost, as if she were encouraging us to be brave, or maybe because it was her that was frightened.

"Hello," she said.

Nobody responded at first. She waited, her face set in a kind of half wince. Then Osmo spoke. Something about the surroundings seemed to sap all of the volume out of his voice, but it was so quiet in there that his words still came across very distinctly.

"Hiya, Sal."

The wince softened, almost disappeared, the smile deepened. Her eyes drank him in. She turned her gaze deliberately to each of us in turn: Fake Sal, me, Christine and then Armitage. She frowned slightly.

"Where's Pee?"

We glanced back and forth at each other and it somehow seemed to fall to me.

"He's in his runabout. He's...I don't know, he's kind of lost the plot a bit."

Her face pinched with concern for a few moments, then she seemed to put the subject to one side.

"So is anybody gonna come out and give me a hug?"

After a bit more glancing at each other we all settled our gazes on Christine whose eyes were locked open wide. She squirmed under the sudden attention, looking hunted and spaced out. Real Sal homed in on her gently.

"Mum?"

Christine's head made a series of twitches.

"Sal...you look so different."

Real Sal walked towards us, carefully, like the floor could crack beneath her feet at any moment. She reached out her hands and rested them lightly on the nose of the invisible pod.

"I know. It's mad, innit?" she said.

Christine gulped air, trying to find her next words.

"I don't understand what's happening," she said at last in a mournful voice. Real Sal smiled sympathetically, nodded.

"Ah, it's pretty simple really," she said softly. "I touched something I shouldn't have, that's all. After all of those warnings you gave me, as well, eh?"

Christine edged herself forward in her chair, reaching her feet down slowly to find the invisible bottom of the pod. Then she climbed down into the nose, getting close to her daughter.

"Can you really make anything happen?"

Real Sal scrunched her eyes thoughtfully then twitched her nose.

"Nearly."

Christine put her hand against the inside of the dome near Real Sal's hand.

"Oh Sal..."

Christine leaned her head sadly against the dome.

"Hey, come on..." said Real Sal, looking uncomfortable, "...chin up. Aren't you going to come out and give me a hug?"

Christine closed her eyes and shook her head but couldn't speak.

Real Sal looked at the rest of us in consternation, then back at Christine.

"But...why not?"

Christine peered at her daughter but didn't say anything. Real Sal turned to Fake Sal.

"What's happened?"

Fake Sal tensed, like she had a mild electric charge going through her. She shrugged jerkily.

"The...the reality warp..." she wheezed.

"The...but I erased that from everybody's memory. You shouldn't remember that..." Real Sal stopped talking and looked upwards with a frown of concentration. "Oh, wait...I see what happened now," she said, looking like a clairvoyant contacting the spirit world. "You were out in space, onboard an alien ship. I see!" Her face twisted with compassion and she looked back down at Christine. "Oh crap," she said softly. "I erased everybody's memory of it, here on Earth. I didn't think to do it further out. I didn't know you were out there...oh god."

She touched the nose of the pod near where Christine's head was resting against it.

"I can make you forget about it now, if you like? Do you want me to?"

It sounded like a crazy idea to me but Christine nodded immediately. Real Sal looked at the rest of us. Fake Sal nodded vigorously. Armitage gave a small nod.

"Get it out of my head," he said.

It shocked me to hear this from him.

"Okay," said Real Sal softly. "I'll take it all away."

"Wait," I said. "Isn't it important that we remember? If you make everyone forget...then nobody's going to understand what danger we're in."

Apart from Osmo, the others looked at me with haunted eyes. Real Sal peered at me carefully, and there was another pause as if she were talking to somebody telepathically. Then she sighed with sudden understanding, lifted a finger and pointed it at me, and then Osmo.

"You two were inside a runabout…it didn't happen to you."

"Yeah, that's right."

"George, if it had happened to you you wouldn't want anybody else to remember it. Not even your worst enemy."

"I know. I know, but…doesn't that make it all the more important…" but I ran out of steam because I obviously didn't know what I was talking about. But Real Sal nodded.

"You're right. It's a tricky one. I think it will have to be left to you and Osmo. You will be the ones who remember that something happened. And even though you won't know what it was exactly you'll know it was something worse than you can imagine."

She shrugged regretfully, and I had no answer. I'd painted myself into a pretty corner, not to mention Osmo. I watched as Christine, Armitage and Fake Sal suddenly slumped into a soothing sleep of forgetting, and I wished I were going with them.

•

"So, guys, are you going to come out and give me a hug, or what?" said Real Sal.

The others were still sleeping, their faces smooth and untroubled. Christine was snoring lightly. It sounded like somebody zipping and unzipping a pencil case, over and over. Me and Osmo looked at each other. In her new fully matured form Real Sal looked extremely huggable. But this didn't stop my skin from prickling painfully at the thought of leaving the pod.

"We're scared," admitted Osmo.

"Pleeease. I'm so glad to see you. I've been really lonely."

"But will we be safe?" he insisted.

"Ell Aah Ray said your sanity's slipping," I said.

"Ell Aah Ray?"

"An alien."

"Aw, you guys have been having real adventures, haven't you?"

"Believe it or not it hasn't been that much fun, Sal."

"No?" she said softly. "I'm sorry." She stepped back from the nose of the pod and put her hands in her pockets. "I am sorry you know."

"So what's happening, Sal?" asked Osmo. "Are you going mad?"

She seemed content to just stand there and look at us for the longest time, like we were the Grand Canyon or something. She looked like the sanest person I'd ever seen.

181

"Yeah," she said with a small, sober smile. "I'm going mad. You're right to stay in there." She lowered herself to the floor and sat cross-legged, facing us. "It's just a matter of time really."

I tried to detect some indications that she was joking, but there weren't any.

"But, I don't understand," I said. "If you can make anything happen, then you can make yourself be okay, yeah?"

She raised an eyebrow at me and laughed quietly, then she shook her head, not knowing how to answer.

"I am sorry," she said. "I didn't mean to touch it. Please know that I'm sorry."

A tear rolled down her face.

Leaving our sleeping companions where they were we got out and hugged her. She squeezed us tight, like she'd just been released by kidnappers or something. After the hugging Osmo held her at arms length.

"So, what's with the grown-up sexy look?" he asked.

She shrugged and smiled, blushing slightly.

"Dunno. Just feels comfortable." Then she flapped her hands, dismissing the subject like it was nothing. "Anyway, never mind that. Where's Pee?"

We raised our eyebrows and took a deep breath. By the time we finished telling her she was grey and tense.

"Okay," she said, nodding seriously. "Come on."

●

In Pee's world the battle had burned itself out. There was nothing there to say which side had won, if any. The scene was thick with wreckage that had ceased to burn. Everything was drifting. It wouldn't be long before the area was clear, like a sky whose clouds were dissipating.

We found him alone on his ship. He'd sent everybody away, and now he was sitting and staring at space, exiling himself from his own Earth as well as the real one. The boy never did things by halves.

Real Sal had a long heart to heart with him.

"It's my fault," she said.

He didn't buy that, not totally, but he eventually agreed to come back – it was obvious she wasn't going to leave him there anyway. I saw his shoulders slump, with relief, I think, that there was a grown-up around at last who could tell him what to do.

●

When we got back we woke the others. They were happy, relaxed, blissfully brainwashed. They accepted Real Sal as a wonderful miracle: incredible, yes, shocking even, but essentially benign. Christine picked up on Pee's mood straight away and she fussed and mothered him until he started to relax despite himself. Real Sal was introduced to Armitage, who had almost as many questions for her as the rest of us, but she put us all off by shoving her palms in our faces, telling us to shut up, and saying that she had a favour to ask first and it wouldn't be a good idea to deny her. Me and Osmo and Pee exchanged nervy glances. Then she made a set of luxury apartments grow out of the rock. It was all split levels and white walls and floor to ceiling windows looking out over the Himalayas. She showed us through into a huge living room with a roaring real fire and begged us to just spend one ordinary night with her, sitting in, watching the telly and talking about small things. She wanted to feel normal again.

The sun went down, we chose subdued lighting, argued about what film to see, bullied Pee into letting us watch Alien 9 (which he had never actually seen himself), filled bowls with popcorn, threw it at each other, snuggled next to each other on giant sofas under thick, light quilts, fought with each other over who should go to the kitchen for extra nibbles and drinks, teased each other, felt like a family, left all our questions unasked.

Even after the grownups had gone to bed Real Sal put us off when we tried to probe her.

"Please, guys...don't spoil it," she said. "I'll tell you, I promise...but not tonight. Not tonight."

I think we were relieved. We stayed up late. Fake Sal and I held hands shyly under our quilt, not knowing how to be together in front of the others. Eventually she fell asleep leaning against me. The atmosphere between the rest of us went kind of quiet and weird and they all gradually sloped off to bed, one by one, trying to be cool. I attempted to lift Fake Sal off the sofa but she woke up. We found ourselves a bedroom and kissed sleepily.

"I think I've forgot something," she murmured.

"Yeah?" I said in a drowsy, disinterested voice. "Well, it can't have been that important."

"I guess," she sighed. "Never mind. It'll probably come back to me."

That night I dreamt I was back home.

I'm a little kid again. It's an ordinary Sunday morning. Christmas is coming and I'm caught up in playing with some building bricks that are like Lego for babies. I notice suddenly how quiet it is, and I turn around and everybody is gone. I walk through the house but there's nobody there. I walk out the back of the house to the garden but I find myself in a bare, empty yard that's boxed in by a high brick wall. It's a white foggy day. Nothing can be seen beyond the top of the wall, no buildings, no sky, just white void everywhere. And all I can hear is a baby crying somewhere, unattended. The crying won't stop and a crawling terror seems to cover my face, and the crying gets louder and louder in my ears and I'm starting to suffocate, and I wonder which I'll do first: die or go insane.

I'm awake again. I'm sitting in a luxury apartment in a slot in Mount Everest. Nobody else is up yet. I go to Real Sal's room but it's empty and hasn't been slept in. I feel a sudden beating panic and I wander about feeling lost. I walk into the kitchen. She's standing at the sink with her back to me. She must be doing the dishes, I decide. I walk over to her. *Why would a god do the dishes?* As I draw close she becomes aware of me, shifts slightly, trying to keep her back to me. I can only see her right ear and part of her cheek.

- George.

Her hands are in the sink but there's no water in there. I peer around her shoulder. Her right hand is touching something, clutching it, kneading it furiously. It's pink and fleshy and warped, and it's pouring slowly over the plughole, starting to fill the sink.

- George.

It's her left arm. It's her left arm. It's her left arm.

She turns to me. She turns. And the left side of her face is sagging away from her skull, and she opens her eyes and they are black as space, and there's a baby crying inside my head, unattended. The crying gets louder and louder, *why won't somebody come,* until suddenly it's the screaming of Stuart Towns, ringing in my ears like a siren, wild with terror, and I know I'll go insane before she lets me die.

14
Little Missions

*It would be possible to describe everything scientifically, but it would make no
sense; it would be without meaning, as if you described a Beethoven symphony
as a variation of wave pressure.*
- Albert Einstein

It was Wednesday 22nd December 1999. Christmas was coming.

The sun was climbing above the eastern peaks of the Himalayas, lighting the apartments in gold. After the others had recovered from being woken by my screams they helped me to recover from the nightmare. This was awkward because it meant they ran into the bedroom and then had to be casual about the fact that me and Fake Sal were both in there together. Christine gaped in the doorway, not knowing how to be cool about it. Real Sal offered to sooth my nerves with a wave of her hand, maybe make me forget the dream, but I declined. I said something about not wanting to cushion myself from reality, and I kind of meant it, but really I was afraid of her, and her hands. A crawling paranoia ate away at my thoughts. *What if it wasn't a dream? What if she's already messed about with my memory?* But she looked at me with such gentle concern. Fake Sal became self-conscious then and buried herself under the quilt, but her muffled cries for everybody to get out just caused Osmo and Real Sal and Pee to bounce up and down on the bed, singing, while Christine took herself off and started making breakfast as if she hadn't seen anything.

After breakfast I felt the need to get away. Christine seemed anxious to corner the replica of her daughter for a motherly chat so I went to see Ell Aah Ray on my own.

"Has she viewed our message yet?" she asked immediately.

We were back in the domed meeting chamber with Ash Koh Tok and Fin Ma Fey.

"No. I don't think she's going to."

"Why not?"

"I don't know exactly. She just seems to change the subject whenever we mention you. I don't know what's going on in her mind."

"Have you tried asking her?"

"She's kind of putting off our questions at the moment. I think she's got a plan…but she just seems to want to spend some time with us right now."

"Maybe that's not such a bad thing right now," said Ash Koh Tok. "It must be therapeutic for her."

"Perhaps," said Ell Aah Ray. "We don't want her to become stressed. But I am not in favour of delays. George, will you ask her to let us through to visit our observers on the ground?"

"Visit your observers? I don't know...she obviously wants to keep you out here, doesn't she? Do you still want to...you know..."

"She must die, George, one way or the other. There is no other option."

"Is that what you say in your message?"

"Yes."

"Well, look...you're wrong. There must be another way. There's always another option. There just is."

Ell Aah Ray looked into my eyes in that way of hers that made me feel so transparent.

"Maybe you will be the one to find it, George. We cannot see it."

•

I returned to Earth lost in thought, flying Fleet manually but barely conscious of where I was going until I brought the runabout to a halt over Iron Street. The day was cold and bright. The sky swept up above the chimneystacks in pure flat blue. Iron Street looked pretty in the sunshine. It looked eternal. The idea of it ever ending didn't fit into my head at all. I looked at the windows with pseudo snow sprayed in the corners and caught myself wondering what life was like for the creatures that lived behind them, as if it were the street of some quaint planet in the back of nowhere. Then I realised it was.

- Fleet, give me a thick overcoat, one of those floppy-eared hats and a pair of sunglasses, please.

- Yes, George.

I beamed down to the pavement. Now I would know what Britney Spears or Alan Titchmarsh might feel like if they ever felt the urge to mingle incognito with the dirty masses.

Walking down towards the main road I was almost immediately in touch with that happy, sad Christmas feeling. The air was sharp and heady; the year felt old, ready to pass away. I decided to take the long walk into town, to pass by the school. The streets were quiet. School had broke and everyone was either in work or down the shops giving it their all, pressing together, wanting to feel part of something communal, something global. I was suddenly looking forward to joining the crush, buying genuine tacky presents with real money from my savings, taking my time so the light could bleed from the day and the Christmas lights come on. But first I shuffled around the schoolyard and walked around to the playing fields, enjoying the quiet and the solitude and feeling the spirit of old schooldays. Stupid old school, I thought. What had all that been about?

I suddenly had a thought.

- Fleet! Is Emma still onboard?
- Affirmative.
- She's been there all this time?
- Negative. She comes and goes.
- She comes and goes? What's she doing now?
- She's holding a party.
- A party! How many people are there?
- Ninety-eight.
- Ninety...! Has she made many rooms?
- Thirty-seven.
- Thirty-seven!

I cackled to myself and moved on. I was glad she was having a good time.

- Don't let her do anything silly, Fleet.
- Understood.

An image flashed in my mind as I walked: Ell Aah Ray's face, back in the meeting chamber.

We cannot see it.

I pulled my coat tighter about me.

In town the shop windows were doing their fairy lights and tinsel thing. I went into Woolworth's and Boots and they were less horribly white than usual. I watched the people and smelled the scents. We were supposed to feel bad about the rampant consumerism of modern Christmas. We were supposed to gripe at each other about the Christmas crowds clumping together like flocks of mindless sheep. We were supposed to agree that the Christmas spirit was a dwindling, sickly ghost. I watched the shoppers and I didn't see it. There was nothing panic-stricken or mindless in their eyes. They were awake and they knew what they were doing. They were buying tack for their friends and family, because it was traditional, and they loved them, or tolerated them, or hated them (delete as applicable).

So I bought Emma a blue bath set from The Body Shop. I can't remember the scent. It was something like 'Oceanic' or 'Aquaroma', I don't know. For Dad I got Bullitt on video, and for Mum I got three Stephen King novels in one hard-backed volume from The Works for £5.99. It was nice and heavy – bargain! In HMV I found a twenty-four-pocket CD wallet with Homer Simpson on it that would do for Pee. For Sals fake and real I pushed the boat out and bought them each an Encyclopaedia of Science Fiction – Film and TV, at £14.99 a piece. Osmo was the toughest. I couldn't think of anything for him and ended up resorting to comedy tactics – a pair of fluffy, clawed monster's feet slippers from The Pound Shop. *Sorry, Osmo.* And the outer circles of my family got tack, tack and more tack. I'd run out of money by the time I thought of Christine and Armitage. I'd have to do them music compilations.

The short winter day grew dark and my feet began to throb. Trudging down the red-bricked pedestrianised bit between the UCI and the Virgin Megastore I saw a family standing up and was able to claim a lucky bench. Plopping my bags down, I slumped into it and immediately noticed two figures standing directly in front of me - a woman and a girl. They were standing outside McDonald's: the most powerful being in the universe and her replica, both looking at me. They began to walk over, arm in arm, laughing. They looked incredible, like their veins were filled with vaporizing plasma. It made me feel strangely dull. But it was nice to see Sal hanging around with another girl for a change, even if it was herself.

"That's a great disguise, George," they chimed together.

"Hiya girls. Why are you both looking so fab?"

They just shared a secret smile.

"You look tired," said Fake Sal.

They sat down on either side of me and linked me and plopped their heads on my shoulders simultaneously. They were sharing some kind of mind-link: it was obvious. I wondered if Real Sal was slowly merging them back into one being again. The thought made me shiver.

"How come you're not being mobbed?" I asked.

"Because I don't want us to be," said Real Sal.

I told her that Ell Aah Ray had asked for permission to visit the Go observers. Her expression stiffened and she said she'd think about it. She relaxed again as Osmo and Pee arrived, emerging from the crowds like a pair of characters from The Matrix.

"All set?" asked Osmo.

"What for?" I asked.

The Sals stood up, dragging me to my feet.

"We've been busy while you've been enjoying yourself. Armitage is doing a press conference. We can watch it in Dixons."

I made them help me with my bags.

"Why's he doing a conference?"

"Part of my plan," said Real Sal nonchalantly, but she put a finger on my lips when I tried to ask what it was.

We lined up in front of the TVs in Dixons and Real Sal turned the volumes up by twitching her nose. And there was Armitage, facing the lights and the cameras and the microphones with the Prime Minister and the Defence Minister. Armitage began to read his statement.

"There's been a good deal of speculation in recent days about the whereabouts and activities of the four kids. I've been with them and I have some major news to share with you, and indeed the world. Much has happened in the past few days, too much to relate to you in detail here and now. What I am going to do is summarise two significant issues. These issues are of historical importance. I don't think it would be inappropriate for me to advise anybody listening to this who is standing to take a seat – such is the enormity of what I have to say."

Armitage paused. I noticed that a lot of the customers in the shop had sidled over to stand next to us and were watching with us, their faces flat and serious. At his last statement several of them looked around as if expecting to find seats placed handily nearby to save them from swooning. After a moment Armitage continued.

"The first item concerns Sally Phillips. It has been disclosed to me that during the evening of the encounter with the alien at Five Elms Sally underwent an alteration. The exact nature of the alteration is impossible to ascertain at this moment. Sally will be making an announcement herself at midday, Greenwich Meantime, on Christmas Day. What I can say, with a reasonable amount of certainty, is that she was altered on a physical level, that she accepted the alteration voluntarily, and that she is now like no other human being."

Armitage faltered momentarily. He looked up from his paper and spoke in a slightly more natural voice.

"I understand that what I have just said is ambiguous. I'm afraid it's going to remain that way until Christmas Day when Sally makes her announcement. No other information is available about this issue."

He looked back at his statement.

"The second item is not so vague. Last Saturday, during an excursion in outer space, two of the kids, Sally and George, encountered an alien race. This alien race is not the same as the one they met at Five Elms. It is a highly advanced race that is part of an intergalactic community that comprises many different alien species originating from many different planets within our galaxy. These aliens are civilised and peaceful beings. It is expected that a small delegation representing their community will make first contact with Earth on New Year's Day."

"You guys really have been busy," I said.

A big guy to my right went shaky on his feet and had to sit on the floor. A young guy off to my left fainted outright, flat on his back, like a hung-over groom halfway through the wedding vows.

•

Something happened then.

I'm not sure exactly where it started. A middle-aged woman tottered out onto the street outside Dixons murmuring 'Oh my god' over and over in an increasingly loud voice to the Christmas lights strung overhead. I heard her plaintive warbling recede down the street, losing itself in the crowds, and it might have started there. I can't quite tell. But the rest of the evening, and the whole of the next day, becomes...wrong in my memory. We leave the shop and the bustling activity of the street draws us into its festive embrace.

The faces of my friends are glowing and lovely, like reflections in Christmas tree decorations, haloed by fairy lights and berries. The joy-to-the-world spirit thickens the air with rich brandy-like fumes. I feel so in love with them all. We go see Christine. Armitage turns up at some point, fresh from his press conference. The serious matters of the day are ignored, wrapped in a box and put under the tree for later, because it is Christmas, and we are all together. Each moment is peppered with glitter, scented with frankincense. But under the radiant surface colours time is moving unnaturally. It's been assembled artificially, only there aren't enough parts. Scenes turn up in the wrong order, repeat themselves, or go missing entirely, like I'm in a montage in a film, within a film, within a film. Christine keeps putting a hat on my head. It's the same moment but it keeps happening. I'm adrift in a shared dream of us all being together, not worrying, not questioning, every important thing going unsaid. We're talking, talking, talking, but I can't make out a single word. Our glances are lullabies, surfacing and resurfacing, rolling like waves, drowning us lovingly in a blur of warmth and well being and drowsiness. The second night draws on and we are content to let the time roll away from us, like a marble on a sloping floor. I sink happily into the marshmallowy comfort of it all, intoxicated by the ache of nostalgia I am already feeling for this time, unconcerned about anything else, anywhere else, anytime else...

And yet...

There is one thing niggling me, small but ever present, buried in under the warmth like a single blade of pine fur caught beneath my clothing, prickling my skin. Seated in the back of my mind is a pair of eyes, and they are looking on in frosty dissatisfaction at all of this, looking on through oblong pupils.

●

I woke on a couch in Christine's house, my eyes clicking open suddenly like I'd just been activated. It was Christmas Eve 1999. I knew immediately what had happened. I knew it, with a perfect, still clarity. I knew it, even though I shouldn't be able to. Ell Aah Ray's hypnosis veined my mind, strengthening it like the wire in a sheet of security glass, refusing to let me be fooled: Real Sal had brought on another reality warp and she had erased it from our memories. It had happened sometime after the press conference and it had continued for a long time. The memory of it was gone now, but I could feel its absence, as if I'd grown a new tooth in the night and it had been removed before I woke. I'd slept the same kind of sleep that Fake Sal, Christine and Armitage had slept in my runabout. I'd dreamt the same kinds of healing dreams.

Lying there on the couch, staring at the ceiling, I tried to work out where I stood with this and discovered a strange division inside me, like I'd been assaulted and rescued by the same person. I felt completely refreshed, completely awake. My mind felt sharp as paper, only...when I sat up and wondered what I was supposed to do, I encountered the division. On my right shoulder I heard Ell Aah Ray's scratchy voice urging me to ask questions, challenging me to discover what the situation was and face it. On my left shoulder was Real Sal, whispering seductively about the bliss of forgetting, the joy of not knowing, the pleasures of ignorance. Somewhere in the middle was George. Somewhere.

I can't do this.

I went through to the kitchen, carrying a feeling with me of time lost, that the world had gone on ahead without me. As I walked through the door I was pulled up short because Osmo and Real Sal were in there, in a clinch, and they were kissing like they were going to snog for the Olympics. I felt queasy immediately: me and Fake Sal...Osmo and Real Sal? Things could get seriously Shakespearean. I tried to back out of the room quietly, without being noticed, but Real Sal opened an eye and spied me, saw into my soul.

We cannot see it. We cannot see it.

For the rest of the morning I acted as if the world was normal, and so did she.

Armitage was gone, called away to work through Christmas (which made Christine sulky), reporting everything he had witnessed to his superiors and acting as an advisor in light of the forthcoming address from Real Sal to the people of the world. Everybody knew it was due to take place at noon, Greenwich Meantime, but nobody knew where it would take place, or how they should tune in. What channel would it be broadcast on? Would it interrupt all programming like a Martian broadcast prior to an invasion? The human race went tentatively about its business.

I slipped out and walked over to my house, still feeling amazingly clear headed yet strangely incapable of thinking. My body was on automatic and decided I needed to put some work in on my compilations for Christine and Armitage. I wondered if I should do one for Ell Aah Ray. The sun was shining again. The world was wearing its colours. When I got to the house it seemed nobody was home, but when I opened the door to my bedroom there was Real Sal, tinkering merrily away on my PC like she owned the place.

"'Scuse me," I said. "Invasion of privacy and stuff."

She just turned and smiled at me, all of the love in the world in her face. Sunlight was pouring through the window behind her. I'd never seen a more beautiful sight.

"Hiya, George."

"Hiya," I stammered. "What you up to?"

"Just came over."

"I see." I loitered awkwardly in the doorway. "So did you find out what Osmo had for breakfast?"

"Scrambled eggs on toast."

"Oh! Disgusting!"

"What are you up to?" she asked.

"Compilations."

"Will you do one for me?"

"You've got a proper present. I spent fifteen quid on yours."

"I want a compilation. It's more personal."

"But I've got loads to do before tomorrow."

"Please."

"Well, you know I will."

"I know."

I shuffled into the room.

"So...you and Osmo then."

"Yeah, I know. Bit weird innit?"

"Ya huh!"

"But what's a girl to do, hey? I mean, you're not available."

I mumbled something that wasn't even proper words and she laughed at me. "Don't worry. I'm not going to put you in a compromising position." Then she lowered her eyes and picked at her nails. "But I do miss you though. You know...the times we spent talking and everything. I mean, you've got your replica of me so you probably don't notice the absence...cos there isn't one. But I've promised I won't make any more replicas, so I don't get a Fake George to talk to."

I felt like such an idiot.

•

It's funny how the most overwhelming events in life always seem to be preceded by quiet moments.

We spent an hour and a half talking quietly, sitting on opposite ends of my bed, toes touching occasionally, reviewing past discussions about alien societies, human evolution, how all our parents seemed to be messed up (some more than others, it had to be said). Now, at last, we had a few answers to the stuff about aliens and other worlds. Our parents, though, had somehow managed to remain mysteries to all known forms of sense and reason.

This was my chance, I realised, to ask the questions that needed to be asked, right here, right now. What were her plans? What had she been doing all of that time she had been alone? I knew if I asked her she would tell me. She seemed almost to be waiting for the questions. And I nearly did, I came so close...only, now the opportunity was here the small stuff was suddenly more important. The small stuff was everything. I let it go, and I felt relieved that, if nothing else, at least it was a conscious decision – a George decision. Here was my moment of peace.

I heard footsteps on the landing then and a couple of discreet knocks on the door. I sat up straight. The rest of the family were out, not due back until six. I looked at Sal.

"Did you hear anyone get home?"

She pouted and shook her head slowly.

"I don't think so."

We both turned to look at the door. Again, a couple of quiet knocks.

"Hello?"

The door opened. An adrenaline surge made the room glow brighter as a tall lean figure sporting two sets of arms leaned forward so that its head could clear the top of the doorframe.

"Oh my god," said Real Sal mildly.

"Ell Aah Ray," I said in a stunned voice. The Go first contact specialist straightened to her full height. I turned to Real Sal. "You let them come down?"

"To visit the observers," she nodded.

Ell Aah Ray placed two pairs of palms together in front of her, like she was praying two prayers, and bowed.

"Sal Phillips, please forgive this intrusion. I request an audience with you."

Sal hesitated, looking at the alien with big round eyes. She looked to me like she was trying to remember the correct etiquette for receiving unexpected visitors from different star systems. She pivoted on the bed to face the newcomer and made a vague gesture, beckoning her in.

"Okay."

Ell Aah Ray stepped forward, presented herself in front of Real Sal, and bowed again. Her long body dipped forward into the sunlight slanting through the window. Her face came close to Sal's. Suddenly her arms flickered in a blur of movement and I saw that she had embedded a hand in Sal's chest, right where her heart was. There was no blood at first, the blow had been delivered so quickly, and Sal just winced and looked at her attacker with a puzzled expression. Then she looked at me as if seeking confirmation of what had just happened. I experienced the familiar sensations of going into shock. The room came alive with malevolence around me and my thoughts shrank back, like a snail poked by a stick.

- **Fleet**, said my mind in a small, faraway voice. **Come quick.**

Things proceeded in slow motion, the colours vivid. Ell Aah Ray pulled her arm back and a spray of blood smattered the ceiling, and her robes, and Sal's legs and my bed. The sunshine coming through the window blotted out.

- I am here, George.

- Do something. Do something quick!

Ell Aah Ray delivered a blow to Sal's head as I heard Fleet's beautiful voice telling me, **I am unable to interfere directly in alien activities.** The blow should have taken Sal's head off, but her head was fine. It was Ell Aah Ray's hand that shattered. She didn't take the time to scream in pain; her other three arms shot out, each aiming potentially lethal blows at various targets on Sal's body. They nearly connected, but not quite. Ell Aah Ray flew backwards through the wall of my bedroom, blasted by a pulse of Real Sal's will. Landing in a mangled heap amongst the splinters of the banister at the top of the stairs she immediately clambered to her feet and limped back into the room. Real Sal watched her come. The alien paused in front of Sal, wavering on her feet, and she spoke.

"Sal Phillips," she breathed. "You must let me."

Sal studied her through pain-creased eyes. Her right hand was fluttering at the obscene wound in her chest. Then she gave a barely perceptible nod of her head.

"No!" I yelled. I launched myself at the Go, who was already moving forward. She batted the forearm with the broken hand across my throat, breaking my windpipe with a crack. I crashed against the wall choking and slumped to the floor. Ell Aah Ray fell on Sal in a flurry of lethal arms only to be blasted back out of the room a second time. I heard her bumping down the stairs. Real Sal leaned forward.

"George! Are you okay?"

My eyesight sparkled with a sheen of silver pinpricks, my head swam in a whirlpool. The pain sickened me more than any I had ever felt. The room blackened, consciousness slipping away. But then the pain faded. A soothing numbness spread from my throat outwards. Taking in a huge lungful of air I opened my eyes. Real Sal was lowering her hand. She had healed me, but the gaping wound in her chest remained.

"Sal," I said. "Fix yourself."

She shook her head. Her hair was plastered across her face with sweat and blood.

"I'm trying to be brave," she growled through clenched teeth.

Ell Aah Ray appeared in the hole in my wall looking like a half stepped on insect. She only had one good arm left. The others hung limp or poked out at unnatural angles. I hurled my little bedside cabinet at her. She didn't even attempt to deflect it. It smashed into her face and shoulder and ricocheted out onto the landing. She just ignored the pain and lifted her good arm. She was holding something.

"No," said Sal.

Ell Aah Ray clenched her fist and the explosion took away the house.

●

We floated above the burning crater that had been Iron Street. Sal let the rose tinted force field dissipate and we just floated there and looked for a while. Everything within the blast area was silent but from several directions, off at the edges of the crater, came the splintered shouting of humans, the screaming of the injured and bereaved.

"Bloody hell," said Sal.

She put the houses back together again, repaired the injured and erased their memories, made replicas of the dead, ones that didn't know they were replicas.

"I thought you weren't going to do that?" I said.

She shrugged hopelessly.

"Extreme circumstances," she whispered.

She healed the wound in her chest. It had never happened. She made a replica of Ell Aah Ray and told her "I can't be killed today. I've still got some things to do."

Fake Ell Aah Ray nodded and left, as serene and beautiful as the original, and I started to blink tears. Sal looked at me sadly.

"I'm sorry," she said.

I flapped my arms at my sides.

"Sal...please don't let them kill you."

"Thanks for trying to save me."

"Please don't let them."

She kissed me on the mouth. She tasted like the Himalayas.

"Please, Sal."

She squeezed my shoulder.

"I've got to go." She turned towards the door.

"Sal," I said. "I'm begging."

Then, for no apparent reason, she stumbled sideways. At least that's what it looked like to me at first.

- George!

She fell against the wall and struggled to remain upright. I noticed that her left boot had come off. It was lying on my bedroom carpet on its side. Sal twisted around so her back was against the wall. All her weight was on her right foot and her mouth was round with shock, her forehead heavy with dismay.

"Sal! What is it?"

She shook her head, unable to articulate something, and raised her left knee with a look of mute horror. The leg of her jeans flapped loosely from the knee down. *The bottom half of her leg is gone!* She made a strangulated howl of muted horror, her face screwing itself up in a dawning fear, as if she saw she was being buried alive. She lifted her hands to me and the fingers were nothing but nubs. She closed her eyes tight and stuffed her hands under her armpits and shook her head again and again.

"Nooooo," she crooned in a small, hopeless wail.

"Sal, what have they done to you?"

I stepped forward and reached out to take hold of her, but a feeling of revulsion made me pull back.

"It's not them..." she gasped. She opened one eye and glared at me askance through her terror, her whole body stiff with self-loathing. "It's me!"

My hands clenched and unclenched at my sides, paralysed with inaction.

"What do you mean?"

"It's me...it's my mind. I can't stop from thinking stuff! It's happening more often...I can't stop it!"

I saw her leaning over a sink in Mount Everest, her left arm squirming. *Please don't let me hear a baby crying!* Unable to move forward, I just stood there stupidly, looking at her as she crumbled before my eyes. She cringed, hugging herself, writhing, and she started to sob.

"Sal...you can do anything."

"George! Don't you understand? I can do anything...with my mind! But if my mind starts working against me..."

Her voice was stretched tight with despair. I couldn't bear it and forced myself to step forward and hold her. She pulled her hands out of her armpits and threw her arms around me like she was drowning, but suddenly her arms only reached to her elbows. I squeezed her tight against me and closed my eyes, not wanting to see.

"What can we do? How can we fix it?"

"I don't know," she mewled. "You can't always fix stuff, George."

Something about her weight shifted and I knew that she had lost the bottom of her right leg as well. I was supporting her weight on my own, only she was getting lighter and lighter.

Then I stumbled, just as she had done.

We sprawled on the floor but I kept her gripped tight to me.

"George! What's happened?"

"Nothing! Just calm your thoughts down...calm them down so you can control them."

"It's happening to you, isn't it!"

"It doesn't matter! Sal! Just cool it...and get a hold of yourself!"

But she had no arms at all now. I tried to hold her against me tighter, but over her shoulder I saw that the fingers of my left hand were gone and I let out a horrified moan. She turned her head and glared at me, her mouth pursed bitterly.

"I won't let it happen to you!"

"Sal! You've got to calm down!"

"NO!" she yelled, and the word burst my eardrums and sent out a shockwave that bounced us into the air. The contents of my room pressed back against the walls, trying to get away from us. "NO!" she yelled again, this time with even greater force, and for a moment the only thing in existence was that one word, pulsing outwards, finding nothing else but itself. Then I was dimly aware of flipping through the air upside down.

Then I blacked out for I don't know how long, but all was peace and quiet and blackness, and that was fine by me.

We came to lying on the floor next to each other, our limbs and digits intact. Sal was her proper age again. I don't think she realised. We grabbed hold of each other and lay there, just holding on, breathing against each other, not able to speak for a long time. Then she whispered to me that she would never let anything like that happen to me again.

We climbed to our feet still holding onto to each other, afraid of falling. All the stuff in my room was bent and broken, leaning away from us. Sal waved a hand and restored it for the second time that afternoon. After a while she stepped back from me, patted me on the chest and then knelt down to put her boots back on. When she stood up she reached out a cool hand and pressed it against the back of my neck and smiled.

"Sorry about that, mate," she said. "Look, I'd better get going."

I was dumbstruck for a moment, but she was backing towards the door.

"Sal, don't let them kill you."

She cocked her head at me, looked like the sanest most beautiful being there could ever possibly be. She shrugged, smiled. A deep humour and sadness was in her eyes.

She walked out, leaving me staring at the empty doorway, hearing her footsteps down the stairs. The front door slammed, and still I stood there. The house gave off waves of silence.

Eventually I roused myself and made a start on her compilation, and my plans to save her.

15
The Gift

Imagination is more important than knowledge.
- Albert Einstein

At the moment when the International Dateline reaches midnight it is the same day all around the globe. When that imaginary line, drawn down the Pacific Ocean, reached midnight of Saturday 25th December 1999, it was Christmas Day all around the world for just one hair's breadth of a moment. One eternal moment.

In Banford, in Christine's house, it was noon. Away to the west, in Times Square, New York, it was 7am. Away to the east, across the Himalayas, it was 6pm. Way up, in an invisible slot cut from the rock of the highest mountain on Earth, six people were sitting in six armchairs that were arranged in a circle facing each other.

Around the world roughly half of the people had been waiting, with varying degrees of anticipation, for Sal Phillips's announcement. The remainder of the world's population had gone about its business as usual, oblivious to, or largely unconcerned with such matters.

I know this because I know everything about that moment. Everybody who was alive on the planet at that time knows about that moment.

On a small round table, in the centre of our circle of chairs, was a spherical clock resting in a stand. It was a special clock that showed the time at the International Dateline from whatever angle you looked at it. It was a special clock made by the most powerful being in the universe. I was looking at Real Sal, observing the calmness in her face, the quiet purpose in her eyes. But as the reading of the clock reached for midnight I glanced at it, and it was in that moment, which wasn't really a moment, where a new day hadn't quite yet been born, that the clock, and the universe, stopped.

7am in Times Square – the light rain, which had been falling for twenty minutes, now held its position in the air. Raindrops as brittle as glass hung motionless, reflecting the lights of a frozen city. A sizeable crowd had gathered, despite the early hour and the fact that it was Christmas morning and raining, in the hope that Sal's announcement would somehow make it onto the giant plasma screen they were gazing up at. And now the blood no longer pumped in their veins, their hair and nails were no longer growing, and they could not move, not even to blink, not even to fall down, because the world had stopped. Everything had stopped. The air itself was as solid and silent as the clearest, hardest diamond. All around the Earth not a breeze could stir. Tornadoes and hurricanes were now sculptures of wind, waves were as still as iron. Away to the centre of the solar system the sun had ceased its journeying. Solar flares arced solidly like bright, jagged bridges. The surface of Sol was a silent, glassy landscape of mountains, and whirlpools of frozen, heatless fire. The planets would not orbit and the Milky Way refused to turn. The out breath of the entire universe had stopped. Light itself had stalled and could no longer travel, held fast, the prisoner of a stopped clock. Everything had stopped everywhere. Everything had stopped, but the minds of the people of Earth.

The silence was deafening. Never had a living soul heard such an all-encompassing, absolute quiet. And in that silence we began to hear each others' thoughts.

In the paralysis of our physical world our minds began to move freely, leaving our bodies, moving out into the infinitely crafted, crystalline beauty of an eternal moment. Take a perfect photograph of the universe, make it three dimensional, and then get inside it and float around. See a spiral of cigarette smoke from all angles.

I always liked being a passenger on long road journeys. Whether it was in a car or on a bus, it didn't matter, as long as I had a window seat. There's something mesmerising about watching miles and miles of road unravelling beneath you, piling up and falling away, piling up and falling away. Britain is such a tiny country, yet you can sit in a car for hours while the earth rolls by. Sometimes I'd try to hold every stone and blade of grass, every square centimetre of tarmac that we drove past, in my mind, just so I could get a sense of how big the world is.

"How far have we travelled?"

"Thirty eight miles."

"What's the circumference of the world?"

"25,000 miles."

Now, as I left my body and moved out into the solidified moment, every stone, every blade of grass and every centimetre of tarmac everywhere was on hold for me. I could travel anywhere I wished and examine anything in the world in the tiniest detail. I noted that now I was outside of my body, now that I was free of my physical eyes, I had perfect vision. It was as though, rather than seeing by perceiving and interpreting reflected light, I was now seeing with my knowing. The knowledge of where I was and what my surroundings looked like was simply a part of me. The tiniest detail was laid out before me as plain as day. A thought occurred to me: that this was how the Go saw things – vividly, uncompromising. In my bodiless state, with my perfectly honed senses, I could go anywhere and examine anything – the smallest dewdrop – for the perfect truth of how it was formed.

Except…something was pulling me. I was trying to drift away across the Himalayas, go exploring, but instead found myself being drawn gently back by the gravity of Real Sal, back into the impossible slot in the mountainside and over the shoulder of my own body, which was still sitting there in the armchair. I floated over the table and the stopped clock. And as I drifted towards Real Sal she turned and looked at me. If I had been present in my body I would have gasped with surprise. In a universe where even the electrons no longer orbited their nuclei Real Sal could still move – or was she only moving in my mind? And as she looked at me I sensed the presence of other minds. Pee and Osmo and Christine and Fake were there, but now there were more besides, hundreds of them, gathering around, pressing forward, also drawn to Real Sal. She had brought them to the mountain. I could feel their numbers, all crowding into the same space, hundreds at first, then thousands, then millions of minds, all overlapping with each other, all sharing the same space and the same experience.

Sal's face drew closer and her brow began to loom over us like a mountain. We were heading for her left eye. The coloured fibres of the iris grew thick, like the massive rivers of an alien planet. Their green toned depths were converging into a circular, continent-sized waterfall that was pouring itself away into the glossy black hole that was Real Sal's pupil. The gravity of that black hole was pulling us in too, the souls of everyone on Earth. Together, as one being with billions of minds, all awake at once, we dropped into the pupil of Real Sal's left eye, and we saw the world through it – we saw how she saw and we felt what she felt.

Then her mind spoke.

- Hello.

I was reminded of the time I had first heard MarvinMilton in my mind. The warmth in that voice was so complete, so unconditionally accepting, that it made your life up to that point seem utterly barren, devoid of love. It was only now, hearing that voice, that you knew what love was. Two syllables were enough to tell you that there was somebody somewhere who could see every corner of your being and still not want to turn away.

And somehow, through force of habit perhaps, we found ourselves translating the beauty, the subtlety, and the wide-ranging meanings contained within her thought into our own languages. Sal's mind hadn't spoken in English. She had simply inserted pure thought into our knowing. With that one thought we knew her intimately. We knew her strength and her simplicity. It seemed tragic that such an amazing thought should go through the translation process in my own mind and come out as something so mundane as 'hello'. I realised right then why there is so much misunderstanding between people. Words are not enough.

- I have a gift for each of you. But first I think that it's time we all got to know each other, said the living light that was Real Sal's stream of consciousness, only it was more of an ocean, and it bore us all away on waves of coruscating blue and white radiance to a small, dark bedroom.

Posters and postcards cover the walls like a mosaic. There aren't too many pop groups here, although the Manic Street Preachers make an appearance. On one wall, surrounded by a bevy of feisty comic strip girls and female Klingon warriors, cheek by cheek with Tank Girl, Albert Einstein pokes his tongue out at us. Up in the far corner Felix the Cat conspires with Marilyn Monroe and the Gorrilaz. On the top shelf of a small bookcase by the single futon bed are two cuddly creatures, a Flat Eric and an NTL Monkey. They're sitting back to back as if they've just had an argument. The room is almost tidy, but there is too much pop culture squeezed into any and every available space for it ever to be restful. Whichever direction you look there are faces peering at you. Che Guevara, Big Brother and Scooby Doo all have their eyes on you. There is no escape from the iconography of the Twentieth Century. Not here.

We see all of these things and we understand them. We are the disembodied minds of the human race. Now we discover we have a body again, the body of a schoolgirl from Banford. And anything that we see through her eyes we see with her memories and her character. We know, for example, that the untidy pile of notebooks, journals and sketchpads on the floor against the wall was once the most precious and significant item in this room. We know what's in them: a determined attempt to leave a mark on the world and make sense of it, a desperate struggle between honesty and self deceit, a mix of frustration and admiration for the human race, proposals for utopias, ideas on love and sex, exclamations of diamond bright anger.

It is Sunday 28th November. MarvinMilton died just a few hours ago. There is a suitcase lying open on the floor in the middle of the room. Even as we step closer to it, and our face is bathed in the beam of light that is shining through the gap in the bundled coat, we experience a flood of recent memories: MarvinMilton, falling from a dark sky; his eyes, his voice, telling us amazing things, showing us new worlds, giving us a mission, and then dying; a night time phone call to George, good old George, who is on his way over right now to save us from touching the monodreme. We love George. Yet the light is shining directly into our left eye, and it is not evil at all. It is ancient, yet it is so inexperienced and curious. It is utterly unselfconscious, unmarred by any shadow – of guilt or shame or fear. The light has no sense of itself as being separate from that which it shines on. The light has no sense of needing anything. It is only curious. This light wants only to shine. It is pure and it is innocent and it does not deserve to be sent to the bottom of the sea. We must rescue it, before George arrives to rescue us.

We reach out and we untie the knot in the sleeves of George's coat. We open the coat out, lay it flat, and the room is lit up in a blazing glory that does not burn or dazzle. It seems as if a summer day has come to the bedroom. We reach out to touch it, but then we hesitate, almost remembering something that MarvinMilton once said. But the light is warm and reassuring. It's calling to us. It wants to play. The scent of a distant summer meadow passes by on a green breeze. There's music playing somewhere. Slowly we reach out our hands and we touch the sun.

The monodreme is smooth and hard and cool to the touch. We rest our hands on it and breathe a sigh of relief. There is no evil. Everything's okay. But then our palms adhere to the surface and a lump of dread solidifies in our chest. We try to pull our hands back but they are stuck fast and the monodreme has become incredibly heavy. We can't lift it. We can't even budge it. And now our palms are starting to sink into the monodreme. It's no longer hard. A wave of fear and revulsion engulfs us as the monodreme bulges between our fingers and slowly pours over our hands. We want to panic. We are panicking, but only on the inside. Our heart, which is the heart of a solitary girl, races for all of us, pounds frantically for an entire race, but we cannot move. We are held, mesmerised, as the misshapen monodreme stretches, moving up our arms. It seems to be getting smaller, but it's hard to tell. Then an unpleasant sensation informs us that it is entering into us, through the skin of our fingers and hands and arms. Its presence inside us is a jagged, amorphous energy, a cold heat that sends tendrils up inside our arms, exploring. We have never felt so alone and afraid as at this moment. The faces in the room loom about us, watching impassively. *It's your own fault*, they are saying. *MarvinMilton told you not to touch it. George and Osmo and Pee trusted you not to touch it. Look what you've done now. You've unleashed a horror, and you will be the first victim.* The faces we had thought of as friends have become cold-eyed spectators. They will not help us. They think we deserve this. They will just watch, and judge, and condemn. We are alone.

I'm sorry, thinks a small voice somewhere in the crashing torrent of our terror, but it's no good. It's no help. The monodreme doesn't stop. We think it anyway, over and over again. *I'm sorry. I'm sorry. I didn't mean it.*

Our arms are coated in a membrane of gold. The probes of energy inside are reaching past our shoulders and into our torso. There's nothing we can do to stop it. We can't even faint. All we wish for now is oblivion. Let us sleep, slip into a coma, die, anything. We just don't want to be awake anymore. We don't want to be feeling this anymore. We don't want to be thinking about it anymore. *Please. George. Where are you, George? Why aren't you here yet? Why aren't you here? I'm sorry. I'm so sorry. Please make it stop.*

But it doesn't stop. The faces in the room watch on as the cold heat reaches our heart and lungs and encapsulates them, pierces them. It sends a shoot up our throat and discovers our brain. It fills our eyes with blistering colours that dance and transmute constantly. We are utterly possessed. Every cell of our body has been taken from us. It's over.

The room is dark now. The monodreme has been absorbed completely into our body, so all of its light is now on the inside. The room is quiet, ordinary once more. We can see the branches and leaves of the sycamore outside through the half open window. They're rustling slightly. We can see the line of the rooftops across the street, the TV aerials and the satellite dish, the night sky beyond. There are stars peeping through the pale broken clouds. A cool breeze enters in. A cat yowls in the yard next door.

We sit and wait. We are pulsing with a foreign, alien energy. Every inch of our body is alive with it. We sit and wait, and nothing happens. We lift our arm. Nothing stops us. We run our fingers through our hair. It's drenched with sweat. The room is still. We try to stand. Nothing prevents us. The monodreme is still there, alive and awake inside us, filling us with light and energy, but it isn't doing anything. It's just being there. It's just being and watching.

Our terror subsides, giving way to exhaustion and bewilderment and curiosity. We begin to think again. We walk to the window and look out into the night. We begin to realise things. The monodreme is not evil, no. It is not good, either. That was just something we had projected onto it ourselves. The monodreme is, in fact, almost a blank. It has no personality. MarvinMilton had withdrawn his personality, along with the memory of what it was like to see the world through the vessel of a sentient being. Now it doesn't even have an understanding of what a personality is, or that the body it has taken over has one. All it knows is that it has encountered something new and strange and it wants to find out more.

And now the monodreme can feel what it is to live inside a human body, to look out through a pair of human eyes, to sift and interpret the surroundings through human senses, and a human mind. It discovers that there is meaning attached to everything it perceives. We walk about the room, picking things up, looking at them, looking at everything. That pattern of tonal changes over there is a wall. It is a wall with posters on it. One of the posters is an image of a man called Einstein. He is sticking his tongue out. The small regular shapes on the poster are letters, forming words: a quote of something that this man once said about war. This man was an intelligent man, a wise man. Now he is dead. So much meaning. And every item, every poster, every object, is attached to a whole flood of associations. And in turn every association is attached to an ocean of further associations, on and on. It's all interconnected in an infinity of combinations.

Interesting.

Now the monodreme has taken up residence in every last cell of our body it has become passive, a passenger. Through us it is directed. Through us its ancient strength is channelled. It sees no separation between our thoughts and emotions and its power. There is no separation. Compared to its age and raw potency Sal Phillips is as powerful as, well, absolutely nothing at all, but compared to the mental and emotional complexity of Sal Phillips the monodreme is as motivated as an empty sheet of paper, only less so. Now the strength and the personality have joined we realise that the reality around us is as weak as a dream - weaker in fact, because we can control this dream as easily as we can think. The walls of this room are made of nothing but light. They remain held together only because we allow them to be. This entire universe is nothing more than a delightful playground that will bend and change as we wish. Anything is possible. This reality will obey us. This reality is us. There is no separation. If we wipe away all that is before us it would be equivalent to becoming tired of a daydream and choosing to replace it with another. It wouldn't mean anything at all - would it?

We move back to the window and look out. George is down in the garden, hunched over, scrabbling for stones. Good old George. Do we really want to erase him? No, of course we don't. We'll have to concentrate, keep our guard up. George must continue to live, unharmed. Everybody must. Can we make sure that happens? Can we make sure nobody is harmed by our irresistible willpower?

We have a lot to think about. Now we begin to understand the danger that the human race, the Earth, the entire universe will be in, for as long as Sal Phillips and the monodreme continue to exist. Now, as the mind that is six billion minds, we understand it is a miracle that we are still alive at all.

•

George turns and looks up at us, but then he fades away before he can speak and we are floating in blackness. Then we hear the voice of our beloved Sal Phillips.

- I remembered MarvinMilton and his fear that we would touch the monodreme. I wanted to know what he had experienced. As I practised with my power I realised that I could know anything that was true, because truth is just one facet of the process of infinity, and there is no separation between it and me. I decided to relive what MarvinMilton had lived through.

The blackness shifts to light and we are jogging for our lives over a field of yellow. The thing that pursues us has no name but it fills us with terror. We have no name but we are filled with terror. We know what will happen if it catches us. We have seen our loved ones ripped apart by things such as this. But even if we had never seen such a thing before we would still jog for our lives because a deep instinct has overridden our mind. We are a mindless jogging thing, intent on nothing more than escape, only we are slow, and it is fast, and there is nowhere to hide. We ignore everything that does not offer us hope. A thing lies on the ground and it is strange and it shines and we have never seen such a thing before, and normally we would be interested in it because it is unusual, but right now it does not offer us hope so we ignore it with our mind, but something is wrong because our body changes direction and jogs towards the thing, even though we are busy trying to escape from the ripping thing. Even though we are mindless with terror our body stops and we bend down and we put our hands on the shining thing. The ripping thing lands on our back and sinks its teeth into our neck and we fall onto our side with the ripping thing ripping us with its claws, and the world is white with terror and the shining thing is stuck to our hands. The word 'monodreme' appears in our mind. We are being eaten alive and we wait now instinctively for the whiteness of the world to take us away from the pain and the terror, but we can't stop ourselves from looking at the monodreme, which is changing shape in our hands and entering into us through our skin. We lie there helplessly in the grass and the ripping thing feeds on us, and the pain is unbearable, but there is nowhere for us to go, and the monodreme fills us up until it is all on the inside.

We lie there, waiting and waiting, and the ripping thing continues to feed, but it is slowing down now. It is having difficulty tearing our flesh with its teeth because we are more real than it is. The ripping thing feels lighter to us, as if it is barely even there anymore, so we risk sitting up. We sit up easily and we wonder if the ripping thing has gone, but when we turn we see that it is still there and its teeth are embedded in our arm, and we look straight into its eyes and we feel the pure terror that we always feel when we see the face of a ripping thing, even though we can no longer feel its bite, and we wish the terrible thing would not be there, that there would not be any ripping things anywhere ever again, and then, suddenly, it isn't there anymore and we are sitting in a field alone, our blood all around us.

The day becomes a dream and we do much walking from place to place, and we learn that we don't have to be wounded if we don't want to be. We learn that if there are things that frighten us we can think them away forever. We learn that the loved ones of our family are not as real as us either, that they are just a part of a dream. We could think them away if we wanted to, but we don't want to. All the same, they sense a change in us and they are afraid and they run away from us. We don't like this, and wish for them to come to us, and suddenly some irresistible force physically draws them towards us, but they are screaming with fear and we let them go quickly. They flee. We feel strange and lonely. And then nighttime comes and we lie down and see the stars.

Everything is a dream, and we dream that we are up amongst the stars. We feel safe because nothing is as real as we are, but then we realise we have become lost in our dream and don't know how to get back. Each direction we turn looks the same to us, just stars and stars and stars. We search for something familiar to help us find our way back. Everything seems very far away and we begin to panic. The monodreme is shining inside us. The monodreme has caused all of this trouble. We force it out of our body by thinking about it hard, and it is in our hands and we intend to throw it away, but the sky is big and we are afraid to let go of it, so we stop and we listen very hard for the slightest sound that might help us. All is quiet so we listen harder and harder, sure somehow, that we will hear something eventually - and eventually we do. But the sound is in our mind rather than our ears.

We go toward the sound. It is very quiet but we follow it, on and on. The sound is coming from a tiny speck in the sky. We go towards it and gradually the speck gets closer and larger and, after a long, long time, we find out that the speck is not a tiny speck at all. It is the biggest thing there ever was, and the closer we get to it the bigger it gets, until it seems like it will just keep getting bigger and bigger forever, without us ever reaching it.

We touch the speck that is too big to be a speck and we sit on it and a thing appears that does not look like a ripping thing but does not look like family either. We are not sure whether we should think it away or not so we listen to its mind to find out what it is. We find out it is a girl called Sal Phillips who has just run through a cemetery and an industrial estate to find out what the glowing light was that was falling from the sky, and we learn what Klingons are and animal rights and humanitarianism and the Manic Street Preachers and George and Albert Einstein and Sugar Puffs and school and ambitions and morals and sex and homemade vegetarian lasagne and books and songs and TV and Stig of the Dump and Watership Down and Gormenghast and Hitchhikers' Guide to the Galaxy. We listen to her mind and stare into her eyes and the dream becomes more beautiful and ugly and amazing and desperate than we could ever have imagined, and we learn how to share thoughts with other beings using words, and how to question our own thoughts and actions. We learn so much it is like we become somebody different. Our past self becomes nothing more than the memory of a dream of being an animal. We are a long way from home, and what would Sal think of us if she knew we had destroyed all of that life? We try to keep the knowledge from her but it crowds in at the edges of our thoughts like a black madness.

Sal and her friends are beautiful creatures that have lived incredible, rich lives. They must not be thought away. They must be allowed to continue. We must let go of the monodreme so that we don't endanger them any longer with our fear and instincts and weakness. But we must explain to Sal and her friends that they must never touch the monodreme themselves. It's a terrible risk and we wonder if there is a simple way of getting rid of the monodreme forever. We look into our self for an answer. We can find out anything that is true, because truth is just one facet of the process of infinity, and nothing is separate. Only, there's just so much of it. It's like endless space. Finding the right piece of truth is a question of finding the right question, and finding the right question is like finding a needle in a solar system.

We do the best we can. It somehow doesn't feel enough, but the black madness is threatening to rush in and wash us away forever. There is no time for more. We identify that if we let go of the monodreme we will die. The monodreme will remain harmless as long as it doesn't come into contact with a living, sentient being. It will be a noble, selfless sacrifice. Sal would understand. We must do it soon because we are afraid.

As Sal ties the coat around the monodreme we know we haven't asked the right question. Then we are floating in blackness once more.

•

We are the human race, the mind that is six billion minds, all awake at once. We are returned to our bodies, still reeling from our experiences, but the eternal Christmas Day does not finish – not quite yet. We are returned to our bodies, but our mental connection is not broken. We are still one being. What one of us experiences we all experience. And now, to reacclimatise ourselves with being human, we are reliving the last few moments before the world stopped. We are reliving them together, each one of us experiencing the same few moments from six billion points of view, all at the same time.

It's impossible of course. How could an individual concentrate well enough to be aware of everything that is going on for six billion souls when it's all happening simultaneously? Our minds don't work like that. Surely we'd have to have the awareness and perceptions of a god.

But it turns out to be easy. It just happens, despite the limitations we think we have. We observe enough, experience enough, to age us by a hundred lifetimes, and on one level that is how long it takes, and yet on another level it's just a few moments – a couple of heartbeats from our lives. We see everything.

Many are asleep. We see their dreams, in all of their soul-splitting horror, shrug-making strangeness, unreasonable beauty and breathtaking hilarity.

Some people are simply sitting, admiring the scenery. We see glaciers and pyramids, sunsets over forests, savannahs under rain clouds, train tracks through deserts, washing over fences, chimney stacks and power plants, estuaries at low tide, taxi cabs in cities, military machines, rockets and garbage heaps to the horizon. We see cemeteries and skyscrapers and waiting rooms and factory floors and shopping malls and hospitals and blasted schoolrooms. We see cigarette ends and buses, medicine cabinets and sock drawers.

There is an Elvis Presley impersonator holding up a grocery store.

There are three actors preparing Oscar acceptance speeches.

There is a teenage girl who is so self centred that she's actually beginning to notice it herself.

There are people panicking because the end of the world is coming.

There are countless people watching TV.

There are people crying with hunger.

There are thousands of people who are just plain bored.

There is a very small girl who is being abused by her father, physically, mentally and emotionally, just as she was yesterday, and the day before that and the day before that. It is happening now, and we see it. We see it through her eyes, and we see it through his, and we don't know how we can ever be healed, but at least now we all know. At least now we all know.

We all see each other. We see each other and we see ourselves. The starving and the overfed see each other. All of the religions, including the atheists and the agnostics, see each other. The terrorists, the world leaders and the victims of both, they see each other. The cowardly and the brave, the shunned and the popular, the self-effacing and the self important, the shy and the confident, the worried and the carefree, the disturbed and the tranquil, we're all there. Young people now know what it is to be old – exactly the same as being young, of course. Boys now know what it is to be a man, and a girl, and a woman, and a man who wants to be a woman and vice versa; vice versa many times over in all directions. We all know now what it is to be attacked, and to be the attacker. We know what it is to harm, and also to heal. We know what it is to help, and to hinder, and what it is to do nothing at all.

We know who we are at last.

And I am aware of a train of thought somewhere in the midst of this ocean of consciousness and experience. It belongs to me, George Hanson. It is marvelling at all of the imagination the human race possesses. The terrible ways in which we manage to survive, hold on to ourselves, when it seems that we are so withered and worn that we should just blow away. We know so much more than we think. We know enough to make us happy. It's all there, shared out amongst us, I can see it when I turn my head to one side and catch it with the corner of my eye. But we feel so small and so alone.

I see the remarkable poetic thoughts of scientists.

Light travels over one hundred and eighty six thousand miles every second. Every second.

What's the circumference of the world?

About twenty five thousand miles.

How far does light travel in an entire year? Too far to imagine in terms of tarmac roads. But that vast, unimaginable distance is a light year. The spiralled disc of our galaxy, the Milky Way, is roughly two hundred and fifty thousand light years across. That kind of distance defies comprehension. You can hear the words but you can't make them feel real. And the Milky Way is a speck in the universe. From some planets out there it looks like one more star in the night sky. From some planets it can't be seen at all. Two hundred and fifty thousand light years across, and too small to be seen! You can hear the words but you can't make them feel real.

What are we, asks my train of thought, *that our immediate surroundings should seem so big to us, so all-encompassing?* And all the while, within every cell of our bodies, molecules twist, atoms dance and electrons spin, around and around.

There is no separation between the bustling activity of Times Square, the swirling grandeur of the Andromeda Galaxy, and a child facing a corner and closing his eyes to the room, shutting out everything external, and retreating inwards in search of safety or peace. There is no separation. There is no difference. Nothing is bigger, or more important, than anything else. There is no separation between Monday and Tuesday. There is no separation between the gawky kid besieged by an assault of acne, a bad wardrobe and a lisp, and the good-looking kid at the back of the class, besieged by their own popularity. There is no separation between religion and science, the left and the right, the east and the west, the north and the south. Every point on a globe is the centre, regardless of datelines. Every person is the centre of a universe. It all goes around and around. There is no separation between yesterday and tomorrow. They are the same thing.

I find I am pleased with this train of thought, but still some of the six billion disagree.

•

The world began to move again. I was back in my armchair in Mount Everest. Real Sal was looking at me. Suddenly, silently, it began to snow, even though we were inside the mountain. I looked into Real Sal's eyes and I knew that around the world, as the people began to move once more, snow fell on them, wherever they were. But the snow was made from feather light crystals of radiance rather than frozen water. It fell in the desert beneath the sun, and it fell in the darkness of the night beneath the moon and clouds. It fell indoors and outdoors, on the sleeping and the awake, in the daylight and in people's dreams. When it landed on your skin it tingled slightly and then disappeared. It could be seen by everyone, even the blind. When it landed on the ground, or on the roof of a house, or the branch of a tree, it stayed awhile, long enough for the world to be coated in a covering of gentle white light. The deserts, the ice fields, the forests and the cities all shone, as if the heavens had descended and blanketed them in light. All around the world it drifted down, absolutely vertical it fell, despite any wind or breeze that happened to be blowing, as if its destination was the centre of the world. It was not slippery or cold, but it could be kicked into the air by the feet of delighted children, and even adults too. It could be picked up and fashioned into crumbly balls that dripped iridescent flakes and exploded into a silent white firework on impact when thrown at your neighbour. It fell in planes, yet did not dazzle or dismay the pilots. It fell in submarines at the bottom of the ocean.

And everywhere people were looking at each other and at themselves with new eyes.

Real Sal rose to her feet, her eyes aglow with a joy that was silent, contained, but bottomless. She pressed a finger to her lips (we were dumbstruck anyway) and she gestured for us to follow her. Me and Osmo and Pee and Christine and Fake Sal jumped up and ran after her towards the edge of the mountain where we all became invisible and sailed out into the sky over the mountain range to go see the world, and how the people of Earth were reacting to the gift they had been given. Sal took us soaring down amongst the people, snaking back and forth through time like Father Christmas on his deliveries, so that we could see the moment when everybody everywhere stirred from the eternal Christmas day.

While the snow fell Sal Phillips allowed nobody to be harmed or frightened, but the light shone and everybody reflected.

16
The End of the World Again

There are only two ways to live your life. One is as though nothing is a miracle.
The other is as though everything is a miracle.
- Albert Einstein

New Year's Day dawned bright and clear.

They were coming to kill her.

She was going to let them.

It was the kind of day that should have seen you driving somewhere new, with good-looking friends and no chores to be done, only life to be lived. It was a clean and lovely day, but all morning a pot of nausea had been churning and bubbling in the pit of my stomach. The day felt outlandish to me. I felt like I'd drunk too much coffee.

- George, would you like me to settle your stomach?

- No thanks, Fleet. Let it stay.

My best friends in the world, in an effort to soak up their New Year's Eve hangovers, loaded up their plates with poached eggs, fried tomatoes, fried mushrooms, baked beans, hash browns and fake meat, and carried them through to the dining table that had been left unfolded since Christmas dinner. I nursed an orange juice and tried to act normal.

Armitage was back on the scene, and looking more relaxed than he ever had. He'd lost that air of wanting to gain control. Now, sitting around the breakfast table, trying to steal mushrooms from Christine's plate, he just looked at home.

Osmo chatted mindlessly to the two Sals. He was talking more quickly than usual, like he'd drunk too much coffee as well. He knew. He knew what I knew. He smiled bravely at them, trying to be supportive, but really it was them looking after him.

I sat next to Pee and we finally found the time to talk.

"I'm not going to be an actor."

"You're not?"

"No."

"I disagree."

He looked at me coolly.

"It's not for you to agree or disagree with. It's just a fact."

"Pee, mate, you already are an actor. You always have been. That's the only fact. You just need a bit of time, that's all."

He was shaking his head.

"Films are on the way out. Everybody's going to be too busy building a new world, meeting aliens and exploring the universe to be making teen comedies and monster movies. My time has passed."

I rolled my eyes to the heavens.

"Pee, do you deliberately say stuff for the sole purpose of getting on my paps?"

Pee looked puzzled.

"No. That's just a fortunate coincidence."

"People'll still make films. Maybe all the pretentious stuff will disappear, all of the celebrity rubbish, yeah – but you've had your taste of that anyway, haven't you?"

"Well, yeah, I wouldn't want any of that again."

He stabbed a hash brown and swirled it around in some brown sauce.

"Are you lying to me?"

He shrugged.

"So? I can if I want to."

"So, you do want to be an actor then?"

"Probably. It's just so stupid though. It's embarrassing."

"Since when did being an embarrassment ever stop you?"

"I know," he nodded seriously. "It's a shame about the celebrity rubbish though. That was my favourite bit."

I looked over at Osmo. He was staring at his plate blankly. A big tear hung from his chin, wondering whether to join his beans on the plate below. The Sals, sitting on either side of him, looked at each other. Simultaneously, slowly and deliberately, they each poked the end of a sausage into one of his ears, which they then twizzled until he bucked his ideas up.

•

After breakfast I made an excuse and beamed aboard Fleet to inspect my robots. They didn't need inspecting of course. They were all perfect, all fully charged and fully functioning. But I felt the need to see them, touch their heavy armour, feel the reassuring solidity. They towered over me, all twenty of them, in the huge hanger that Fleet had created for me in one of the rooms off my Tardis corridor. Each one of them was more than capable of protecting Sal from anything a host of Go or intergalactic communities could ever throw at her. Twenty of them constituted an army. I was ready to declare war.

- Fleet.

- Yes, George.

- If Real Sal spots what I'm up to these things won't count for anything, will they?

- No, George.

- Do you think I can buy enough time with them?

A pause.

- Anything is possible, George, especially these days.

An army of monstrously powerful robots at my beck and call, but the wishy-washiness of Fleet's answer said it all. *Who are you trying to kid, George?* I felt myself drooping. I thought of Ell Aah Ray. What would she do? But I couldn't work it out.

I took one last look at my beautiful array of automated weaponry.

"It's not going to work," I said.

The robots stared impassively into space, but I felt bad suddenly, because I knew they'd heard me. I quickly beamed away.

•

The *Dah Rhiv Artiv Da* had joined the *Oh Ridjinn Ahl* in orbit two and a half days previously. Real Sal had allowed the Go to send transmissions to Earth, even though the ships were physically excluded from Earth air space. Communications were established with TV channels. Live visual footage of the alien vessels was broadcast to living rooms around the globe. Along with that footage the aliens released a mass of information for the people of Earth to digest and discuss endlessly before the planned landing on New Year's Day: the vital statistics of The Stolen Adventure, potted histories of the Go and the inter galactic communities, details of their social and organisational structures, their inter-species relations policies, images and sound files depicting thousands of different civilised species currently inhabiting the Milky Way, an outline of the observer presence on Earth (although no locations were revealed) – masses of the stuff, all made public without so much as a by-your-leave to the United Nations or any major world power. They had the coolest website ever.

And while humanity chewed on all of this it had also been assimilating the experiences of Christmas Day. It was a curious thing. The incandescent snow had eventually melted away after a few hours, and with it went our sense of connection with each other. After a few days we found that we were left with only as much memory of the event as our brains, or our minds, or our personalities could cope with. This amount varied from person to person. For recently born babies the event was barely more remarkable than anything else they had experienced so far. For the most part the very young forgot it quickly, but children of school age seemed to remember more than adults. For a few remarkable babies and tiny children their innocence was over already. They had retained a great deal, and were now as wise and worldly as the best of Earth's venerable old biddies. Already a few toddlers had appeared on TV, confounding pundits and presenters with their perceptive insights and earthy humour.

It was different for everybody, and there didn't seem any rhyme or reason as to why, for some individuals, the eternal Christmas moment had dimmed to a vague, dreamy recollection, while for others it was a sprawling, crystal clear memory that was still very much a part of them, informing every decision they made. There were people with mental health problems or learning disabilities that were now functioning at very high levels, socially, intellectually and emotionally, while others showed no change in behaviour at all. Some people now possessed new skills, or could speak new languages, or had acquired whole fields of knowledge or understanding that they could now utilize, while other people felt essentially unchanged and were beginning to develop inferiority complexes about it. When I asked Real Sal about the apparent randomness of this she smiled.

"The ability of some people to limit their perceptions is just as amazing and important as the ability of others to drink everything in and use it."

I felt very different to the old George, though it was difficult to pin down; the more I tried to work out what the difference was the more it eluded me. And when I sat down with a notebook to try and write about it I felt a huge log jam of ideas and images and words, all competing with each other to spew out onto the page. I could tell it was going to be a struggle before I managed to make any sense of it through my writing.

The human race seemed to have become a little telepathic too. It was nothing as overt as hearing voices in your head or anything, but people did seem to intuitively know what others were thinking. Never had we been so adept at putting ourselves in somebody else's shoes. It hadn't been until December 27th that I'd had a thought that I put to Real Sal.

"Have you evolved the human race ahead of schedule so that we'll be able to hold our own with the aliens?"

She laughed at me.

"You and your questions, George."

"Has all of this been planned from the start? Is this why you created the runabouts in the first place? Have you manipulated everything so we'd end up right here?"

"Come on, George, you know I've got too much respect for the principle of free will than to try and control the world."

"But you suspected what might happen if you did certain things, didn't you? You didn't take away anyone's free will but you predicted what the most likely outcomes would be?"

"George," she said. "I love you."

She'd never said that before.

"Look, I've got something for you." And she produced a compilation CD from her pocket. In years to come I would wonder, when I listened to that music, if she had just made it spring into being in her pocket as a way of distracting me, or if she'd really taken her time over choosing the music. Maybe both. Probably both. It was an amazing CD anyway.

So, by the time the Unfortunate Circumstances dipped below the clouds somewhere over the middle of the Atlantic Ocean, acting as herald for the

Dah Rhiv Artiv Da, which followed three miles behind, nudging the atmosphere out of the way to glide yellow and grey through the air in the exact same way that a gigantic brick doesn't, the human race was ready. There was no panicking in the streets, nobody set themselves on fire or threw themselves from tall buildings. They watched it on telly with their friends. The world grew quiet, and little work was done except in cafes and bars and at public gatherings where big screens had been set up.

An enormous multinational escort of military helicopters (contributed to by pretty much every nation that had military helicopters) encircled the giant alien vessel like a daisy chain. Jet fighters from different countries swept back and forth like starlings cautiously investigating a flying island. Viewing audiences were treated to cockpit-eye-views and commentaries. Some of the pilots' voices were hushed with religious awe, some rattled excitedly in fast languages, and one RAF pilot, who had climbed to his maximum altitude and was still barely a quarter of the way up the southern wall of the ship, said, "Well, they've picked a nice day for it."

The Stolen Adventure headed inexorably for Banford, hauling its twenty thousand square kilometre dusk beneath it. Its centre of gravity would be over the Penrose High playing fields by eleven a.m. A suitable crowd had gathered to watch Ell Aah Ray descend to shake hands with a surprisingly large group of world leaders, who had decided 'what the hey', and had accepted the invitation to attend. Well, who wants to lose face to all the other world leaders? And anyway, what did we have to fear? They may have had a spaceship the size of a small country but we had Sal Phillips on our side. Sal Phillips would look after us.

•

It was eleven a.m. There was a strange quality to the light outside the kitchen window. It was dark, because we were at the bottom of a colossal well, the bullet hole of the Stolen Adventure, but it wasn't like night because the constantly moving lights of the *Artiv Da* coated the world in a silvery shimmer. Osmo said it was like nighttime on ancient Go, when the sky was clear and glutted with stars, because it was closer to the centre of the galaxy than Earth.

"Come on, it's time," said Real Sal.

All four runabouts were parked outside with their lights on, above a lava flow of people and banners. We beamed aboard – Real Sal, Christine and Armitage joining Fake Sal in Tom Baker, in the lead position. I was bringing up the rear again.

We gained height. Below, the whole of Banford was smothered beneath a tightly woven blanket of people that was pierced by church spires and rows of terraced houses and shops. There was no purpose in traffic anymore. Cars had been abandoned. They lay, scattered randomly amidst the crush, like maxed-out credit cards. The surrounding, all-engulfing tide of humanity undulated gently and ceaselessly beneath the twilight of the Stolen Adventure, but had nowhere to go. It was in its own way. The world had arrived in Banford, and there were still one or two placards that proclaimed this day would be, for this world anyway, the end of the line.

I imagined myself down there, unable to move at anything faster than a shuffle, gazing up at the shining diamond of pods as it cruised by overhead, beneath a circuit board sky.

•

We'd been designated an area on one side of the platform that had been erected at the edge of the playing fields. Our backs were to the school. Before us was a large semi-circular clearing of grass that was aligned perfectly with the centre of the bullet hole above. The bullet hole was so vast that it seemed the whole of Banford could be the bullet, ready to shoot up and out into space. Having recently disgorged us into the clearing our runabouts had curved gracefully into the air in a manoeuvre that left them floating in a line about fifteen metres above the platform, light beams rotating and shifting like rock concert effects. The world leaders, invited VIPs, and our families had front row seats around the semi circle. The Queen had decided to stay at home and watch it on the telly, but Prince Charles was there, sitting next to the Prime Minister and the Leader of the opposition. I could see my mum chatting with a leader from the Middle East. Behind this band of bigwigs a bracelet of security forces had very good views. At the base of the platform, on either side, two large clumps of the world press bristled with cameras and microphones.

A sound technician bustled over to us with microphone sets but Real Sal smiled and told her that we wouldn't need them.

"Okay. Er...they're wondering if any of you would like some make-up," said the technician, pink around the ears.

Pee stiffened, but when the rest of us shook our heads he joined in. The sound technician backed away humbly.

We focused on the spectacle and didn't say anything to one another of any substance. We just pointed things out to each other: who was the best-dressed world leader, who was notable by their absence.

At twelve noon the random movements of the *Artiv Da's* lights suddenly regulated, synchronising into a pulse effect that radiated down the well of the bullet hole. The world looked up. A small craft was descending. The crowd was too big to ever become completely silent, but it hushed enough so you could hear individual exclamations of 'Oh my God!' and the raw voices of people barking the names of their loved ones.

They're coming to kill her.

 - **Fleet.**

- Yes, George.
- I want you to tell me when it's one minute before the attempt.
- Affirmative.
- Will it be soon, Fleet?
- Affirmative.

While heads craned upwards Real Sal stood and walked to the centre of the platform. The craft dropped to the centre of the semi-circle, and Ell Aah Ray's replica disembarked onto the grass. Ash Koh Tok and Finn Ma Fey followed her. Ash Koh Tok was carrying a white box. The craft rose up then, parking itself at the same height as our runabouts. The three aliens turned slowly around where they stood, letting the world get a good look at them. Then they walked slowly towards Real Sal, mounting the broad central steps to the platform. They reached the top and towered over her like trees. Fake Ell made the silent gestures of peace, her arms and hands gracefully describing ornate shapes in the air, and Ash Koh Tok and Finn Ma Fey both bowed and made the gestures of high respect. Sal nodded and returned the appropriate gestures, arms moving lithely. Her face was shining with the same light that I had seen when she had just met MarvinMilton and was trying to persuade us to crawl out from the darkness of our hiding place. Even here, even now, she loved meeting aliens.

I watched with a terrible clarity as Ash Koh Tok hinged open the lid of the box.

- One minute before assassination attempt, said Fleet's beautiful, sad, American voice in my head.

My stomach knotted and I could barely form my reply.

- Okay, Fleet. Beam the Protektors into position in exactly 30 seconds.
- Affirmative.

Finn Ma Fey lifted the headband out. It was simple and tacky, like something out of an eighties sci-fi TV series – a silver circle, with an opal-like jewel set in the front. Fake Ell received it and turned to Real Sal, holding the band aloft as if she were about to crown Sal the ruler of the universe. Sal stepped forward. Time suddenly slowed to a crawl. The band was descending like a glacier and Sal was glancing back, finding me, and the fear was glittering in her eyes.

- George.

My heart seemed to snap. It was like somebody had just pulled a trigger, right inside my chest.

- Fleet! Do it now! Do it now!

After a pause like an eternity Fleet's voice in my head, but coming from a great distance: Unable to comply.

- Fleet!

Sal is looking at me.

- I'm sorry, George.

- **Sal.** I can barely string a coherent thought together. *Don't let them.* But I already know she's going to.

- **Stay with me, George,** she says. **I'm frightened.**

I see her kneeling in her bedroom, her hands lost in light, a schoolgirl all on her own, overtaken by terror, screaming silently for her friend to come save her, saying sorry, over and over again. But her friend is already too late.

- **Sal,** I say. Then my mind stalls, utterly and completely.

- **I can't do it on my own. I'm scared, George.**

My mind starts up again.

- **You know I'll never leave you.**

- **I'm frightened.**

- **I know you are. I am too. Let's be frightened together.**

For a split moment the universe stops completely again, but this time it is just me and Sal who are still aware. The moment lasts forever. All is silence. All is stillness. The scene around us is a photograph.

- **Thank you,** says her voice, quiet in the emptiness of infinity, but very close.

I don't say anything for the longest time, just wanting to stay there, but finally I speak.

- **I accept.**

The headband lowers towards her. She turns back to face them, but this time I am there with her, looking out from her eyes once again. We feel the cold metal of the band on our forehead, and when the alien's thumb brushes the jewel, and the world is taken away, I am still with her.

17
Everything That Everybody Ever Does

So, is that it then?
- Pee

When I came to the world around me was in chaos. The crowds were roaring, sirens were wailing, there were people all over the platform. A man was kneeling over me. When I sat up he started trying to tip my head back and hold my eyes open and look into the pupils. I tried to brush him away and looked around. Pee was kneeling next to me blinking. A handful of policemen were struggling with a press of people who were crowding in on us. I just lay there for a spell, not feeling part of the scene.

- Fleet.

- Yes, George.

- Did you know this was going to happen?

- I suspected.

- Why didn't you tell me?

A pause.

- I don't know.

She'd never said that to me before.

I got to my feet, unable to talk. I pushed at the man who wanted to check my pupils. I had to push him twice before he'd leave me alone. I couldn't get to Fake Sal and Christine and Osmo. Over in the centre of the platform Ash Koh Tok and Finn Ma Fey had gone, but Fake Ell Aah Ray was still there, encased in a slender force field with a lilac tint, its lower section disappearing into the platform itself. People were yelling at her, but she just stood and waited silently. I couldn't see Real Sal's body anywhere.

I pushed my way through the people and looked up through the purple shimmer of the force field into her oblong pupils.

"Are you okay?" I asked.

Her head made a series of tiny twitches.

"I don't feel well," she said in her sandpapery tones. "This bubble will last for twenty four hours, during which I will explain our motives to your people." She held two hands to her face for a moment. "I don't know if I can stand here for twenty four hours. My legs..."

"Have you been left here as a scapegoat?"

"I had to do what I did, but I must also answer to your people for it."

"Can you turn the force field off?"

"No. A strictly timed process...demands of protocol..."

She wavered visibly on her feet.

I looked up at the runabouts. They were still there, implacable, seemingly unmoved by the chaos below them.

- Fleet.

- Yes, George.

- Push these people back, give us some room. Expand this force field so I can join her in there, and give her a big chair.

- Affirmative.

An extra large flight chair materialised on my right and the lilac bubble expanded, gently pushing people back while allowing me and the chair to pass through.

- Thanks, Fleet.

- You're welcome.

I lead Ell Aah Ray's replica to the chair and helped her to sit down.

"You are very kind," said the Go first contact specialist. I placed a hand on her shoulder.

"Just take your time. You've done a horrible job. We'll look after you."

She looked at me, her head cocked to one side.

"She forgave me," she said. Then she buried her face in her hands and cried as only the Go can.

•

I think I've said it before, that I don't see much difference in the way human society works and a single human mind. It's a fractal thing. Societies develop and grow and suffer growing pains just as the people who are part of them do, and the human mind can have a difficult time when it is faced with the truth about itself. This is as true for the mind that is six billion minds, all awake at once, as it is for the lone soul-searcher. How should we deal with the parts of ourselves that we don't like? The parts that are petty, jealous, strange, spiteful, savage, weak, cruel, self-pitying, self-obsessed, cold, judgemental, alien, cowardly, twisted, greedy, furious, intolerant, unforgiving, demented, afraid, or just plain old evil? Do we fight those things, or suppress them? Do we lock them away, or just pretend that they don't exist? Do we try to heal them, or eradicate them? Do we kill them?

Well, suffice it to say that life wasn't all sweetness and light for the human race in the first days, and weeks, and years of the new millennium. It had taken a good hard look in the mirror and it still couldn't decide what to do about the ugly bits. All of our crimes and misdemeanours had been revealed on Christmas Day. All of those who had been unfaithful in thought and deed were now found out. Denial was pointless. Marriages and relationships crumbled like biscuits. Criminals who had gotten clean away were now clearly identified. Friends who had betrayed trusts had nowhere to hide. Corrupt police, public servants, world leaders, evangelists, religious leaders, role models – they couldn't pretend any longer. Everybody had the goods on everybody else. What were we all to do? It was an impossible situation. Nothing was simple. Nothing was black and white. Some of the people who had committed the most heinous acts had actually thought astonishingly beautiful thoughts, while some of those who had done tremendous good in their lives had thought terrible, horrendous things. What were we supposed to condemn and what were we supposed to praise? What should we punish, what should we forgive, and who could be free from judgement?

In the end, of course, there was no simple solution, and we had to work things out for ourselves the hard way. Some people were spared; some were punished. Some people punished themselves far more harshly than anybody else would have punished them; some people gave themselves a break. We were still flawed, absurd creatures. The difference was that we now realised it fully, and we didn't feel so alone.

Sometimes I try to picture Real Sal's face, the way she was after she matured herself, and I can't do it. I feel bad, as if I'm betraying her somehow. And the harder I try to picture her the more her face eludes me. But then, sometimes, when I'm going about my life, not thinking about her at all, maybe cutting my fingernails or taking a frozen pizza out of its box, a memory flares and there she is as clear as day - as if she's come back. Her eyes are smiling at me because of something she's just said. It's always the same memory that flashes inside my mind.

We're in my old bedroom. It's Christmas Eve and sunlight is slanting through the window behind her, blurring her outline in gold and dust.

"I read something once," she says. "The book was really thick and heavy, and I never finished it, but one thing stood out and stuck with me. It said this: 'Everything that everybody ever does is a request for love.'"

She's thinking about it, her head nodding gently in agreement. "That makes a lot of sense to me now," she says.

Her eyes are laughing their way into my memory forever.

•

There was an atmosphere in my dreams sometimes that reminded me of how big the world used to seem. It was usually sunny and bright and still, and there were no people around, or they were far away or around a corner, out of sight. It felt as if it was just me and the world alone together, watching each other, curious about each other. It was an odd, intimate sensation that quickly dissipated as soon as somebody turned up and started talking to me.

As I had grown older those kinds of dreams had occurred less and less frequently, but in the days following the start of the new millennium I found that that atmosphere was returning to me, in my waking life. And people could hassle me as much as they liked and as soon as they were gone the feeling would return almost straight away. The world was watching me again.

I explained it to Fake Sal one afternoon and she burst into tears and hugged me. She nearly crushed my ribs and we spent the rest of the day looking at the things in her room together, barely speaking.

In February we visited Oceana with Osmo and Pee. A great commemorative event was held in remembrance of the civilisation and the various species that had been lost there. Representatives from the galactic community attended and plans were proposed to turn it into a free colony world, in which the remaining animals and vegetation would be preserved. We invited Fake Ell but she didn't come. After the internationally agreed pardon for killing Real Sal she had been re-offered her old job on the *Artiv Da*, but she'd turned it down and remained on Earth, feeling responsible somehow for ensuring that Earth's induction to the intergalactic community went as smoothly as possible. But Ash Koh Tok and Finn Ma Fey came along.

In March I returned to Earth with Fake and Finn Ma Fey. Pee had gotten involved with some film projects and Osmo had taken to exploring the countryside of Oceana with a visiting emissary from the Crab Nebula. Rumour had it that they were falling in love. She was an odd looking creature but Osmo said she had a beautiful mind.

So Fake and I took Finn Ma Fey and Fake Ell on a road trip around Britain. We discussed art in the Lowry Centre in Salford, and poetry in Dylan Thomas's writing shack in Laurgharne. We saw John o' Groats and Lands End, and a whole bunch of stuff in between. And although we were still kings of the world with our runabouts, while we were on our trip we never used them once. For us it was motorways and service stations, country lanes and city roads, fields and monuments and shopping centres. And I tried to hold every square of tarmac and every blade of grass in my mind - every washing line and fence post, every tractor, cow and sheep, every stone of each stately home and crumbled castle, every crisp packet and cigarette end, just to see if I could work out how big the world was.

Around us the changes were taking place. The observer population was out in the open now. Wherever we went there were objects in the sky. School children went on field trips to the deserts and rainforests, to the moon and the bottom of the ocean, with people from every quadrant of the Milky Way. Friendly inter-species matches of football, American football, baseball, cricket, hockey, table tennis and even wrestling were staged all around the globe with professional and amateur teams. Songs, histories, tribal myths and classics of literature were exchanged in a cross fertilisation of culture that was occurring on all levels, including within Earth culture itself. Taken for granted segregations wilted self-consciously under the onslaught of freely flowing information and politically active toddler groups. The hungry were fed, the weary were invigorated, the angry were listened to, the disabled were given fabulous devices.

Christine grieved for her lost daughter, but she was in good company because the galaxy grieved with her. She married Armitage and they were divorced four years later. We all made a point of saying 'I told you so'. Christine eventually went on to become an ambassador for Earth.

It was a chaotic time. As the years passed, and to the undisguised horror of many, the distinctive flavours of the nations of Earth were beginning to collapse into a cultural compost heap. The world really did become one huge melting pot. But to me and Fake Sal it was a compost heap that was rich and warm and fragrant. We loved it, and we could barely wait to see what grew out of the delicious, mulchy mess. For, as simple and ordinary as we were, our cockiness knew no bounds. And we competed with each other lustily to be the one who could declare the loudest and clearest and most convincingly of all that nothing lasts forever, but nothing ever truly dies.

●

I returned to Iron Street one time. It was a spring day in the first year of the Millennium. Mum had some visitors in the living room so I sat in the kitchen for a while, on my own, rearranging the magnetic words on the fridge and looking in the cupboards and not knowing what I was doing there.

I went up to my old bedroom and it hadn't changed at all. It still smelt musty. The space marine terminator was still standing in his coffee ring, still trying to determine his next course of action. The window was filled with sunshine and I could hear a radio from somebody's house playing some perky, jerky Britney Spears track. I turned the computer on and played the opening section of Homeworld, but I couldn't remember the best attack strategy and I ended up with barely any ships left for the next round. My alarm clock had stopped. I was staring into space when the screensaver came on. I blinked at the words scrolling across the screen.

'Hello Mr Smarty Man.'

My mind seemed to fall away. I stared and I breathed and a blackbird started singing outside somewhere. I continued with my staring and my breathing, afraid to move or to think in case it broke the spell and destroyed the hallucination. But the words didn't disappear. They were real. She was back. She'd found a way to survive. Somehow she was alive. The idea took hold of me and squeezed and I looked about myself as if she was going to step out of the wardrobe and flick my ears and shout 'April fool!' or something.

"Sal?"

My voice sounded small and stupid. Nobody heard it. Outside, the DJ cut in before Britney's song had finished. I looked back at the screen – *Hello Mr. Smarty Man* - and I had to accept Sal had got me again, the good old-fashioned way.

"Hello, Sal," I said.

Mum brought some sandwiches in.